T0369325

THE ARCHANGEL

PREVIOUS BOOKS BY ALAN REFKIN

Fiction

Matt Moretti and Han Li Series
The Archivist
The Abductions
The Payback
The Forgotten
The Cabal
The Chase

Mauro Bruno Detective Series
The Patriarch
The Scion
The Artifact
The Mistress
The Collector

Gunter Wayan Series
The Organization
The Frame
The Arrangement
The Defector

Nonfiction

The Wild Wild East: Lessons for Success in Business in Contemporary Capitalist China
By Alan Refkin and Daniel Borgia, PhD

Doing the China Tango: How to Dance around Common Pitfalls in Chinese Business Relationships
By Alan Refkin and Scott Cray

Conducting Business in the Land of the Dragon: What Every Businessperson Needs To Know About China
By Alan Refkin and Scott Cray

Piercing the Great Wall of Corporate China: How to Perform Forensic Due Diligence on Chinese Companies
By Alan Refkin and David Dodge

THE ARCHANGEL

A **MATT MORETTI** AND **HAN LI** THRILLER

ALAN REFKIN

THE ARCHANGEL
A MATT MORETTI AND HAN LI THRILLER

iUniverse books may be ordered through booksellers or by contacting:

iUniverse
1663 Liberty Drive
Bloomington, IN 47403
www.iuniverse.com
844-349-9409

ISBN: 978-1-6632-6272-1 (sc)
ISBN: 978-1-6632-6271-4 (e)

Library of Congress Control Number: 2024909587

Print information available on the last page.

iUniverse rev. date: 05/06/2024

To my wife, Kerry
and
Mark Iwinski and Mike Calbot

CHAPTER I

IT WAS TWENTY MINUTES before midnight when the man and woman entered the vast expanse of Vyšehrad Park, steps from Prague's city center. The thin layer of snow, which had melted during the day and turned into ice in the thirty-degree Fahrenheit nighttime temperature, cracked beneath the boots of the two intruders. With the stars and moon invisible under the dense cloud cover and guided only by the dim light from the map illuminated on one of their cellphones, they cautiously weaved through the forest of dormant trees, trying not to stumble on their thick rope-like roots that protruded to the surface but were hidden beneath the slick opaque ice.

Their midnight meeting was to take place at the Devil's Column, which became a tourist attraction based on an eighteenth-century legend that a priest made a bet with the devil that he could celebrate mass before the devil could bring him a column from St. Peter's Basilica in Rome. The devil lost and, in a fit of rage, threw the marble pillar at the ground, breaking it into three pieces as it impacted the earth. A thousand yards behind the protruding pillars was the Basilica of Saint Peter and Saint Paul, constructed three centuries after Bernini's masterpiece in Rome.

The man was in his mid-thirties, bald, six feet three inches tall, and had the broad shoulders and narrow-waisted athletic build of a swimmer. The woman was in her late twenties, five feet ten inches tall, blonde, and had the slender athleticism of a jogger. They arrived at the rendezvous spot two minutes past midnight, but instead of seeing their contact, they only saw darkness.

"It was a mistake to do this without backup or being mic'd up," the man said, his voice laced with tension, knowing that even if they used their cellphones to call for help, they were too deep in Vyšehrad for the CIA Rapid Response Team, which was waiting on the park's perimeter, to arrive in time to save them.

"You know the ground rules for the meet," the woman reminded him. "Our spy told their handler they'd be a no-show if he saw anyone but two agents, and would walk away if he found a recording or transmitting device on us. That they don't trust anyone is why they're alive."

"I'd like to avoid us becoming gold stars on the Memorial Wall at Langley."

"I have to give it to him. This was a smart place to meet because he could easily spot anyone following us, and the low cloud cover, which he probably knew would occur tonight or was typical for this time of year, prevented us from putting a drone overhead," the woman said.

"He has the tactical advantage since we're on his home turf," the man said as he unzipped his parka and pulled a handgun from the shoulder holster with practiced precision. After disengaging the safety, he chambered a round and put the firearm in his jacket pocket. The woman mirrored his cautious preparation.

As the minutes passed, they became increasingly agitated. The absence of their contact and the isolation and unsettling silence of their surroundings intensified their sense of foreboding. They periodically exchanged a glance, wordlessly acknowledging the apprehension that gripped them.

"Remind me again why they chose us," the man said, posing a rhetorical question.

"Since we only arrived at the embassy a week ago, none of the intelligence agencies in Prague knows our faces, and if they did, we're too junior to be of concern," the woman answered.

"In other words, we're too unimportant to be followed. This guy could have had second thoughts and canceled the meeting, and there'd be no way to find out. We should leave and have the Chief of Station reschedule," the man said, referring to the CIA's top in-country official.

"That's a winning career move that's sure to get us transferred to Dirkou, Niger, or some other career-ending garden spot. It took us thirty minutes to trek here. Let's give the spy until half past the hour before we blow this off," the woman responded with unsuppressed irritation that they call it a day because the situation wasn't to their liking.

The man reluctantly agreed. Fifteen minutes later, they saw a light in the distance coming toward them.

"Showtime," the woman said.

As the light got brighter, a five feet six inches tall man in his early fifties, with a salt and pepper beard and carrying an extra thirty pounds of weight, approached.

"My apologies for being late," he said in broken English with a Russian accent. "I was watching from a distance and needed to ensure you were alone. Please unzip your jackets," he asked, after which he frisked each for a wire and, finding their weapons, tossed them on the ground.

"Do you mind if we reciprocate?" The man asked.

The spy had no issue with the request and unzipped his jacket, the man seeing that he wasn't wired nor carrying a weapon.

"The COS wanted me to ask why you didn't use one of the Agency's drops and requested this meeting instead?" The man said. "He feels this meeting unnecessarily risks your exposure."

The spy answered with a question. "Have you heard of a Russian spy code-named Archangel?"

"We wouldn't tell you if we did," the man answered.

"The looks on your faces say you haven't."

"If that's what you believe," the man replied, knowing the spy was right.

"Archangel is Moscow's most important spy in the United States, their access to highly classified information so extensive that it's not unlike the Kremlin having a seat at Situation Room briefings."

"Given security protocols and background checks, that seems impossible."

"It's not impossible if it's a fact," the spy said.

"What's their name?" The woman asked, wanting to cut through the BS and know who they were talking about.

"By practice, the identity of the spy of this importance is only known to two people in the Russian Federation—Putin and General Grigori Abrankovich, the director of the FSB," he said, referring to the Federal Security Service, the successor to the Soviet Union's KGB. "Even the use of their code name is tightly controlled and never put in a communique nor mentioned other than in face-to-face discussions."

"If that's true, how did you learn about Archangel and, better yet, discover their identity, assuming you, Putin, and Abrankovich aren't vodka-drinking buddies?" The man asked, expressing skepticism at what he'd heard.

"Somebody mentioned their code name in a highly classified

intelligence briefing where they were credited with the data presented. A few in the briefing had heard of this spy but most, like me, hadn't."

"And you haven't previously told the COS about Archangel?"

"No."

"Why?" The man continued.

"To protect myself."

"You need to explain that statement," the woman said.

"If the Agency starts looking for him, Archangel will learn about the investigation and inform the FSB, who will interrogate everyone who'd ever attended a meeting where their code name was mentioned, beginning with the most recent. Their methods of getting to the truth are very unpleasant but get results."

"You're saying that Archangel is a man," the woman stated, receiving a nod in reply.

"How did you discover their identity?" The woman continued.

"I saw him make a drop in this park and retrieved the flash drive."

"How do you know the person making the drop was Archangel?"

"I'm an FSB colonel and my embassy's chief of counterintelligence, meaning I have free rein to detect, exploit, and neutralize spies. I'm also responsible for retrieving dead drops," he said, referring to a coordinated handoff by one party who leaves a physical object in an agreed-upon hiding spot.

"Keep going," the woman said.

"Just as your country has dead drops throughout Prague, so does the Russian Federation, both of us having one in this park several hundred yards apart. When Archangel made his drop, I knew it was him."

"How could you because you don't know what he looks like?"

"Because a red circle was drawn on his flash drive, and my

5

orders, which came directly from General Abrankovich, were to immediately put any drop with a red circle into a diplomatic pouch and send it to Putin. In the numerous drops I retrieved, no other had a red circle, and none were sent directly to Putin. What would be your conclusion?"

"And you made a copy of the flash drive?" The man asked.

"Of course, I'm a spy for the American government. I make a copy and look at whatever I retrieve from a drop."

"How long ago was the drop made?" The man asked.

"It's been several months."

"If I understand correctly, you waited to give us this information fearing the FSB would find out and come hunting for whoever divulged the identity of their top spy and what was on the flash drive he left."

"I can't emphasize enough that they have a very unpleasant and thorough investigative process."

"Why now? What's changed?"

"I'll get to that."

"One thing doesn't add up," the man interjected. "If this person is as senior as you allege, they'll have a security detail. How did you see the drop, and they didn't see it or you?"

"Some time ago, I hid a remotely controlled surveillance camera in the tree behind the bench where we make our drops. That gave me a clear view of the person and what they were leaving."

"How does a camera remain unseen in a park that hundreds must frequent when the weather is right?" The man asked, skeptical of the spy's claims.

"Thousands of people enter this park daily," the spy countered. "The camera is smaller than a koruna," he said, referring to the

Czech coin, "and impossible to see because it's wedged into the cracked bark of a tree."

"What about the security detail?" The woman asked. "If this person is as important as you've alleged, they'll be seasoned professionals. They're not going to miss seeing him make a drop. For me, that's where your story falls apart."

"Archangel was escorted into the park by six security personnel, who created a perimeter around the bench where he sat. They were very vigilant, but they weren't watching him. Instead, once they'd secured the area, they were facing away from the person they were protecting and looking outward for a threat."

The man and woman admitted that made sense.

"He had a flash drive in his gloved hand and, as he grabbed the right arm of the bench to sit down, he lifted the armrest a fraction and pushed it inside the recess with his thumb. It took no more than two to three seconds. I should mention that as proof of this person's identity, along with a copy of the flash drive, I have a photo of him making the drop, but pixelated the face using a robust Russian encryption algorithm to which only I have the key."

"Why would you do that?" The woman asked. "We're on the same side."

"In addition to why I waited until this meeting to tell you about Archangel, I'll soon explain that."

"Get there now," the man replied, losing his patience. "What was on the flash drive?"

"Highly classified information on a United States weapons system known as Vigilant."

The man and woman said they'd never heard of it.

"Let's get back to why you pixelated the face of the person you claim is Archangel, and while you're at it, give us their name," the man demanded.

"First, we need to make a deal. As I said, once the FSB discovers their top spy is under investigation, they'll interrogate everyone who knew of his existence. I'll be high on that list because I retrieved his drop. Even though I've been generously paid, per my agreement with your government, I need to be extracted from Prague now and put in the protective program promised to me. I want to spend the rest of my days doing something other than the sewer of activities I've been involved in for the past thirty years."

"If we do this, will you give us his name, the flash drive, and the pixelation key so that we'll have proof of Archangel's identity?"

"Yes."

"Let me call the COS," the man said. "He's the only one who can make this happen. It would have been easier if you'd let us have a wire."

"Both our countries have extensive intercept capabilities in Prague and will detect those transmissions. I didn't want my colleagues to come here while we were conversing. Make your call; we'll be gone before my embassy's duty officer sends a team to investigate why someone is calling your embassy from this park in the middle of the night."

The man phoned his Chief of Station, the conversation lasting thirty seconds.

"We're to escort you to the Prague-Kbely Airport, where a US military aircraft will take you to the States so you can enter the witness protection program," the man said. "However, as a condition for getting on that plane, we'll need Archangel's name, the flash drive, the photo, and the key to remove the pixelation before we leave this park."

"I'd prefer to have a little leverage," the FSB counterintelligence officer said, offering to give them Archangel's name now and the rest of the information when he boarded the aircraft.

The man again called his COS, who agreed to the revised terms.

"We have a deal," the man said. "What's his name?"

The counterintelligence officer told him.

"That's impossible," the woman gasped. "He's a legend."

"An attitude which allows him to remain above suspicion and operate undetected. We should leave. Our intercept capabilities are very good; by now, the duty officer will be tasking a team to come here and photograph what they believe is a clandestine meeting of your operatives. Once they see us, if I can't be captured, they'll try and kill me to keep you from learning what I know. They also won't be discriminatory when they start shooting, if you get my meaning."

"Point taken. Let's go," the man said as he picked up the guns and handed one to his partner.

"He's meeting with a man and woman at Vyšehrad Park."

"That means nothing to me since I'm in Moscow."

"It's a big space near the center of the city with a lot of trees."

"Are you trying to be funny?"

"I'm being factual," he responded.

The person in Moscow knew he had a problem with authority and only tolerated his disrespect because he was extraordinarily good at his job. "Do you have a good view of the three?" He asked.

"I'm a thousand feet away in a church tower and looking at them through the night vision scope on my rifle," the ex-sniper responded, not bothering to explain that he was in one of the twin one hundred ninety feet towers of the Basilica of Saint Peter and Saint Paul.

"Do the man and woman look to be American?"

"I don't know about American, but they look Western. Since neither seems to be affectionate toward the other or brought alcohol, meaning they didn't come here to get laid or party, and because they both have weapons, I'd say they're intelligence assets."

"Did you see an exchange?"

"No, but one of the Westerners made two calls. I could kill the man and woman and leave the intel officer for you to interrogate, or kill all three. The decision is yours."

"I can't take a chance that the Americans have a team waiting outside the park and that they'll get to our counterintelligence officer before us. Kill everyone, take anything of intelligence value off the bodies, and make it look like a robbery."

"Robbers don't use sniper rifles; they use handguns. The police will trace the angle of my bullets and see they came from this tower, which will tell them that this wasn't a simple robbery."

"Do as you're told and call me after it's done," the person in Moscow ordered, after which the line went dead.

The killer removed a tripod from his backpack, put it on the ledge, and rested the silenced Lobaev SVL sniper rifle atop it. Calmly looking through the night vision scope, he centered the crosshairs on the spy's forehead, exhaled, and put a round into him. The next bullet found the back of the man's head, and 1.67 seconds later, the third round entered the left side of the woman's back, exiting her chest after piercing the heart.

Afterward, he methodically disassembled his rifle and placed it inside the backpack, along with the tripod, and descended the long stairway to the bottom of the tower. Using a flashlight, he walked to the Devil's Column. He put the man and woman's guns into his pocket, along with the weapon the intelligence officer kept in an ankle holster, and removed everything from the victims' pockets. When he finished, he called Moscow.

"The man and a woman are from the American Embassy, and neither they nor the late counterintelligence officer had anything of intelligence value on their bodies," the killer said.

"You're telling me that I no longer need to worry about the traitor or the Americans?"

"Not unless there's an afterlife," the killer replied, ending the call.

The nondescript ten-car train, with ninety-seven intermodal containers stacked on its rail cars, left the Genesis Corporation's plant, a facility known for developing advanced weapons systems for the Department of Defense, under heavy security. In civilian clothes aboard the train was a detachment of Marines, while two CH-53K King Stallion helicopters, each carrying twenty-five Marines, followed high above, unable to be seen from the ground in the black of night.

Four hours and one hundred eighty-one miles later, the train entered the docks of the Norfolk International Terminal, or NIT, and stopped beside the *Resolute Eagle*, a Panamanian-flagged cargo ship on which its intermodal containers were hoisted aboard. Despite its lack of markings, and although its crew wore civilian clothing, the *Eagle*, as most referred to it, was owned by the United States Navy and used for covert operations. Twenty minutes after securing the last container, the vessel departed.

The top secret system that the *Eagle* was transporting was known as Vigilant, consisting of two command and control consoles and ninety-seven capsules containing ICBMs, which were to be lowered to specific spots on the deep ocean floor where, in some areas, the depth exceeded eighteen thousand feet, and the water pressure was over five tons per square inch. Each capsule contained a Trident D5 ballistic missile, which was slightly over forty-four feet long, nearly seven feet in diameter, weighed sixty-five tons, had a range of seven thousand five hundred miles, and was tethered to a self-leveling weight that kept it anchored to the ocean floor. A MIRV, or multiple independently targetable reentry vehicles, carried on the front end or the bus of each ICBM, contained several warheads programmed to strike different targets. Collectively, there were four hundred eighty-five warheads within the ninety-seven missiles.

The capsules in military parlance were referred to as Upward Falling Payloads, or UFPs. Although seemingly misleading, the description of the upward-falling payload was accurate. Once a missile received a launch code through a system of undersea communications nodes, the capsule would release from its tether and ascend, or fall upward, opening near the surface to release the Trident. UFPs had a strategic advantage over ballistic missile submarines, which undersea listening devices and other submarines could track, because they were silent and their locations undetectable at the extreme depths at which they sat.

Shadowing the *Resolute Eagle* as it left port was an Air Force RQ-4 Global Hawk drone, which could stay aloft for thirty-four hours while watching the ship from an altitude of sixty thousand feet. When it ran low on fuel, another would take its place, ensuring the ship was under constant surveillance. On the ocean, the *Eagle* was protected by the *USS Florida*, a Seawolf fast attack submarine with Navy SEALs onboard. In addition to forty-eight torpedoes, *Florida* carried Razorback uncrewed underwater vehicles or UUVs.

Shot from a torpedo tube, they could visually and electronically surveil an area and return to the sub, ensuring the sub commander received a visual of the *Eagle* and its environs at all times.

Vigilant's project manager, Rear Admiral Michael Baird, was the commander of the Office of Naval Research in Arlington, Virginia. The admiral was fifty-seven years old, had yellowed teeth from the copious amount of coffee he drank, and was six feet five inches tall with short gray hair combed straight back. He considered the undetectable undersea missile system a game changer, estimating that the Russian Federation and other technologically advanced countries would need at least a decade and ten billion dollars to replicate the proprietary innovations of the Navy's UFPs. However, unknown to him, one country had initiated an audacious plan to eliminate that technological gap without waiting a decade or spending the ten billion dollars.

CHAPTER 2

THE POLICE CAR WENT to Charles Square, a twenty-acre area of Prague with over two hundred brothels, at six in the morning in response to a call from Madam Irenka, who owned one of the houses of ill repute. They entered without lights or sirens, having long ago established an agreement with the madams that, as long as no one was harmed or robbed, and their clients weren't selling drugs within or around the establishments, they'd treat the brothels as any other business and keep their interactions lowkey unless it was an emergency. Driving this coexistence was the police's realization that there weren't enough law enforcement officers to monitor the estimated twelve thousand sex workers within the square, nor sufficient room in the city's jails to hold a fraction of those they could arrest for prostitution. For their part, the madams maintained an adage similar to that of Las Vegas: What happens in the brothel stays in the brothel. Therefore, this morning's call asking the police to pick up a patron who couldn't leave without significant help was unusual.

"We're not a taxi service," the desk sergeant gruffly explained upon receiving the request.

"It's Adamik," Madam Irenka replied.

"Doesn't he live there?"

"He's having some issues and can't get to work without significant help," she answered.

"We'll be right there," the desk sergeant said, requiring no further explanation.

14

When the two officers arrived at the two-story structure, the madam guided them down a first-floor hallway to the end room, which had the word *private* on a metal plate affixed to the door. Opening it, the officers saw the subject of her concern lying naked and unconscious on the bed with an empty bottle of the plum brandy Slivovitz beside him. The man was in his mid-thirties, five feet eleven inches tall, with a solid physique and black hair that was graying. He had a chiseled face with a firm jaw and a slightly crooked nose, courtesy of the person he was about to arrest who hit him in the face with a brick. Had his eyes been open, they would appear to be golden brown.

"Why did you let him drink so much?" One officer asked.

"He brought the bottle to his room. Many of our clients like to have a drink. I didn't think he was going to consume all of it."

"As I recall, you sell liquor downstairs," the other officer said.

"I make half my profits from the sale of alcohol."

"For which you don't have a license."

"If you're getting technical."

"Was he with one of your girls last night?" The other officer continued.

"That was before he got drunk. According to her, he did his business in fifteen minutes and sent her away saying he wanted to be alone," the madam replied.

"But he still lives here?"

"He rents this room," she said, irritated that she had to answer questions rather than the police taking Adamik to his duty station.

"How long has he been like this?"

"The girl he was with left the room at eleven last night."

"And no one checked on him until now?"

"We were busy. Adamik and I usually have a cup of coffee in the kitchen before he leaves for work. When he didn't stop by this morning, I went to his room, saw the empty bottle, verified he was alive, and called the station."

"You're a saint. Hold the door open," the other officer said as he and his partner wrapped Adamik in a blanket, got him to his feet, and dragged him to their patrol car while Madam Irenka followed with his clothes.

As the officers strapped him in the back seat and covered him with a blanket, she put his clothes beside him and rushed away before any of her customers saw her with the officers or near their vehicle. As she was leaving, another police cruiser pulled beside the patrol car, and an elderly man in a suit and tie exited the vehicle.

"Drunk?" He asked upon seeing his detective's condition.

"You could get inebriated by smelling his breath," one officer commented.

"Get him dressed and take him to the diner across from the station so he can get something to eat. Pour all the coffee you can into him. I need Adamik to be sober, or at least coherent, when you bring him to the station," Colonel Lubos Laska said.

The officer, who wanted to say that it was a miracle Adamik didn't have alcohol poisoning and that he had no idea how long it would take for the detective to put a coherent sentence together, instead told the colonel that he and his partner would do their best.

Laska was forty-two years old, five feet eight inches tall, and had a medium build and close-cropped black hair beginning to gray. As the operational commander of Prague's National Police of the Czech Republic, he was charged with investigating crimes within the city.

At this moment, he was looking at his best investigator, Detective Juraj Adamik, snoring in the rear of the police vehicle.

Once the colonel left, the officers broke an ammonia capsule under the detective's nose, triggering an inhalation reflex that brought him to consciousness, afterward helping him get dressed. They brought him to the dinner, eventually managed to keep some food down him, and got the semi-alert detective to the police station at 7:30 am.

"Did the wheels come off last night?" Laska asked, handing Adamik a bottle of water and three aspirin tablets.

"My ex is getting married."

"I didn't know. You need to move on."

"I know."

"She's not the only fish in the sea."

"She was for me."

"You're the best detective I've ever known, with a perfect record for solving crimes. But you're a trainwreck outside the office. Do you remember why your wife filed for divorce?"

"Because I'm a workaholic who spends too much time at the office and Madam Irenka's."

"Right."

"She deserves better."

"I don't disagree. Do you know why the mayor, nor anyone else at City Hall, has demanded that I fire you?"

"Because I'm brilliant and irreplaceable," Adamik answered after finishing the last of the water and accepting another bottle from Laska to diminish his hangover.

"Also right, even though they think you're a loose cannon who shouldn't be allowed to interact with government officials or the public, much less speak at a press conference. With your record, you should be a major or lieutenant colonel instead of a lieutenant."

"I speak my mind."

"Which is a bad habit for a public servant. Your candid opinions, which you frequently give the press or anyone else who asks, often make city officials and lawmakers look inept."

"They are," Adamik said.

"I don't disagree. I know their only skills are oration and making promises that, although they won't be kept, will get them reelected. Do you know why you're, at least for now, irreplaceable?"

"Because I solve crimes."

"Which the city officials take credit for, making them look good and helping them get reelected. That keeps my budget from being slashed."

"I have my job, you keep your budget, and they get reelected. Some would call that synergy. Why am I here?" Adamik asked.

"We have a triple homicide."

"Where?"

"A jogger found the bodies early this morning at the Devil's Column. The medical examiner estimates the time of death between 12:30 am and 1:30 am."

"How were they killed?"

"One was shot in the head. The others in the back."

"Robbery?"

"There were no wallets or cellphones on the bodies."

"Which means we don't know the identities of the victims."

"Their faces are being run through the national database."

"Are the bodies at the morgue?"

"I told the medical examiner to leave them in place until you arrived. An unsolved triple murder will cost the city tens of millions of dollars in tourist revenues and lost conventions. If these murders go unsolved, the mayor may think it's time for both of us to retire."

"I'll solve this."

"I know. The officers who brought you here are waiting to drive you to the crime scene. Where's your gun?"

"In my desk. I was depressed last night and decided not to take it home."

"Good decision. Take it with you."

"It took you long enough," the medical examiner said as Adamik approached the bodies.

"I had some issues this morning."

"I heard. How's your head?"

"It hurts like hell."

"Take these," he said, handing him two pills.

Adamik dry-swallowed them, not bothering to ask what they were, as he looked at the bodies.

"What do you think?" The ME asked.

"Somebody killed them as they were leaving the park," Adamik responded as he continued to stare at the corpses.

"How can you tell?"

"The position of the bodies is linear."

"What does that mean?"

"They were walking, more or less, in single file, or linearly when they were killed. If they were having a conversation, the bodies would be grouped."

Adamik knelt and took a closer look at the wounds. "There's no stippling," he said, referring to the burning of the clothing or skin by the fire emitted from the gun as the bullet left the barrel. "The killer shot them from a distance."

He next examined the shape of the wounds, explaining to the ME that if they were round, the gun would have been perpendicular to the target. Because these were ellipse-shaped, the killer fired at an angle. He went on to say that standard forensic procedure for determining where the murderer was standing was to put a trajectory rod into each wound and extend a string from them, the merger of the strings giving the location of the shooter. Not having either the trajectory rods or string, Adamik eyeballed from the shape of the wounds the angle at which the bullets entered the bodies, extrapolating that they came from the left tower of the Basilica.

"I'm going to the tower," he told the ME.

"Can I take the bodies to the morgue? I'd like to get started on the autopsies."

"Not yet," he said without elaborating as he started toward the Basilica.

Adamik found the heavy wood door to the left tower had been pried open and left ajar, the wooden jamb around the metal lock splintered and pulled away from the casing. Pushing the door aside, he began climbing the forty-one-step spiral passageway that led to a nearly vertical second flight of stairs. Upon reaching it, he looked up the stairway but couldn't see where it ended. "This is going to hurt," he said as he took a deep breath, exhaled, and stepped onto the first stair. By the time he reached the viewing platform, his head was throbbing, his legs were on fire, and he was out of breath. He didn't so much as sit as collapsed onto the icy stone floor because his legs were wobbly, and he could no longer stand. He wanted to puke but kept it under control, closing his eyes and taking deep breaths. Feeling better several minutes later, he opened his eyes and looked around the platform, seeing numerous footprints on the thin dusting of snow that covered the ice, some of which appeared to lead to where he was sitting. Realizing that he was sitting on evidence, he stood. Trying not to obliterate any more footprints than he already had, he carefully walked to the platform's edge, avoiding stepping on the rest of the evidence.

He noticed that somebody had scraped the snow away from the stone capping in two spots, which appeared to be the perfect width for a tripod. Believing this is where the killer stood because it faced the direction of the bodies, he tried to find the shell casings. He believed that in the dark, the killer would miss or didn't want to look for them since there were three dead bodies a thousand yards away which, from their lack of identification, he'd searched.

That assumption proved correct when, after a ten-minute search, he found three casings in a crevice between the stone floor and the wall enclosing the viewing platform. That they were almost invisible in daylight meant that even if the killer had searched for them, they'd be impossible to find at night. He called one of the officers who accompanied him to the crime scene, asking them to bring gloves, evidence bags, and a roll of crime scene tape to the top of the Basilica's left tower. As he waited, Adamik photographed the area.

When the officer arrived, looking no worse for wear than if he'd walked across the street, the detective put on the latex gloves and placed the shell casings in an evidence bag, using the tip of his pen to remove them from the crevice.

"Tape off the entrance at the base of the tower," the detective said, afterward calling forensics and telling them to send a team.

When Adamik returned to the bodies, Colonel Laska was waiting.

"Did you find anything?" He asked.

"Three 7.62x54R rifle cartridges," the detective replied, handing him the evidence bag. "The killer used Russian ammunition."

"How could you know that?"

"These casings are the same type I found outside the home of the murdered Russian dissident."

"I recall the case but not the cartridges. Why do they have to be Russian?" Laska asked.

"They produced this munition for over half a century because it's an incredibly accurate bullet and, with a weight of one hundred fifty-two grains, delivers an absurd amount of energy on impact. It was the standard ammunition for Russian and Eastern European snipers during the Cold War. Professionals only use ammunition they trust and with which they're familiar."

"You're saying this killer is a former Russian or Eastern Bloc sniper?"

"That would be my guess. Because the killer took his shots from the tower, they either followed their targets or knew ahead of time they'd be at the Devil's Column."

"Someone didn't want these three talking," Laska said.

"Did the facial recognition database give us their names?"

"The younger victims are Deborah Miller and Paul Shepherd. Both are attachés at the United States Embassy."

"And the third?"

"Egor Lisov, a diplomat at the Russian Embassy rumored to be their senior FSB agent."

"Not a good day for diplomatic immunity."

"I was hoping they'd be tourists," Laska lamented. "Everything gets complicated when foreign governments and politicians are involved, especially when diplomats are killed."

"Do you still want me to investigate these deaths? When I try to question those at the Russian and American embassies who knew the deceased, they'll claim diplomatic immunity and toss me out the door. If they provide information, it'll be a lie to divert me from the truth. Therefore, since I can't speak with anyone who might know what this is about, wouldn't it be better to let them handle the situation?"

"The Russians and Americans?"

"Yes," Adamik replied.

"They might not know any more than you. Given you suspect it was a professional hit by a Russian or Eastern European assassin, this seems to fit the FSB's mentality of silencing those who know too much and are now a liability. They would have contracted the hit without telling anyone at the Russian embassy; the two Americans included in the contract or collateral damage."

Adamik knew Laska had a point in that the FSB had a reputation for getting rid of its problem people and those with whom they were involved by putting a bullet in them. At the same time, the Americans preferred to send their problems to a foreign rendition site where they could be interrogated and forgotten about.

"If you don't find the murderer, the president is going to offer someone's head to appease the press and our unesteemed politicians," Laska continued.

"You'll be the one decapitated."

"Not if you solve the murders."

"I'll need to go outside the lines and bend the rules."

"You always break the rules; you don't bend them. That's why I live on Maalox when you're on a case."

"Considering I'm dealing with two embassies who won't cooperate, and an assassin likely contracted by the FSB, I'll need to be more aggressive than usual."

"What does that mean?"

"You don't want to know."

"You're right," Laska said. "Because this investigation involves two countries, try and be discreet for my sake. I'd like to retire at my present rank and not as a desk sergeant," he commented as he turned and went to his car.

Adamik returned to the two officers, who were standing beside their vehicle. "Back to the station?" One of them asked with anticipation.

"Not yet. We're following the van to the morgue," the detective replied, pointing to the coroner's vehicle. "I want to have another look at the bodies before the medical examiner performs the autopsies."

A coroner is generally a person without medical training who's in charge of the morgue and works with law enforcement to investigate unusual deaths in their jurisdiction, sign death certificates, return belongings to the deceased's family, and perform other related functions. In contrast, a medical examiner is a physician with advanced pathology and forensics training. Therefore, the coroner relies on the medical examiner for the cause of death.

Although distance-wise, the morgue was relatively close, it took forty-five minutes to get there in dense, early-morning traffic countering the typical Prague driver. Czech drivers are widely considered some of the worst in the world because of the high rate of car accidents per capita caused by habitual speeding, tailgating, texting/talking, and a disregard for pedestrians. That Adamik was in a police vehicle didn't matter because drivers knew that law enforcement for traffic violations was notoriously lax, police electing to focus on crime rather than violations, letting drivers and their insurance companies sort out the responsibility for accidents.

The police vehicle followed the van to the morgue parking lot and pulled in beside it. As the bodies were taken into the building, Adamik received no argument when he asked the officers to remain outside, both men happy to smoke a cigarette rather than watching three corpses being cut open.

Once in the autopsy room, the cadavers were placed on adjustable-height stainless steel tables and stripped of their clothing, the tables having raised edges to prevent blood and fluids from flowing onto the floor and slanted to facilitate draining.

"Don't you want to watch?" The ME asked, seeing that Adamik was preoccupied with the victim's clothing.

"Go ahead; I have something I need to do," he said as he began slicing the man's parka with his pocketknife.

"Why are you doing that?"

"Each victim was likely an intelligence operative. I want to see if they hid something in their clothing."

"Even a rookie police officer knows that anyone with a diplomatic passport, including dead intelligence operatives, still retain diplomatic immunity and can't be searched, making what you're doing illegal."

"They must have taught that after I left the academy," Adamik said, continuing to take apart the man's garment.

"Don't destroy it; press the fabric together so you can feel if there's something inside. How's the coroner going to explain their clothing being ripped to shreds?"

"He'll need to be creative," Adamik answered as he continued deconstructing the parka, after which he removed the stitching from the rest of their clothing, ultimately finding nothing hidden inside the garments.

"Did you find anything?" The ME asked, glancing up from the autopsy table.

"Not yet," Adamik said as he grabbed Lisov's boots. He began to disassemble one by trying to tear off the heel, finding instead that it twisted to reveal a cavity. Within it was a flash drive and a tightly folded piece of paper. The image on the paper was of a man sitting on a bench and wearing an overcoat and gloves—his face blurred to be unrecognizable. He continued with the other five boots, finding nothing hidden within them.

"Is there a computer nearby?" The detective asked the ME, who was extracting the bullet from Lisov's brain.

"In that office," he answered, gesturing with his head to a room on his right.

Adamik entered the small office and inserted the flash drive into the USB port. A couple of seconds later, the word Vigilant appeared in the center of the screen with Top Secret in heavy red block letters below it. He clicked to the next page, bringing up an annotated color map of the Atlantic Ocean, the same security classification appearing at the top and bottom of the screen. Extending across the ocean was a solid red line, along which were a series of X's, each having a latitude, longitude, and date below. Successive pages on the drive, which were similarly classified, showed detailed schematics of the interior of a ship named *Resolute Eagle*, a diagram of the vessel's security systems, the stations at which security personnel were posted, and the location of Vigilant's command and control consoles. The following three pages provided the flight path and airborne schedule of the RQ-4 surveillance drone and the depth, standoff distance, routing, and other technical details for the *USS Florida*.

After removing the flash drive from the computer, Adamik took a closer look at the photo and saw that the person with the blurred face was lifting the armrest on a bench and dropping a flash drive with a red circle into the recess below. He suspected his drive was a copy of the original because it lacked the red circle. The detective knew that solving this case was going to be extremely complicated, not only due to the issue of diplomatic immunity but also because he suspected the Russian government was involved in a covert operation involving a top secret system the Americans called Vigilant, which he believed was the root cause of this triple homicide.

In beginning to piece this puzzle together, Adamik assumed that the person who stole this highly sensitive information from the Americans and put it on a flash drive was, because of Lisov's nationality, a Russian asset. Not believing in coincidences, he also assumed that Lisov was an American spy because he not only photographed the drop but made a copy of that flash drive, and was in the process of delivering them to the embassy attachés when Moscow decided to clear the playing field and get rid of him and anyone with whom he had contact so they could protect the identity of their American spy. What he didn't understand was why Lisov had blurred the face in the photograph since he obviously saw it. Given these assumptions and where he knew his investigation was headed, and the diplomatic issues his accusations would cause, he put the picture and drive in his pocket and went to see Laska.

"You shredded the diplomat's clothing," Laska exclaimed. "That's the same as searching them. Their diplomatic immunity applies even if they're dead. How am I going to explain to the ambassadors three naked corpses and a pile of material that used to be their garments?"

"I sent the officers who drove me here to a thrift store with my credit card. The ME said he'd change his records to reflect that's what they wore when they arrived."

"Minus the blood splatter and the bullet hole in the woman's clothing because she was shot in the back."

"I realize there are a couple of flaws in that plan, but regardless of how I got the information," Adamik said, "it looks like we know the reason for the murders."

"Which we can't tell anyone because if my boss at the Ministry of the Interior or the Minister of Foreign Affairs learn of how you got this information, both would have our asses because of the embarrassment it'd cause, notwithstanding that they'd never let us give your theory to the media as it would make Prague look like a place where intelligence agencies settle their differences. I'm also certain the Americans and Russians don't want to air their dirty laundry and would be pissed at us for disclosing what we know," Laska said, grabbing the bottle of Maalox from his desk and taking a long drink.

"What I said will never be in a report. I'll write it as a triple homicide."

"Which mayor will demand we solve because of its impact on

tourism. However, since we can't solve the crime because it'll drag in the Russians and Americans, we're screwed either way."

"What do you want me to do?"

"I'll tell you after I have coffee with a friend."

CHAPTER 3

AMBASSADOR ROBERT IWINSKI WAS six feet five inches tall, had short salt and pepper hair, a thickset build, and spoke with a crisp, distinctive speech that evoked confidence. The call from Colonel Laska on the deaths of Miller and Shepherd hit him hard. Although he knew they were CIA operatives whom the State Department let carry the embassy title of attaché, he couldn't recall the last time someone with diplomatic credentials, even if they were a known intelligence agent, was killed. The unwritten policy among governments was that foreign operatives were free to operate unharmed, even on another country's soil, as long as they had diplomatic credentials, which gave them the same immunity from arrest or detention as the ambassador and their staff. That hands-off policy prevented bloodshed and increased scrutiny by the host country, which would make it exponentially more challenging to conduct covert operations.

Miller and Shepherd were at the beginning of a two-month assignment, their cover being that they worked for the State Department and were conducting a routine audit of the books. Because not everyone at the embassy worked for the CIA, it seemed a reasonable ruse. When not at their job, they appeared to be bureaucrats who took advantage of their overseas assignment by being tourists who wandered through parks after work and visited the city's landmarks and museums.

Upon hearing the news of the attaché's deaths, Iwinski called

Mark Calbot, the CIA's Chief of Station, and informed him of the murders.

"I've heard," Calbot said.

"Who told you?"

Calbot shrugged, indicating he wasn't going to get an answer.

"And you didn't tell me?"

"Don't take it personally, but you're a terrible actor. I wanted you to sound surprised when the police called."

"What can you tell me about their deaths?" He asked, believing the COS, with whom he had a reasonable relationship, wouldn't disclose much. To his surprise, Calbot told him significantly more than he expected, making the ambassador wonder what the future tit-for-tat would be for these revelations.

"Miller and Shepherd were going to escort a Russian defector to a waiting US military aircraft at the Prague-Kbely Airport that would transport him to the States where he'd be debriefed and afterward enter the Federal Witness Protection Program. When they didn't show up, I sent an NOC to look for them. She found the three bodies and called me."

Iwinski knew that NOC meant non-official cover—one of the Agency's operatives working in a covert role outside the embassy, and therefore without diplomatic protection.

Calbot removed the phone from his pocket and, after a few clicks, handed it to Iwinski. "These are photographs of the bodies taken at the murder site."

Iwinski looked at them and returned the phone. "The killer knew about the meeting," he said.

"It looks that way."

"Why didn't you or the NOC go to the meet instead of the rookies?"

"You can appreciate that, in Prague, every COS knows every other COS because we sometimes cooperate against adversaries when it's to our mutual advantage."

"And the NOC?"

"She's our top in-country asset and too valuable to risk. If I sent her to meet with Egor Lisov, who the police will tell you is the third victim, she'd no longer be useful to me, and I might as well put her on the morning flight to Dulles. The newbies were the perfect cover. Either Lisov was careless, and someone learned of the meeting, which is doubtful given his experience and that we never had an issue in the past, or there was a leak on our side."

"What was Lisov giving you?"

"That's out of bounds," Calbot replied.

"What will be the Agency's response?"

"Nothing. We're in a risky business, which is why we have one hundred forty stars carved into the marble of the Memorial Wall at Langley. We have no desire to add more. If we find out who pulled the trigger, we'll put a star on their wall or barter for something that will be painful for the Russians to give us."

"Why meet in the park in the middle of the night when I know you have safehouses?"

Calbot cleared his throat. "That wasn't my call. Lisov wanted to meet someplace other than one of our safehouses in case they were under surveillance. Normally, I'd tell him to stick to our protocols, but he said he had information vital to our national security. I gave in since he was an invaluable asset and had always been reliable. Looking back, I believe he thought it was only a matter of time until the Russians learned of where one or more of our safehouses were. He wanted to play it safe since he knew he'd leave the country following the meeting. It's unusual that he was killed and not captured and interrogated to find out what he'd given us. However, given he was with two of our agents, the Russians may have felt they didn't have the time or the manpower in place to extract him."

"Three murders in a city park in the middle of the night will get tremendous play in the media. The mayor, along with the other bureaucrats in City Hall, will put the screws to the police to find the killer. They'll start by asking the Russian ambassador and me questions, which we don't have to answer because we're diplomats. That lack of response will be leaked to the press, who seeing that the victims were from the American and Russian embassies, will make this into a spy incident. They'll do their best to create international intrigue to increase their readership," Iwinski pointed out. "The CIA will be dragged into these killings by implication."

"I can't let that scenario unfold. A better story would be that Lisov had a heart attack and died far away from Miller and Shepherd, who were killed by robbers while being stupid enough to walk through a park at night because it was a romantic place to watch the stars or for some other bullshit reason," Calbot offered.

"That may be possible. Colonel Laska will be under a lot of pressure to solve these murders, and he owes me a favor. But I don't think he'll falsify a police report for three embassy officials unless he also benefits."

"How about doing away with the murders and making the deaths accidental? Tell him the American government will go along with Shepherd and Miller dying in a car accident. He can tell the Russians, who I'm sure he's already informed of the Lisov's murder, that the on-scene officers were wrong about his cause of death and that it wasn't a bullet to the head that killed him but a heart attack."

"Everyone will see the hole in his head when he's returned to Moscow. The families of the American attachés will also see they've been shot," the ambassador said.

"Not if the three are returned in urns. We'll have the bodies cremated at an Agency-friendly mortuary."

"Won't the Russians go postal when the coroner gives them an urn instead of a body?" Iwinski asked.

"They'll be happy to get rid of the corpse and not have to answer questions about how Lisov died."

"And Colonel Laska won't be under pressure to solve these crimes because car accidents and heart attacks aren't his fault," Iwinski added.

"Which is how he benefits."

"I'll speak with him."

"I owe you," Calbot said.

"Yes, you do."

The call from Laska surprised Iwinski, who was going to call him later that day. The two had a good relationship, which started the week after the ambassador arrived in Prague when he phoned and asked for a meeting to establish an open-door policy between them. Laska, largely ignored by Iwinski's predecessor, liked the affable American, and the relationship between the two strengthened with time.

The colonel suggested they meet at the Café Slavia, where they first met. Founded in 1884, it had a magnificent view of the Charles Bridge, Prague Castle, and National Theatre. Iwinski arrived early and was sitting at a table with two cups of double espresso when Laska entered the café. The ambassador stood as he approached, the two men shaking hands.

"I took the liberty of ordering you a double espresso," the ambassador said.

Laska took a sip without adding a sweetener. "The caffeine helps. It's been a rough morning for both of us. What can the Prague police do for my friend and, by extension, the American government?"

"I have a proposal regarding the disposition of the bodies of our embassy attachés and the Russian," Iwinski began, getting straight to the point.

"The CIA told you about Egor Lisov?"

"They knew about the murders before I did," Iwinski said.

"What were they doing in Vyšehrad Park in the middle of the night?"

"You've probably determined that my attachés weren't paper-pushers but worked for the CIA."

"The detective I assigned to the case figured that out," Laska said, explaining that Adamik believed Lisov was an American asset based on what was hidden in his clothing. If the ambassador was upset that Adamik had violated diplomatic immunity, he didn't show it.

"Your detective is right," Iwinski acknowledged, providing more detail on Lisov and that the attachés were going to escort him to an aircraft waiting to take him to the States.

"Any thoughts on where we go from here? I only ask because the mayor is going to roast me when I can't find the person responsible for a triple homicide, which is unlikely given that I suspect the Russians contracted for the murders," Laska said.

"Interestingly, Mark Calbot, the CIA's Chief of Station, gave me a possible solution to this dilemma. He and I believe the Russians don't want the scrutiny of someone making this into an incident that would put a spotlight on their activities in Prague. He's suggesting that you change their cause of death so that the Americans died in a car accident and Lisov of a cardiac arrest. The Russians will go along with a heart attack because they'd like to hide these killings as much as the CIA. His age and the hypothetical assumption of over-exertion in cold weather would make his cause of death believable. I'll go along with a car accident for the attachés."

"Our country's policy is to return bodies to the families or next of kin of the deceased. They or someone at the mortuary will see they've been murdered."

"That can still happen, but instead of a coffin, their bodies will be in urns," Iwinski replied. "Calbot says he'll handle the cremation so you won't be involved."

"I suppose your attachés could have been mutilated beyond recognition, so an open casket viewing is impossible. I can also add there was a bio-hazard risk from blood and exposed organs as another reason for the cremation. But are you sure the Russians will go along? This will blow up in our face if they don't."

"I think they'll go along with cremation because they want to hide this incident, and the lack of a body makes that possible. I'll have Calbot coordinate with his COS counterpart at the Russian Embassy to ensure we're all on the same page."

"The mayor wouldn't mind three fewer homicides. Murders aren't the best advertisements for tourism," Laska admitted.

"That leaves the autopsy, forensic, and crime scene reports—which will need to be changed," Iwinski said. "How will you handle that?"

"Není náš problém," Laska replied.

"That's not our problem," Iwinski, who was somewhat familiar with the Czech language, translated.

"We used this saying during the Cold War, meaning we'll forget about the incident, wipe it from our books, and never discuss it. Occasionally, we still practice what you would call turning your head in the other direction."

"Will everyone go along with re-doing the documentation?"

"We're a team with the singular goal of doing what's best for the community. The absence of a triple homicide, which has nothing to do with civic crime, will make the public feel safer, and it will keep the politicians out of our business."

"Does that include the autopsy reports?" Iwinski asked to clarify if Laska's definition of team extended beyond the police department.

"The ME is a close friend. The three autopsies will reflect our version of their deaths. Once I receive them, I'll close the investigation."

"About that. I'd like you to find out who's behind these killings and, if possible, identify the killer," Iwinski stated, surprising Laska. "I'm saying, if possible, because Moscow may have used imported talent."

"I thought you wanted this to go away?"

"I do. But I don't trust the CIA because I'm not convinced they've given me all the facts. Their story could be a plausible explanation of events meant to obfuscate what actually happened. In the future, if what we've done comes out, they'll claim we thought of this on our own, and we'll be sacrificed to protect the Agency. Having the facts will allow us, if needed, to hold something over their heads and come out of this with our skin attached."

"That you don't fully believe anyone's story would have made you a good police officer," Laska said, handing him the flash drive and the folded piece of paper that Adamik discovered.

"What are these?"

The colonel explained how his detective discovered them hidden in one of Lisov's shoes. "The flash drive contains information on a classified United States project called Vigilant."

"I never heard of it," Iwinski said before unfolding the paper and looking at the pixelated photo. "The face must have been blurred for a reason. It's another mystery to add to what we don't know. Did you make a copy?"

Laska confirmed that he'd made a duplicate of the photo and flash drive and put them in his office safe. "Are you going to give those to your Chief of Station?" He asked.

"Not yet. The CIA can be heavy-handed. I don't want them interfering with your investigation."

"I appreciate it."

"Who knows about what you found on Lisov?" The ambassador asked.

"You, me, and Adamik."

"Let's keep it that way. Is your detective good enough to get us the facts behind these killings?"

"He has a one hundred percent success rate in solving crimes," Laska stated.

"How will you explain an investigation into three non-suspicious deaths where no crime has been committed?" Iwinski asked.

"I think I have a way. As soon as we finish, I'll go to the brothel and speak with Adamik."

"Brothel?"

CHAPTER 4

THE *RESOLUTE EAGLE* WAS anchored in the choppy waters north of Bermuda after having lowered the first of the ninety-seven UFPs to the ocean floor nineteen thousand feet below the ship's hull. Technicians were now going through the two-hour process of activating the underwater communications link and the missile, after which the ship would raise anchor and move to the next insertion point.

Because they were in a prime fishing area, before hoisting the capsuled missile from the hold and onto the deck, affixing it to the tethered weight, and lowering it to the seafloor, a process that took four hours, the captain needed to ensure that no vessel was close enough to see what they were doing. As the ship's radar only had a range of twenty-five miles, and he needed a one-hundred-mile vessel-free privacy zone around the ship, he relied upon the visual and electronic feeds from the RQ-4 flying overhead to give him this information—the drone's camera providing a three hundred mile circular view around the *Eagle*.

Once the privacy area was verified, the captain authorized the insertion process to begin. Two hours later, with the missile halfway to the seafloor, the Global Hawk showed a vessel breaching its one-hundred-mile exclusion zone, projecting that its course would eventually take it less than a hundred yards past the *Eagle's* bow. As the Global Hawk's cameras zoomed in on the offending vessel, a twin-craned trawler towing a long fishing net that extended seven miles behind it appeared on the captain's LED screen.

"How long until it passes our bow?" The captain asked the crewman charged with syncing the drone's feed who, although he couldn't pilot the aircraft, could change its camera angle and magnification.

"At present speed, four hours," came the reply after several taps on his keyboard.

"We should be done by then. Let me know if they change course or speed," he said, returning to Vigilant's command and control consoles, which showed the depth and status of the UFP capsule that was being lowered.

Sixty feet below the water and ten miles from the *Resolute Eagle*, the captain of the *USS Florida*, Commander William Quinn, who was ordered to protect the unmarked Navy vessel and keep it within view at all times, watched it through one of two photonic masts, which sent color, high-solution black-and-white, and infrared imaging to the large LED screen in front of him. He could have maintained visual contact with the *Eagle* from as far as fifteen miles away but decided that ten miles made him inconspicuous enough for any fishing vessel that saw the masts to conclude that his boat was watching another ship. Like the *Eagle*, the *USS Florida* received the Global Hawk's visual and electronic feeds.

Quinn didn't like the idea of a ship getting close to the unmarked Navy vessel, but there was nothing he could do to get it to change course without calling attention to his boat. He thought about calling the *Eagle's* captain *to* warn him of the approaching ship. However, since they both received the Global Hawk's feeds, he believed that wasn't necessary. Therefore, for nearly four hours, he followed the trawler's progress.

"When will the ship pass over us, how long is their net, and how deep does it go?" Quinn asked his executive officer in rapid succession, knowing that some nets extended miles behind a vessel and were weighted to go as deep as five thousand feet.

The XO checked with sonar, receiving the answers seconds later.

"The trawler will pass over us in eight minutes and twenty seconds," the XO repeated, adding that its fishing net extended seven miles behind the vessel and twenty-five feet below the surface.

The *Florida* was neutrally buoyant, meaning its density was equal to that of the fluid in which it was immersed. Therefore, it neither rose nor sank. If it wanted to go deeper without using its forward motion and dive planes to submerge rapidly, it needed to become negatively buoyant. It did this by pumping water into the ballast tanks, thereby increasing the sub's weight and exceeding the weight of the volume of water it displaced. Therefore, because the trawler was on a course to pass over it, Quinn needed to decide whether to get underway and move out of the trawler's path, go deeper, or maintain his position, the bottom of the fishing net estimated to pass thirty-five feet above it once he lowered the masts.

"We'll maintain position. Retract the masts and inform me if the net settles deeper," the captain ordered.

Minutes later, sonar advised they had a problem in that, while the trawler had passed over *Florida*, the net hadn't.

"What precisely does that mean?" The captain asked.

"The trawler lost its net as it passed over us, and it's draped over our boat."

The captain knew from experience that a small commercial net weighed between one and a half to two pounds a foot because he'd used one that was fourteen feet in diameter to go saltwater fishing for a small fishery before joining the Navy. He believed this was less than the deep sea commercial net that engulfed his boat because he hadn't been fishing as deep. However, if he used those same numbers, with a length of seven miles, the weight of the net draped over *Florida* would be a minimum of twenty-eight tons.

Trying to see what was on top of them, Quinn attempted to extend the starboard mast which, although unable to protrude above the sail, showed the net entangling it. The same occurred when he tried to raise the port mast.

"Launch the Razorback so I can look at the boat from a distance," he told the XO.

Once the torpedo room received the order, the breech door in one of the eight torpedo tubes was opened and the Razorback pushed inside, after which the tube was sealed and flooded, and the pressure equalized. The next step in the launch process should have been opening the muzzle door, which would dart the Razorback into the water once a ram with thousands of pounds of water pressure pushed it out of the tube fast enough for the main motor to start. However, when the button to open the muzzle door was pressed, a red light appeared on the fault panel, indicating it remained shut. Not bothering to find and correct the problem because time was always of the essence when launching anything from a torpedo tube, the crew quickly moved the Razorback to an adjacent tube, receiving the same fault indication. Determining the problem may lie with the muzzle doors, they attempted to open the remaining six, receiving the same fault indication. The torpedo room informed the XO, who told the captain that all eight torpedo tubes were inoperative.

"Surface," the captain ordered, figuring that was the fastest way to remove the net and survey the boat for damage.

However, as the controls were engaged to bring *Florida* topside, the boat jerked sharply to starboard, causing the chief engineer to quickly shut down propulsion to prevent the system from being damaged. He contacted the bridge, saying that his indicator panel showed excessive torque on the propeller and that the diving planes were jammed.

Quinn turned to his XO. "Have the SEAL team leader inspect the outside of the boat for damage and the extent to which the net has become entangled with our systems," the captain said.

Five minutes later, two special forces operators entered the sub's airlock. After securing the interior hatch and waiting for the chamber to fill with water and the pressure to equalize, one opened the outside hatch. Even though the visibility wasn't the greatest, they couldn't miss the enormous nylon fishing net that enshrouded the submarine. The divers, fighting their way between the weighted net and the hull, surveyed the boat and reported that the net jammed the diving planes, wrapped around the propeller, and was sucked into the boat's water inlets, the latter important because they were vital for pumping salt water into the sub's distillation equipment—producing the fresh water that was critical for cooling the nuclear reactor.

"How long do you estimate it'll take to clear the net from the boat?" Quinn asked the divers through the comm link, which he put on speaker so that he and the XO could hear.

"Not long if my entire team works on it. Once we pull or cut it from where it's become entangled, the remainder should fall away from the boat and sink to the ocean floor under its weight."

"Get started, beginning with clearing the water inlets," the captain ordered, prioritizing getting coolant to the reactor. He then turned to his XO, telling him to check with sonar to see if the *Resolute Eagle* had moved.

"It's still at anchor, but the trawler that lost the net has stopped beside it," the executive officer reported.

"What?" The captain said.

"Maybe they think the Eagle's crew can help them retrieve their net," the XO remarked.

"That net is too heavy to do anything but sink to the ocean floor."

"Should we inform command and the *Resolute Eagle* of our situation?" The XO asked.

Because Quinn believed the Global Hawk had the ship under surveillance, he thought command saw the trawler pull alongside the *Eagle* and they had been in contact with the ship's captain to determine if there was a situation that required *Florida* to take action. Since he hadn't received a distress signal from the ship or orders from command to dispatch the SEALs, he assumed there wasn't a problem.

However, the overriding reason he wasn't anxious to call the *Eagle* or inform command of his situation was self-preservation. Even though the entanglement with the net wasn't his fault, he'd screwed up in not moving his boat and allowing the fishing vessel to pass over *Florida,* breaching his orders of keeping the *Resolute Eagle* under constant visual surveillance when he lowered his masts instead of repositioning the boat. Although his actions didn't impact the ship he was to surveil, he'd still violated orders. He expected the Navy to make an example of him so that anyone who thought they could unilaterally override orders without consequence would find themselves, as he expected, riding a desk and being removed from the promotion pool. Not eager to immediately end his career by calling command, Quinn put the incident in his log where he believed that if *Eagle* accomplished its mission and returned safely to port, no one would bother to read it, especially if he didn't flag the incident.

As the *USS Florida* became enshrouded in the fishing net, the *Eagle's* captain was focused on the video feed from the RQ-4 that was circling forty-thousand feet overhead, zooming in on the trawler which was now ten miles away and on a course that would take it perilously close to his ship. The approaching vessel was in the center of his LED monitor, the resolution so good he could see the ship's bow cutting through the light ocean waves, when the video suddenly disappeared, replaced by a *signal lost* notation.

"What happened?" The captain asked, unhappy that he'd lost the visual on the trawler that was on a course for his ship.

The crewmember standing beside him, who had the military occupational special or MOS of an electrical technician, which was a catchall for just about anything on the vessel that had a wire connected to it, had no idea because he was unfamiliar with the drone surveillance system installed on the ship. Grabbing the troubleshooting checklist, he scrambled for an answer to the captain's question about what went wrong. However, what no one on the *Eagle* knew was that minutes before, two of the trawler's crew had removed the tarp covering the 150-kilowatt high-energy rotating laser weapon on the ship's bow, which was beneath a steel plate that hid it from aircraft and spy satellites. Controlled by several techs in a compartment one deck below the bridge, the laser synced with the trawler's tracking radar and locked on the drone, emitting a massive number of photons that struck it at the speed of light and disintegrated the aircraft within milliseconds. In the daytime, and from eight and ten miles away, the distances from the *Eagle* to the drone and *Florida*, the stream of photons that struck the aircraft were invisible. The Global Hawk exploded, sending fiery debris cascading into the ocean. Its pilot, flying the drone from Creech AFB in Nevada, knew the aircraft was a goner when the RQ-4 became non-responsive and every fault light on his display panel suddenly illuminated, indicating the Global Hawk met a catastrophic end.

The pilot's initial thought was that a missile had struck the aircraft. However, he discounted that belief because the drone had a sophisticated missile detection system that hadn't sensed an air-to-air or ground-to-air threat locking onto it. Therefore, what caused the demise of the two hundred twenty-two million dollar aircraft was in limbo when Rear Admiral Baird, upon learning that he no longer had aerial surveillance of the *Resolute Eagle*, ordered the launch of a replacement RQ-4. He was confident that the ship was safe because the *USS Florida* had it in sight and would have sent a message if there was a problem. That it didn't, and there was no distress signal from the *Eagle*, led him to believe the mission was proceeding smoothly, an assumption he failed to verify by calling either the ship or the sub.

Onboard the *Resolute Eagle*, the loss of the Global Hawk's video didn't alarm those on the bridge because everyone believed tech glitches happened, a presumption they wouldn't have made had someone seen the aircraft explosion or the falling debris. That they didn't was because their visual perception extended only to the horizon which, because of the height of the bridge above the ocean, was eight and a half miles away, the destruction of the Global Hawk occurring a miles and a half beyond that limitation.

Now relying on radar, the captain watched on the green screen as the trawler continued toward his vessel. Because he was at anchor, which took seven minutes to raise because the ship employed a 7:1 ratio, meaning the length of its chain was seven times that of the ship, and the trawler was an estimated six minutes away, he couldn't move the *Eagle* fast enough to avoid the impact that would occur if the approaching ship didn't change course. Believing that no one wanted a collision at sea and that the trawler's captain was oblivious to what was happening or he would have changed course, he decided to give the trawler an audible warning.

"Sound five short blasts," the captain ordered, which was the international signal for danger.

Despite the one-hundred-fifteen decibel blast from the ship's horn, which could be heard two miles away, the trawler's course remained unaltered.

"Why isn't it changing course?" The first officer asked.

"Everyone may be working below deck, their radar could be non-functional, or they may be drunk," the captain replied, the tension in his voice betraying his nervousness. "I'd bet on the latter. It wouldn't be the first time a fishing crew returning to port set its controls on automatic and, knowing they were in a large ocean where the likelihood of striking another vessel was minuscule, were below deck drinking. Sound emergency and order the crew to brace for collision."

Immediately after that, the ship's horn sounded seven short blasts and one long, followed by the first officer's order to brace. Everyone onboard grabbed onto something immovable and waited for the impact. However, because the trawler had earlier cut power and turned to starboard, instead of its bow striking the Eagle amidships, its port side slammed against the hull of the Navy ship. Immediately afterward, boarding planks were extended onto the *Eagle*, and forty men carrying automatic weapons raced onto the Navy ship with lightning speed, securing the bridge and taking the crew prisoner before anyone onboard, believing at first they'd narrowly avoided a collision at sea, could notify command that the *Resolute Eagle* had been seized.

"Forty-two crew members are locked in a compartment below deck, and their phones have been thrown overboard," Major Misha Vetrov said to Rear Admiral Tolya Balandin, who was bent over the *Eagle's* navigation table. Vetrov and the other thirty-nine men who boarded the ship were Spetsnaz—a special forces team within the Russian military intelligence organization known as the GRU, which conducted covert operations outside the homeland. Vetrov was in his early thirties, six feet six inches tall, bald, and had a chiseled face and muscular body. In contrast, Balandin was fifteen years older, lean, and six feet three inches tall. He had seashell ears that seemed too small for his frame, a slightly crooked jaw, close-cropped nut-brown hair, and a stubble beard.

Balandin was looking at a paper chart that laid out the locations where the UFPs were to be placed, ignoring the electronic version on a tablet at the corner of the navigation table. Taking the plotting compass, he laid out a row of dead reckoning positions to Mariel Naval Base in Cuba, afterward leaving it on the table.

"Are the ship's GPS equipment and transponders switched off?" Balandin asked, turning his attention to Vetrov.

"They were disabled, as you predicted."

"We have two hours to transfer everything to our ship. Any

longer, and we risk the submarine cutting itself free and sinking our vessel," the admiral said, reiterating their timeframe.

"We'll be done by then," he confidently stated, leaving the bridge to ensure he kept that promise.

Two hours and ten minutes after the collision, the trawler pushed away from the *Resolute Eagle*. An hour later, the *USS Florida* freed itself from the net and, after failing to contact the ship using several frequencies and not getting a video feed from the Global Hawk, surfaced and brought itself abeam of the vessel, stopping fifty yards away.

"The ship appears deserted," the XO said to Quinn, both standing on the submarine's sail and looking at the *Eagle* through their binoculars.

"Something's not right. Sound general quarters, condition one easy," the captain ordered, sending the crew to their action stations with the implied warning that action was probable and that they lacked precise information on the enemy.

When they left the sail and returned to the bridge, Quinn summoned the SEAL team commander, who had heard the order to go to general quarters and was geared up and looked ready for a conflict when he walked onto the bridge.

"We've lost contact with the *Resolute Eagle*, and the ship appears deserted," Quinn said without preamble, pointing to the photonic mast's video feed on his LED screen. "Take your men, go onboard, and give me a situation report. Do you have questions?"

The commander shook his head, indicating that he didn't. His facial expression remained unchanged by what he was told, viewing his orders as just another day at the office.

"You don't seem surprised," Quinn said.

"If you've been doing this as long as me, nothing surprises you. No one uses us to give advice and step aside. We're the blunt force trauma inflicted on the bad guys to get the desired result."

Quinn nodded.

"My ROE?" The team leader asked, referring to the rules of engagement, which specified the circumstances under which his team could use force to accomplish its mission.

"Weapons free if necessary to keep the *Resolute Eagle* from falling into enemy hands or to protect your team and the crew," Quinn said, giving him the authority to engage any target he deemed a threat.

The SEAL team removed their Rigid Hull Inflatable Boat, or RIB, from *Florida's* dry deck shelter, a module attached to a submarine that allowed divers to access it while submerged or, in this case, on the surface. With the seas relatively calm, it took twenty minutes to get to the *Eagle* and board the ship.

"Do you want to inform Admiral Baird of the situation?" The XO asked the captain, politely suggesting he brief the ONR on what happened as both men looked through their binoculars at the team boarding the vessel.

"Not until I know what we're dealing with," the captain tersely replied.

Fifteen minutes after the SEALs boarded, their team leader called Quinn and said they'd found the crew locked in a compartment below deck.

"What?" The captain involuntarily exclaimed, knowing he'd screwed up by not reporting his boat's entanglement in the fishing net and the loss of contact with the *Eagle*. "What about the cargo?"

"The holds are empty."

CHAPTER 5

"HOW AM I GOING to investigate a triple murder, documented as accidental deaths, without anyone in the office knowing there's an investigation?" Adamik, sitting in Laska's office, asked after the colonel explained what he needed from his star detective.

"Because you'll be conducting your investigation while on vacation."

"Everyone knows I don't take vacations because I get bored when I'm away from the office. They especially won't believe it when they learn I haven't left Prague. A vacation means you go somewhere."

"I've got that covered. I'll announce that after your incident at Madam Irenka's, I ordered that you take time off to pull yourself together, giving you the choice of taking a vacation or being suspended. Therefore, no one will know about this investigation except you, me, and the ambassador."

"I thought there was an agreement to put this matter to rest by documenting these deaths as accidental?"

"They have," Laska said.

"The Americans and Russians will find it suspicious when they discover, because they both have informants and excellent intelligence networks in Prague, that I'm speaking with people regarding the deceased, and I don't think I'll be asked nicely when they demand an explanation."

"Stay below their radar."

"That sounds like good advice."

"It is good advice."

"I'll need to take my office computer home to access the department's databases, labs, files, etc. I don't own a computer."

"I know. The department is loaning you one. It's being installed in your room at Madam Irenka's, and it'll have the same access privileges as the terminal in your office."

"When can I use it?"

"It's being set up now, assuming the technician isn't distracted."

"If I'm up against a professional killer who's put three bodies in the morgue, I'm going to need more than my handgun."

"Below the radar means no one suspects you're investigating. Therefore, there's no reason for anyone to shoot at you."

"Understood."

"By understood, you mean that you agree with me and will use your gun only as an absolute last resort?"

"If that makes you feel better."

Adamik decided to start his investigation by searching Egor Lisov's apartment, which was still covered by diplomatic immunity even though his ashes were about to be placed in an urn. The FSB agent lived in a small two-story apartment in *Bubeneč*, called Little Moscow by locals because the Russian Embassy was located nearby, and its employees rented in that area because of its proximity to their workplace. As they did, restaurants and businesses that catered to their ethnicity followed. Lisov lived in what was advertised as a bachelor space—a six hundred square feet unit on the top floor. Adamik had no trouble finding it because of the yellow police tape his department placed there and the tamper-proof plastic seal with Cyrillic lettering on it that was affixed between the door frame and the lockset, put there by the Russian Embassy to warn those who might want to look inside that the area was off limits because it had diplomatic immunity.

After cutting the seal with his pocketknife and finding the door locked, he removed a small leather pouch from his jacket pocket and took from it a tube of graphite lubricant, squirting it into the lock to loosen the pins. He then gently inserted into the bottom of the plug, or the part of the lock which turned, a tension wrench—a thin L-shaped piece of metal that applied torque to the plug and held the lock pins in place. With the wrench inside the lock, he inserted above it a rake—a piece of metal with multiple ridges along the top. Pushing it to the back and then moving it forward while gently pressing up in a motion called scrubbing, he moved the six internal pins upward, releasing the lock.

Stretching the police tape aside, he entered the apartment and closed the door behind him. Lisov's domicile consisted of a tiny kitchen, living room, bedroom, and bathroom, all of which looked like a tornado had hit it. Every drawer and whatever was in them had been haphazardly thrown on the floor. The couch cushions, club chair, and bed mattress were cut apart, and the polyurethane foam removed from them. The threadbare carpet had been ripped off the floor, and large sections of the plasterboard walls were cut away to see if anything was hidden beneath or behind them.

"What a mess," Adamik said as he stepped through the rubble, marveling at the destructive thoroughness of what he assumed was the FSB, which he thought wanted to remove anything that could remotely connect their agent to illegal activities or the intelligence service.

Not optimistic that the FSB had overlooked anything after such a detailed search, he nevertheless decided, since he was here, to look around. He started with the bedroom and worked his way toward the front door. That didn't take long, and forty-five minutes after he entered the apartment, he was finished with nothing to show for his efforts but the white drywall dust that covered everything within the apartment and now clung to his clothes.

Lisov had no personal photos or mementos, at least none that the FSB left. The only oddities were the dozen dog-eared magazines scattered on the floor. Each was published two and three years ago and focused on such diverse subjects as travel, food, hunting, health, etc. That they were old, perused numerous times, and written in Czech and not Russian piqued his interest. He picked one up and looked at every page, after which he selected another and went through it, noticing that one of its pages, just as in the first magazine, had a black smudge above the page number. Although marks of this type weren't unusual for periodicals this old, it was odd that the smudges on both appeared in the same location and only on one page, each advertising a different apartment complex in Prague. He reviewed the other publications, finding that each also had a single smudge on a page with a similar advertisement for local apartments.

Believing the magazines were significant, he pushed away the debris around him. He then spread the twelve periodicals on the floor, opening them to the page with the smudge to see if they shared a commonality beyond the smear and apartment complex advertisement. However, after twenty minutes of intently studying the pages, the only thing he found strange was that each magazine's publication date was in a different month. He decided to take a closer look at the pages when he got home later that day.

After leaving the apartment, he drove to the Hilton Old Town, where Shepherd and Miller stayed. He showed his credentials to the front desk and asked to see their rooms.

"I can't do that. Other guests occupy them," the front desk clerk said.

"Are you sure we're talking about the same rooms? Both guests died this morning. How could they check out?"

"They're dead?" The startled clerk asked.

"They perished in a car accident."

"Foreigners aren't used to Prague traffic," she volunteered.

"Putting our driving habits aside, if you didn't know about their deaths, and they obviously couldn't check themselves out, who did?" Adamik asked.

"Mr. Calbot from the United States Embassy did, and left with their luggage. He was technically the occupant because his credit card was on file."

"Didn't you find that leaving with their luggage was unusual?"

"I assumed his guests were busy and didn't have much time to catch their flight to the States. You'd be surprised how many, even those who've been here for a while, have told me they're going to miss their plane as they handed me their room key and said they didn't have time to review or get a copy of their bill."

Knowing it would take a warrant to search the rooms and that Calbot wouldn't have left anything, he thanked the clerk. He went to a quiet corner of the lobby and called Laska, asking him to text the passport photo that customs and immigration took of Lisov when he entered the country. He also requested that the photos of officials working at the Russian and American embassies be texted with it.

"I understand Lisov, but why the other photos?" The colonel asked.

"A hunch."

"When do you need them?"

"Ideally, in the next fifteen minutes. I'm going to show them to a few people."

"Since these are embassy employees, please be discreet and polite?"

"As always."

"I was afraid you were going to say that," Laska answered," uncapping a new bottle of Maalox after the call.

Adamik decided to visit one of the apartment complexes advertised in the magazines, selecting the one closest to the Hilton. By the time he arrived, he'd received the photos from Laska.

Pressing the button for the manager's office, he identified himself as a police detective.

"Apartment one at the end of the hall," the woman said, a buzzer announcing the door lock had been released.

When he arrived, he found the door open and a thin woman in her mid-sixties with gray hair standing at the threshold. When she didn't invite him inside, he stood in the hallway as they spoke. "Do you mind scrolling through these photos to see if you recognize any of these people?" He asked, giving her his phone.

"This one has been a visitor on occasion," the woman said after reviewing them and pointing to Lisov. "But this person rents the apartment that man visits," she quickly added, scrolling back thirty photos.

"Tell me about him."

"He told me he travels a lot and that I probably wouldn't see much of him. He also told me his sister would be living there while he was gone and showed me a photo of her. One glance, and I knew she wasn't his sister, not only because there was no resemblance between them but also because she was much younger than him.

Therefore, I assumed he rented the apartment for other reasons if you get my drift."

"Did you notice anything unusual about her?"

"I can tell you that she wasn't bored while he was away, having more than her share of male visitors."

"Did that bother you?"

"I'm not the morality police. The rent was always paid on time, she was quiet, and none of the tenants complained. I figured that whatever was going on inside their unit was none of my business."

"Do you stay in this apartment most of the time?"

The woman said she did.

"Then, how did you know about the sister's visitors and him?" Adamik asked, pointing to Lisov's picture.

She moved aside so the detective could look into the apartment. On a table beside her wall-mounted TV was an LED screen that displayed the feeds from eight security cameras. "I like to know who goes in and out of this complex," she replied.

"Do you keep these feeds on file?"

"I record over them unless someone reports an incident."

After a few more questions, the detective thanked the woman and left, driving to the other apartment complexes and speaking with their managers. All recalled seeing Lisov and remembered the renter, an attaché at the United States Embassy who Adamik suspected was a CIA agent. The managers also recalled that, just as with the first manager, the renter said that his sister would be living there while he was traveling and that she had frequent male visitors.

It was nine at night when he returned to the brothel, where he could hear customers in various stages of their entertainment cycle as he made his way down the long hallway to his room. Madam

Irenk's was designed so that each of the women's work areas would be soundproof, constructed with six-inch air cavities between their drywalls which muted the noise between each room. However, the designer never considered that the wooden doors, which were undercut, meaning there was a gap between the bottom of the door and the floor, would let the sound of what was occurring inside escape. Therefore, since patrons didn't whisper during their entertainment cycle, the sounds of those activities escaped into the hall. Although Adamik heard these cacophony of sounds as he walked to his room, he'd gotten used to them and tuned out what was happening as he passed.

When he entered his room, he saw the computer Laska had promised sitting on his desk. Putting the magazines he'd taken from Lisov's apartment beside it, he called the colonel, who was still at the office.

"You're working late."

"Documenting three accidents is time-consuming," Laska commented.

"I found some things," Adamik said, beginning to tell him about his day when the colonel cut him off.

"I think we should have this conversation in person. I'm leaving the office now and coming to the brothel," he said, ending the call before his detective could comment.

When he arrived, Madam Irenka escorted him briskly from the foyer to Adamik's room, wanting to get the police colonel out of sight before any of her clients recognized him.

"Don't you find this environment distracting?" Laska asked after she pushed him inside the room and closed the door behind him.

"You get used to it."

"I could help you find an apartment, and you could live with me until then."

"This fits my lifestyle, and the girls leave me alone unless I want company. When I'm hungry, I go to the kitchen where there's always has something hot on the stove or in the oven."

"I'm only telling you this because my wife wanted me to ask. I'm saying that if you ever want to leave paradise, let me know."

"I understand."

"I'm here because I'd rather not discuss this case, any more than we must, over the phone. Rumors are that the NSA and their Russian counterpart have tapped into our phone system."

"A good assumption."

"What did you find?" Laska asked.

The detective showed him the magazines and summarized his interviews with the managers of the twelve apartment complexes.

"The same attaché from the American Embassy rented twelve apartments?" The colonel asked. "That's probably not something an embassy employee would do. They're probably CIA."

Adamik nodded in agreement.

"From the smudge marks in these magazines, each above the page number, and because Lisov was seen at these complexes, we should assume these apartments are Agency safehouses."

"They were smart to put what I believe was a prostitute in each unit," Laska said. "If someone from the Russian Embassy saw Lisov enter the building or that apartment, he could say he was paying for a good time."

"It's a great cover," the detective admitted.

"Paying such a person's rent while allowing her to continue

seeing her clients, although there would undoubtedly be restrictions, wouldn't be a difficult sell to someone in that profession."

"And the magazines were given to Lisov so that he could have the addresses of the safehouses without writing them down," Adamik said. "Where they were to meet could be as simple as going to the apartments in their monthly order or employing a code word to indicate which safehouse would be used."

"Why didn't Shepherd and Miller meet Lisov at one of these places instead of the Devil's Column?" Laska asked.

"We may never know," the detective admitted. "He could have believed the Russians discovered the location of one or more safehouses and were watching them. Not feeling secure about going to any, he wanted to meet off the grid. The Russians somehow found out, and everyone was killed to prevent Lisov from defecting or to ensure that what he knew, and possibly told the two CIA agents, went with them to their graves."

"If the Russians killed the American agents to eliminate any possibility he told them something Moscow regards as invaluable, they'll try to kill you if they find out you have his flash drive and the photo."

"The reality is, I can't get the facts that allow us and the ambassador to have the leverage we need to protect ourselves from being a scapegoat in the future without the Russians, and possibly the Americans, trying to kill me."

"I can understand why the Russians might want you dead, but why the Americans?"

"Because I might interfere with their investigation into finding their high-level spy, warning them that they've been unmasked and allowing them to escape capture. If that happened, the CIA would never find out what they told Moscow nor the possibly sensitive information this spy could divulge about the FSB, Russian intelligence, etc."

"How will you get the Russians to come after you?" Laska asked.

"I'm going to poke the bear."

"What does that mean?"

"They'll need to find out that I have the flash drive and photo that will expose their spy. I'll also let it be known that I've only told you about it, making it more believable."

"Mentioning me isn't necessary."

"The Russians will expect it since you're my boss."

"In name only. Feel free to take all the credit and leave me out of this."

"If you say."

"I do. You're not at the top of the food chain when standing next to a bear, meaning it usually doesn't end well for the person doing the poking."

"I know, but it will quickly tell me who's involved."

"How will you let the Russians know you have the drive and photo?"

"I won't, the Americans will," Adamik said. "That's where I need your help."

"Is your detective onboard?" Iwinski asked Laska the following morning as they sat in a corner booth at the Café Slavia.

The colonel said he was, but he needed the ambassador's help to leak what Adamik found to the Russians, hoping to provoke a response to get those involved to reveal themselves.

"To be clear, he wants me to leak that he found a flash drive and photo hidden in Lisov's shoe?" Iwinski asked.

"He's counting on you knowing how to get this information to the Russians in such a way that it doesn't appear to be a CIA setup. It wouldn't hurt to add that he's kept everything to himself and not shared what he discovered with anyone at the police department."

"Keeping your name out of it."

"Please."

"Informing the CIA will be easy. I'll tell Calbot and document our conversation with an internal memo, which I'm sure he'll either classify as Top Secret or destroy. As you suspected, we have a way of spoon-feeding the Russians disinformation," Iwinski confessed. "In the past, it's proven effective. Therefore, your detective will get the response he's seeking, but it will probably get him killed."

"He knows the risks. Tell me how it's done?"

Iwinski didn't hold back. "When the State Department wants me to propagate disinformation to the Russians, I send a couple of my staff to one of several cafés in Little Russia. Our techs have previously visited most of those establishments in the area and, using miniaturized video and sound detection equipment, determined which places are being monitored. I have that list."

"The FSB wants to listen to their employees' conversations away from the embassy?" Laska asked.

"Embassy personnel, along with anyone else at the café."

"Won't they be suspicious of two American Embassy employees eating there? Wouldn't your staff be more likely to go someplace serving pizza or a burger and fries?"

"There are several embassies on the fringe of Little Russia, and ours is not that far away. As an enticement, a handful of cafés offer a thirty percent discount to anyone with an embassy ID. They also serve comfort food from other nations. This includes, I'm told, pizza and a burger and fries. I have to admit, it's a great way to gather intelligence."

"Has providing disinformation in one of these cafés worked in the past?"

"It's worked very well so far. I'll also have my staff add in their conversation that your detective didn't tell anyone because he thought that if he did, you'd demand he'd return anything he'd taken to the Russian Embassy since diplomats and attachés have immunity from search. Instead, he's running a rogue investigation while on vacation."

"That's a good hook," Laska agreed.

"Is Adamik a friend?"

"More a pain in the ass. But yes, a friend."

"Tell your friend I'll send my staff to the café at noon. After that, it'll be open season on him."

CHAPTER 6

IT WAS TEN IN the evening Washington time, two hours and fifty minutes after the trawler left the *Resolute Eagle*, when Secretary of Defense James T. Rosen, Director of National Intelligence Thomas Winegar, and Rear Admiral Michael Baird met in the SecDef's Pentagon office. Winegar was fifty-six years of age, five feet ten inches tall, and had a medium build. He'd served in several intelligence agencies before being appointed DNI and was considered methodical and thoughtful in his analysis of a situation before rendering a conclusion. In Washington, where *going along to get along* was considered a mantra, he was a breath of fresh air for anyone who wanted politics removed from the advice they were being given. Many considered him the Mark Twain of the National Security Council, not only because of his commonsense approach to complex issues and good-natured humor, but because his hair was completely white, and he had the slightly disheveled look of Twain. In sharp contrast, the SecDef was a sixty-four-year-old retired Marine Corps general with a booming voice who'd kept his hair high and tight, just as he did the day he retired from the Corps, and was still fit enough to run the Marine Corps Marathon every year since he retired.

"Whoever did this knew what was onboard the *Resolute Eagle*, exactly where and when to strike, and the security that was in place, including airborne and water surveillance. Therefore, it's difficult to believe those who planned and executed such a complex operation would use a plotting compass instead of an electronic navigation system to set a course to a destination they would need to know ahead of time. That they plotted the course using a chart on the ship they boarded makes this all the more bizarre," Baird said after the captain of the *Eagle* commented on the navigational map's plotting compass marks that led to the Mariel Naval Base.

"They're laying a trail of breadcrumbs to Cuba, hoping we'll focus our search in that direction," Rosen volunteered.

The DNI and Baird agreed.

"Do we control the UFP the *Eagle* placed on the ocean floor?" Winegar asked.

"No one does," the rear admiral replied.

"Why?"

"The setup wasn't complete."

Winegar asked him to explain the process.

"Once the missile, which was secured inside its capsule at the Genesis Corporation's Manassas, Virginia plant, is removed from the transport container, it's tethered to a self-leveling weight. The command and control consoles then perform a diagnostic of every electronic circuit. Afterward, the encapsulated missile and tethered weight are lowered to the ocean floor, where the consoles facilitate an undersea communications link between the Trident missile and the NCA," Baird said, referring to the National Command Authority.

"By NCA, you're referring to the president and the Secretary of Defense," Winegar clarified, knowing that the NCA was the ultimate military authority. Over time, the term was extended to include the commanding officers of the eleven Unified Combatant Commands, each entrusted with a nontransferable operational authority over assigned forces, irrespective of the branch of service.

"And the Unified Combat Commands," Baird added.

"One of those commands, the one in which Vigilant was placed, is under your authority," Rosen said.

The admiral verified that the SecDef's statement was correct.

Although the SecDef and Baird were on the same page, the DNI had no idea what each UCC controlled and segued back to understanding the Vigilant activation process.

"But that link with the NCA was never established," Winegar said.

"No. Therefore, the UFP is inactive and in a waiting mode until it can connect with the NCA."

"Let's go back to what you said earlier," the DNI said with a tone of urgency. "Because these consoles check every circuit in the missile and capsule, are you saying whoever stole our system has the digitized schematics for Vigilant? In other words, they have the blueprint to replicate the system?"

"A single digital integrated circuit contains billions of logic gates, flip-flops, multiplexers, and other circuits, and Vigilant contains thousands of these circuits. If a problem is detected during diagnostics, it would be impossible to find the faulty component without a template or, using your words, digitized schematics. Think of this as a fire station receiving a call for a stove fire but not being given the address. It would be impossible to respond to the fire without a map giving the house address. The template is that map."

"That's a good analogy," the DNI admitted. "What about the launch code?"

"It's inserted through the consoles as the final step in the activation process once the link is established," Baird replied.

"The missile doesn't have a launch code when it's lowered to the ocean floor," Winegar stated, wanting to see if the admiral disputed that statement.

"Correct. Launch codes are constructed in the blind by the NSA, which encrypts and transmits them through the link to the missile. It doesn't even know how many characters are used nor whether it's an alpha, numeric, symbol, or code that involves a combination of the three. They only know that the computer randomly constructing the code will ensure it matches the one in the president's nuclear briefcase."

"Therefore, no link, no code. Since the missile on the ocean floor, and I assume the others because they haven't even begun the activation process, won't arm or launch unless there's a match with the code in the nuclear briefcase, it would be impossible for whoever stole the UFPs to use them to initiate a nuclear strike," the DNI stated.

"That should be true. However, Vigilant is the unintentional exception," Baird answered, his voice betraying his nervousness.

"What the hell does that mean?" Rosen asked, irritated at the rear admiral's slippery language. "I thought you said the warheads wouldn't arm without a matching code provided by the National Command Authority, which generally means the president?"

Baird fidgeted in his chair and cleared his throat before responding. "Without the communications link, the encapsulated missile is a very deadly weapon waiting on the ocean floor for the last box in its activation program to be checked. However, because the consoles can establish that link, it's technically possible for them to create and transmit a launch code to a Vigilant missile and, since that's done in the clear, know and store the launch code it created."

"You're saying that all that's required to launch every one of these missiles is for the consoles to create codes for which it would have the duplicate?" Rosen asked in an unbelieving tone.

"That's the unintentional exception I mentioned earlier."

"That's quite an exception. Didn't you know that your activation process for Vigilant was a huge security risk?"

"My staff and I, apparently inaccurately, determined the consoles were well-protected because of the mission's secrecy, that they were on a Navy ship in the middle of the ocean, a Seawolf-class sub with a SEAL team was always within visual range, and the *Eagle* would be under constant surveillance by a Global Hawk drone."

"Not unreasonable assumptions," Winegar admitted.

"Did the crew provide any clues as to who might be responsible?" Rosen asked.

"Nothing that leads to anything but conjecture. They said the assailants wore balaclavas and gloves. Therefore, we have no fingerprints or descriptions of those who boarded the ship. However, because each carried an AK-74M rifle, the main service weapon of the Russian Army, and their accents seemed to be Russian or Eastern European, we suspect it was a Kremlin operation."

"Something this sophisticated could only be orchestrated by a few nation-states, the Russian Federation being at the top of that list. Learning that we were planning to place nearly five hundred nuclear warheads on the floor of the Atlantic Ocean might have sent them over the edge enough to take this action," Winegar stated.

"Since a trawler isn't fast, and where the attack occurred isn't near land, we should be able to find that ship," the SecDef said.

"The typical trawler can only travel at speeds approaching twelve knots or about fourteen mph. The fastest can reach twenty knots or twenty-three mph. That will define our search area," Baird volunteered.

"If we assume these speeds, can we determine how many trawlers are in this part of the ocean?" Winegar asked Rosen.

"We'll find out."

"How many people knew the *Resolute Eagle's* schedule and insertion points?" The SecDef asked.

"I'd estimate as many as forty to fifty," the admiral answered. "But that's a shot in the dark because the alphabet agencies don't disclose who they've told internally."

"What are you thinking, Jim?" Winegar asked Rosen.

"Thank you, admiral, keep us posted," the SecDef said, dismissing Baird before he answered the DNI's question.

"The only explanation for what's happened is that we have a highly embedded spy," Rosen replied once the rear admiral left the room.

"We need to tell the president in short order," Winegar advised. "Once that happens, he'll call a meeting of the National Security Council. If our traitor is as highly placed as we suspect, they'll then know everything we do, enabling them to not only warn Moscow but also stay ahead of our investigation."

"How do we search for this spy without warning them, especially since we don't know which organization they work for?" Rosen asked.

"By using an outsider," Winegar answered.

"Everyone we know works for or with the government, in one way or another," Rosen replied. "We might be hiring the fox to watch the hen house."

"There's an unintentional exception," Winegar said, employing the term used by Baird which earlier set him off.

It was eleven in the evening when President Ballinger, working on a planned speech in the Oval Office, received a call from the DNI asking if he could come to the White House on a matter of national security, Rosen remaining at the Pentagon to work on what he and Winegar discussed. Knowing he wouldn't ask for a meeting at this hour unless it was an extremely serious matter, the president said he'd have a mug of coffee waiting. Thirty minutes later, the Secret Service escorted him into the Oval Office.

"Have a seat," POTUS said, pointing to the couch as he poured two mugs of coffee from an urn on a side table and handed one to Winegar. The president, formerly a two-term governor and one-term senator from Kansas, was a widower with the Midwestern demeanor of making those around him feel at ease. He was five feet ten inches tall, had brown hair sprinkled with gray, and was of medium build.

"Black, as I remember," Ballinger said.

"Black," the DNI confirmed.

"I assume we have a serious problem," the president said as he sat in the club chair to Winegar's left.

"We do, sir. Are you familiar with the Vigilant system?"

When the president said he was, the DNI briefed him on what occurred.

"If I understand correctly," Ballinger calmly said with an intent look, "whoever has the consoles can place our missiles on any seafloor in the world, where they'd be undetectable, and launch them against us and our allies. They could also sell them to a third party, such as North Korea, Iran, or a Middle Eastern group, who could threaten us with nuclear blackmail, forcing a change to our foreign and economic policies. And, because they have the schematics, in the not too distant future they'll replicate the system and manufacture as many UFPs as they desire."

"That's our nightmare."

"And the prime suspect is Russia?"

"Circumstantially. Only a few governments have the sophistication to conduct this type of operation, and they're at the top of the list."

"But why would they do it?" The president asked. "We both have enough ICBMs and warheads in our arsenals to decimate each other multiple times over. This isn't about blackmail; it's about something else."

"From what I've been told, our UFP technology is a game changer and gives the United States a significant strategic advantage over the Kremlin for at least a decade," Winegar replied. "This theft would level the playing field and save them billions of dollars in research and development monies. They could also threaten us with selling UFPs, ours or the ones they replicate, to an unfriendly country to get economic, political, or other concessions."

"Losing what would have been the ultimate strategic deterrent, ensuring no one would dare attack the United States or our allies, will embolden our enemies. We need to find out how this theft occurred and who's responsible to prevent something like this from happening again."

"Addressing who's responsible, Jim Rosen and I feel the only logical explanation is that there's a highly placed spy in our government. However, finding them won't be easy because, as we've learned, as many as fifty people knew the *Resolute Eagle's* routing and other details that made the theft possible. Moreover, each would have passed an extensive background check to obtain the Top Secret clearance and Sensitive Compartmented Information access necessary to know the details of this project, including the schedule of when and where the UFPs were to be placed."

"I'll provide whatever you require to get the job done."

"What I need are the services of the White House Statistical Analysis Division."

"My bean counters?"

"I've always been curious as to why your analysts are located an hour and a half from here at the Raven Rock Mountain complex, because Site R is an extraordinarily secure military installation with tightly controlled access. Also, someone from an intel agency under my purview had some interesting things to say about them."

"Go on," the president said.

"He told me that your analysts flew to China in F-16 fighters. Curious, he checked with a highly placed Chinese source on his agency's payroll and asked what they knew about the situation. Apparently, your bean counters neutralized two Soviet-era nuclear weapons just before they were to detonate in Beijing and Shanghai."

"That's an interesting rumor. Did he tell the head of his agency?"

"No. He's an ambitious prick who bypassed his boss and came directly to me because he thought it would leapfrog his career."

"What did you tell him?"

"To keep it between us and forget about the bean counters until I've looked into it."

"Did he?"

"As I said, he's an ambitious prick, and he put the names of your team in his agency's tracking system. Not long after, he tracked them to Zurich and, using car rental records, to Davos. Several days later, an avalanche in that town killed those rumored to be members of a covert organization known as The Cabal, some of whom were part of our government."

"I recall the incident," the president commented.

"He called his counterpart at Switzerland's Federal Intelligence Service, who said your bean counters were suspected of sending a cannon shell into the snow atop the mountain, causing the tragic mishap. He also told me to look into the backgrounds of your analysts."

"What did you learn?"

"Most, except for the two ex-NSA employees, are ex-military or law enforcement. Additionally, not one has ever taken an accounting or statistics course."

"I'm sure your intel source wanted you to request a congressional hearing."

"He did, hoping it would make him a household name. Instead, I summoned him to my office and, after reaming his ass for continuing his investigation after I'd told him the ball was in my court, lied by saying your analysts were being used as cover for the real operatives and that his questions had potentially compromised their identities and jeopardized their lives, and might have screwed up any future covert operations for this team. I then transferred him to our listening post in Tierra del Fuego, an archipelago on Antarctica's doorstep, saying that if he spoke about your bean counters again, he'd get a multi-year pass to Leavenworth."

"Why didn't you tell me about this earlier?"

"I figured that whatever you were doing in your Statistical Analysis Division was to protect our country, and I'd give you the same free hand you've given me to protect it. However, now I need their help if I'm going to find Vigilant."

Those words hung in the air for fifteen seconds until President Ballinger broke the silence.

"The White House Statistical Analysis Division is used as cover for an off-the-books group known as Nemesis. It has nine members. Only the vice president, me, Libby Parra at the NSA, Lieutenant Colonel Doug Cray, its ex-commander and currently a presidential advisor, and now you know of its existence."

"Nemesis. That's an interesting moniker for an off-the-books covert team."

"It was named after the Greek goddess for retribution against evil deeds because its mission is to protect this country from foreign and domestic adversaries. Unlike special forces units within the military and operatives within your functions, it can react immediately to adverse situations without the hindrance of bureaucracy or congressional oversight. Needless to say, they're part of the black budget."

"Which is why it's worked. They don't need to brief the Senate Select Committee on Intelligence, which has seventeen members, or the twenty-five members of the House Permanent Select Committee on Intelligence, both of whom are sometimes guilty of Monday morning quarterbacking, political bias, leaking information to the press, and putting a stranglehold on funds for anything to which they're opposed," Winegar stated.

The president then went on to explain what Nemesis had accomplished, surprising the DNI with their unbridled success and that most of what they'd accomplished hadn't reached the rumor mill.

"Without Nemesis, this and other countries would have suffered great harm," Winegar said once he'd finished, his admiration for them apparent in his voice.

"That's why no one outside our circle can learn of its existence. You said that you needed their help to find Vigilant."

"Because I don't know where our spy is employed, I don't trust anyone but your team."

"That's why you need to meet Nemesis and brief them on their new mission."

"When?"

"There's no time like the present."

The team arrived at the White House at 1:30 am and were escorted to the Situation Room, a five thousand five hundred twenty-five square feet conference room and intelligence management center in the basement of the West Wing of the White House. President Ballinger, Vice President Houck, Winegar, and Lieutenant Colonel Cray were seated at the conference table when they entered. No introduction to the DNI was needed as everyone in the room was familiar with him, especially Nemesis' new administrative head, Angela Johnson, who previously worked at the National Counterterrorism Center, which was under his purview.

The team's leader was Matt Moretti. The ex-Army Ranger was forty, six feet three inches tall, weighed two hundred thirty pounds, and had a chiseled-cut face and a thick-chested muscular physique. At the president's direction, he introduced himself and his team, beginning with his wife, Han Li. The five-foot, eleven-inch tall statuesque brunette had porcelain-like skin, an athletic build, and black, opal-colored eyes. The introduction skipped that she was a former Chinese assassin sent to kill her future husband, circumstances dictating that they instead work together to prevent an international incident.

Continuing around the table, Moretti introduced Jack Bonaquist, an ex-FBI and Secret Service agent; Blaine McGough, a

Force Recon Marine; and Kyle Alexson and Mike Connelly, super-techies previously employed by the NSA. Angela Johnson and Rafael Alvarez were last to be mentioned. Johnson, a twenty-eight-year-old African American, was slender, five feet eight inches tall, and had hazelnut skin and black hair cut in a TWA, or Tweeny Weeny Afro. Cray recruited her to assume his in-house duties when he became a presidential advisor. Rafael Alvarez was twenty-six years old, five feet ten inches tall, and a muscular one hundred seventy-five pounds, with black hair in a buzz-cut. He was the team's sniper.

"Who's familiar with the Vigilant program?" The DNI asked. When only the president and the vice president said they were, he gave a brief overview.

"Stationing missiles on the ocean floor seems an inexpensive way to supplement submarine patrols," Cray stated.

"Vigilant was originally conceived because of exponentially mounting costs to design, operate, and support our ballistic missile fleet. The average Virginia-class submarine costs around $2.8 billion. The next generation is estimated to cost $5.5 billion. This doesn't include the billions in expenditures for training, simulators, docking facilities, replacement parts, and so forth," the DNI explained.

"And we're here because something happened to Vigilant," Moretti stated, drawing a nod of affirmation from Winegar.

"At 5:00 pm last night, Eastern Standard Time, the *Resolute Eagle*, an unmarked naval vessel, had just placed the first UFP on the ocean floor north of Bermuda when a fishing trawler slammed alongside it, and a group of heavily armed men boarded and overpowered the crew so quickly that no one was able to call for help. They left two hours and ten minutes later with the Vigilant command and control consoles, ninety-six ICBMs with MIRVs containing four hundred eighty-five warheads, their crush-proof capsules and self-leveling anchors, and the system's documentation. The command and control consoles are particularly troubling in that they contain the schematics and details necessary to replicate the system."

The room was silent; the shock on everyone's faces was as if they'd been doused with a bucket of ice water.

Cray was the first to speak. "Do we know who's behind this?"

"We believe the Russians attacked the ship to obtain the technology," Winegar answered. "However, at this point, that's speculation."

"That's ballsy, even for them," Moretti said.

"This goes beyond ballsy. It's technically an act of war which will have enormous consequences if we can prove they did it," Vice President Houck stated.

"If the Russians knew the exact location of the ship, what it was transporting, and the locations of the drone and Seawolf submarine escorting the *Resolute Eagle*, we have a spy," Moretti said.

"I agree. And they're highly placed in our government," Winegar replied.

"What are Nemesis' orders?" Moretti asked President Ballinger, who alone had the authority to commit the team.

"No matter what, retrieve or destroy the Vigilant system," POTUS replied. "It can't be allowed to fall into the hands of another country."

"What about the spy?"

"Director Winegar will handle that problem."

Moretti said that worked for him, as it narrowed his team's focus.

"Do you have an idea where you'll start?" the president asked.

"With Libby Parra," he answered, drawing a nod from everyone in the room.

Libby Parra was five feet five inches tall, thin, and had short blonde hair. Before being promoted to her current position as head of the Global Issues Analysis Office at NSA headquarters at Fort Meade, Maryland, the Agency being part of the Department of Defense, the forty-nine-year-old spent twenty-eight years analyzing intercepted Russian communications. During that period, she'd been offered her current job five times, previously turning it down because she understood the Kremlin's thinking and predicted what they would do so accurately that it was as if she attended their staff meetings. The Agency's current director, General Parker McInnes, also wanted Parra for this position, desiring to use her analytical skills on a broader scope than her current focus on the Russian Federation. However, he took a different approach than his predecessors in enticing her to accept the job. Instead of telling her about the increase in pay, benefits, and prestige, he emphasized that she would significantly impact national security and that America would be safer if she accepted the position. She left for Maryland the same day.

It was 3:00 am when Moretti and Cray entered building 2B, the NSA's leadership occupying the offices on the top floor. A guard escorted them to her office.

"It's good to see you again," Parra said as she rose from her chair and greeted them.

They apologized for getting her out of bed.

"You didn't. I'm single, a workaholic, and don't have a pet. As part of my agreement to accept this position, the NSA provided me with living quarters within this building. That said, I was in my office waiting for your call."

"Why is that?"

"Secretary Rosen called and told me about the theft of the Vigilant system, that the DNI went to the White House to brief the president, and that he suspects a highly placed spy leaked information to the Russians that allowed them to seize the system. Once the president found out, I knew he'd task Nemesis to get it back."

"Do you want to bring General McInnes in on this?" Moretti asked.

"I'll brief him when we know something. How can I help?"

"Using the imagery from one of your surveillance satellites, find the trawler onto which the system was transferred."

"That's going to be a problem."

"Why?" Cray asked.

"We have no imaging or electronic surveillance satellites over the area of the Atlantic where the SecDef told me the *Resolute Eagle* was boarded. As far as the United States is concerned, there's nothing of strategic value within it."

"I thought the NSA's eyes and ears covered the entire planet."

"That's what we would like everyone to believe."

"We need a way to find that ship before it transfers the missiles and consoles to another vessel or reaches land," Cray said. "Do you have any suggestions?"

"I was thinking about that. The theft occurred approximately eight hours ago," Parra said, referencing the clock on the wall. "I looked up the average and maximum speeds for a trawler about the length of the *Resolute Eagle*, made a back-of-the-envelope calculation, and determined that the distance it traveled is somewhere between a hundred and twelve and one hundred eighty-four miles."

"There's a lot of ocean between those numbers," Cray remarked, "especially since we don't know what direction it sailed."

She brought up a map of the Atlantic Ocean on her laptop, projecting the image onto the LED screen mounted on the wall. "I don't think it went south, west, or north. That would bring it closer to the United States or toward Africa. Given your belief the Russians are behind this, northeast is the most reasonable direction because that takes the ship toward their northern military installations and not the shore of another country. If this assumption is correct, they'll travel through the Norwegian and Barents Seas to the Kola Peninsula, where the Russian Navy has a strong presence," Parra warned.

"The planning for this operation was demonstrably meticulous and based on inside information. Therefore, let's assume that whoever was behind this knew we don't have satellite coverage in that area of the Atlantic and that the theft would be discovered before the ship reached land or Russian-friendly waters. Judging from what I see, that would take days," Moretti interjected. "They also knew we'd go after this trawler with everything we had and put a torpedo or cruise missile into the ship if we couldn't intercept it."

"You're implying they're going to transfer their cargo to another vessel?" Parra asked.

"I would," Moretti said. "After the transfer is complete, they'll make the trawler a decoy, hoping we'll focus on it. This will allow the ship with Vigilant onboard to sail to its destination undetected. We need to find the trawler before that transfer."

Parra began typing on her keyboard, scrolling through several menus before selecting the one that contained the locations of every

US drone. "I can dispatch an RQ-4 Global Hawk from Pope Field in Fayetteville, North Carolina. It's less than a thousand miles from where we believe the trawler is sailing."

"That works. How long until it gets over the area?" Cray asked.

"Approximately two and a half hours. It can stay airborne for another twenty-eight before returning to refuel."

"Two and a half hours is a long time."

"It's the hand we're dealt. However, because this drone is at Pope Field to support the DEA in detecting and interdicting smugglers, that aircraft has a significant enhancement which we can use to our advantage," Parra said before explaining.

"That's very useful," Cray agreed.

"Let's assume you find the trawler. What then?" she asked Moretti.

"We'll board and commandeer or disable the vessel until help arrives."

"That means you'll be parachuting onto it."

"More likely pushing a CRRC out the back of the aircraft and using it to come alongside the trawler," he stated, referring to a combat rubber raiding craft, which civilians called a Zodiac.

"Director Rosen told me the *Eagle's* crew estimated that approximately thirty to forty armed intruders came onboard the ship. That means there may be eight bad guys confronting every member of your team. Quite a bit of firepower could be coming your way."

"One of the perks of the job," Moretti replied.

CHAPTER 7

THE GLOBAL HAWK BEGAN photographing Parra's search area northeast of where the trawler was boarded from an altitude of forty-seven thousand feet; its data stream routed through a series of military satellites until it was received by the NSA's Utah Data Center. Code-named Bumblehive, it was located at Camp Williams near Bluffdale, twenty-one miles from the Great Salt Lake. The UDC was built at a cost of two billion dollars, and an equal amount was added to the government's tab for hardware, software, and other equipment. Within this one-and-a-half million square feet of space was a field of Cray XC supercomputers that worked in parallel, each capable of performing 100,000 trillion calculations per second.

Parra decided to refine her search by having an Agency programmer write an algorithm that instructed the system to identify any two-craned, three hundred thirty feet long black-hulled trawler, a description provided by *Eagle's* captain and first officer, along with her assumptions that its maximum speed would be twenty-three mph and that it would sit low in the water because of the weight of the missiles. The RQ-4 found four ships meeting these criterion. Because the drone had an augmented vision system that could look through the hull and decks of a vessel, the special enhancement she'd mentioned to Moretti and Cray, Parra could view the trawler's holds. Disappointingly, none were transporting missiles, although one ship did have long scrape marks along its hull. She called Moretti, who was with his team in the Nemesis conference room at Site R. He put his cellphone on speaker.

82

"The trawler with the scrape marks sounds like it could be the one that came alongside the *Eagle*," Bonaquist said after she gave the search results. "Are you sure there were no missiles inside that vessel?"

"Three of these ships had their holds filled with fish. The one with the scrape marks was transporting machinery which, for a trawler, is unusual because they're generally used as fishing vessels and not for transporting cargo. That said, ninety-six missiles, their crush-proof capsules, and the Vigilant consoles would fill every hold in these ships and cause each to be, according to my computer model, sailing approximately five feet lower if they were transporting the missiles because, excluding the capsules and anchoring systems, each weighs sixty-five tons. Multiply that by ninety-six."

"I had no idea the missiles were that heavy," Bonaquist conceded.

"Assuming the trawler with the scrape marks is the one we're looking for, which it appears to be because of its location, Vigilant must have already been transferred to another vessel," Moretti said. "What would it take to flag any ship within your search area carrying a heavy load?"

"Changing the algorithm will be easy. However, we're working against the clock because the search area continues to expand the longer this takes," Parra replied. "I suspect that the Russians, who've so far been methodical in their planning, knew this. Therefore, I believe this transfer is the first of many surprises they have in store for us."

"Any idea of what else they could have in mind?" Moretti asked.

"I expect we'll find out soon enough."

When Putin ordered Abrankovich to organize an operation to steal Vigilant, he understood the stakes were high because what he was about to do could be construed as an act of war. But he felt he had no choice because, from the intelligence provided by Archangel, this system would upend their nuclear parity with the United States, putting the Russian Federation in the number two spot for at least a decade and, when they finally did develop a competing system, assuming he could squeeze the billions for its accelerated development from the minuscule amount of money in his treasury, the Americans would already be deploying their next technological marvel, again putting his country in an expensive race to catch up. Eventually, he'd run out of money.

This wasn't about survival because he didn't believe the Americans wanted to start a nuclear war any more than he did. The aftermath would not only be the decimation of their populations but also the destruction of their cities and economies and making large swaths of their lands a nuclear waste zone for the next century. This level of conflict meant both countries would go from superpowers to third-rate nations in an instant, overtaken by China, India, and anyone else who had the common sense not to enter into nuclear war. Instead, stealing this system was about preserving their nuclear parity to maintain the Russian Federation's significant global influence and the political, economic, and military benefits that followed—all of which would gradually evaporate once Vigilant was deployed and its existence announced.

Abrankovich realized that stealing Vigilant wouldn't be easy. Once the United States focused its resources, the trawler would eventually be discovered and, shortly after that, would either be destroyed or boarded by Navy SEALs because the Americans would do everything in their power to retrieve or destroy the system before it reached shore. Therefore, he wasn't about to keep it on the same ship for the time it took to get to the Russian mainland. Consequently, he implemented a three-part plan to counter their anticipated responses, following Putin's directive for absolute secrecy by keeping the plan from his staff until he required their involvement.

His three top deputies previously recommended that he murder the crew and sink the *Resolute Eagle*, reasoning that although the United States would detect its vessel sank because the submarine shadowing it would follow its plunge to the bottom of the ocean on sonar, they'd have no way of knowing for sure whether their system was stolen because neither the sub nor the drone would have visually captured the theft. The deputies further reasoned that the confusion that followed the vessel's sinking would allow the trawler the time necessary to reach Russian soil before the Americans learned the truth and could respond. One deputy even suggested they spin the *Resolute Eagle's* disappearance into a Bermuda Triangle-type incident. Abrankovich scoffed at his staff's naivete, feeling they'd been bureaucrats too long. Although they were good at implementing an operation once given the blueprint for how it was to unfold, sitting behind a desk had taken away their grasp of reality.

The general didn't believe in God and thought the world was a jungle where the stronger survived and the weaker didn't. It wasn't fair, but that was the way of it, and he'd rather be the shark than the minnow. Therefore, he didn't have a problem with killing the crew. However, the Russian Federation wasn't the only shark in the water. The United States was also a shark and, given their technological and intelligence resources, there was nothing that he or his staff could do to spin what happened so they'd believe this was anything but a brazen theft.

"Is your conclusion that the Americans will think two

simultaneous random accidents took away their visual surveillance of the *Resolute Eagle*? That's ridiculous," Abrankovich admonished his deputies. "The Russian military's longstanding cliché that the Western lifestyle has made them complacent and stupid is a misnomer, and underestimating them on a mission of this complexity and importance is at our peril."

His staff was silent, not knowing where the general was taking the conversation.

"Because this encounter was in the middle of the Atlantic Ocean, our trawler won't get two hundred miles before they have one or more drones over the area and find it, after which they'll either send naval assets to retrieve their system or put a missile into its hull. If either happens, we'll have conducted a politically and economically expensive military operation, receiving in return only scorn and mistrust from other nations. To avoid this, I've ordered the trawler to sail south upon leaving the *Resolute Eagle*, which is an illogical direction given that it takes it further from Russia and into the open ocean. With the Americans logically concentrating their search to the north, the missile containers will then be transferred to a fishing factory ship, the *Antias*. This is part two of my three-part plan, which I'll equate to a shell game."

The deputies, who weren't consulted on the general's three-part plan, realized they were being included on an as-needed basis, heightening their insecurity and wondering whether they were about to be shown the door, replaced by someone the general felt had less naivete.

"To stay outside their anticipated search area, the *Antias* will continue south while the trawler sets course for Africa," the general said. "Part three of my shell game is for the factory ship to rendezvous with the Russian Navy cargo vessel *Severnaya* and the Akula-class submarine *Pantera*, K-317. The crew will transfer the missiles and related equipment to the ship and the consoles to the submarine's dry deck shelter, a pressurized and watertight module attached to its deck. Both vessels will then turn north toward the mainland, the *Pantera* submerging to one thousand feet, making it undetectable.

You may ask why I didn't put the entire system on the ship, as the prevailing belief in our military hierarchy is that the United States would never attack a Russian naval vessel. The Americans held a similar belief regarding the *Resolute Eagle*, which although unmarked, was staffed by their Navy. Therefore, I think it's safe to say that notion is antiquated. As a result, I placed the command and control consoles, which I'm told contains the data necessary to replicate this system, on the *Pantera*. Are there any questions?" Hearing none, Abrankovich slid the folder in front of him to the center of the table, telling his deputies to get to work on the logistics.

At two in the afternoon, after seven hours of looking at a steady stream of Global Hawk data feeds showing the interiors of ships that were low in the water but didn't have missiles onboard, Libby Parra called Moretti.

"We need to shake things up. We're either searching in the wrong direction, or the ship we're searching for is significantly faster than we estimated," Para said after telling him she'd failed to find the vessel.

"Who's the genius who came up with the idea of putting every Vigilant missile, along with their consoles, on an unmarked ship? Why wasn't it put onboard a commissioned naval vessel, such as an aircraft carrier, which could accommodate the cargo and is surrounded by escort ships?"

"My boss came up with the idea," Parra answered.

"That was a bad decision from someone as astute as McInnes," Moretti said. "What was his reasoning?"

"He wanted to keep the location of the UFPs a secret, making them impossible to detect in the vastness of the ocean. He felt that sending naval vessels into an area of the Atlantic with no known strategic importance would attract Russia's attention and that they'd send one or more ships from their northern bases, or those on patrol in the Barents Sea, to follow them. Therefore, he recommended the insertion be done by the *Resolute Eagle*, which the Navy routinely uses to lower undersea listening and other devices."

"Either retrieving or destroying Vigilant will be a challenge, and when we do find the system, it's going to get ugly," Moretti said.

"I think losing ninety-seven missiles, four hundred eighty-five nuclear warheads, and the command and control consoles, in which our game-changing technology is stored, already puts us on the far side of ugly," Parra replied.

"I can't argue with that. From what I've been told, while the Russians have a thirty-thousand-foot view of this system's capabilities, they don't yet know the specifics of its operation. That could work to our advantage," Moretti said.

"I'm listening."

"What if it was leaked that a code was required to reactivate the command consoles once the power to them was interrupted and that, if it wasn't entered in a specific number of days, the system erases its software and destroys every chip and circuit board?"

"They'd be manic because their costly and diplomatically perilous adventure would be for naught," Parra said. "Who has this supposed code?"

"It needs to be the ONR," Moretti answered.

"Why them?"

Moretti told her.

The president convened the National Security Council at 3:00 pm. Part of the Executive Branch and located in the White House, the NSC is comprised of those Cabinet members and senior officials who advise the president on national security and foreign policy. At Moretti's suggestion, POTUS invited the NSA, CIA, DIA, and FBI directors to attend.

"This is catastrophic," General Robert Trowbridge, the Chairman of the Joint Chiefs stated, following the DNI and ONR briefings. "The Russians will reverse engineer our technology, and we'll have a new arms race to see who can put the most ICBMs on the ocean floor."

"As the DNI explained, the control consoles self-destruct without the reactivation code," CIA director David Barrett stated.

"Does that apply to the missiles and warheads?" Vice President Houck asked.

"No. The missiles and consoles aren't linked," Baird answered.

"Explain the self-destruction process," Dr. Jim Goodburn, the National Security Advisor, asked.

"Circuit boards are made from insulating materials, such as a fiberglass-reinforced epoxy resin, that provide support, connectivity, and insulation for their components. Vigilant's circuit boards are groundbreaking in that the insulating material is pre-stressed glass," he explained.

"Glass?" Goodburn questioned.

Before the NSC meeting, Moretti spoke to the president, with

Winegar and Rosen also in attendance, and told them about this ruse. With the president in agreement, they brought Baird into their plan, having no choice but to trust the ONR because, as project manager, he was the only one who could credibly sell the existence of the additional code.

"Extremely thin glass, which gives four to five times greater conductivity speeds than silicon PCBs. If the reactivation code isn't entered within one hundred sixty-eight hours from the time the consoles lost power, which is a week, or someone attempts to tamper with or remove components from the consoles, or the temperature sharply drops, such as freezing the circuitry with liquid nitrogen, a capacitor discharges into the glass turning the circuit board into tiny fragments," the rear admiral said, accurately explaining the tamper-proof features incorporated into the PCBs, with the exception of the reactivation code.

"Who has this reactivation code?" The FBI director, Daniel Paterson, asked.

"It's stored within the ONR's computer system," Baird answered.

"The Russians have some of the best hackers on the planet. Once they learn a code is required, they'll attack your system with their most sophisticated technology," Paterson stated.

"There's not a day that goes by when they, North Korea, and even our allies, don't try penetrating our firewalls to walk away with our technology," the SecDef replied, helping Baird out. "However, to get to the ONR's servers, they'll first need to go through the DOD's firewalls."

"Circling back," Winegar said, taking the discussion in another direction, "although we believe Russia is the probable culprit, there's no definitive proof it's them. That assumption is based on the accents of those assaulting the *Eagle*, the weapons used, and that few nations have the resources and intelligence capabilities to pull this off."

The other members of the NSC agreed with that assessment. The meeting continued until 4:30 p.m., after which the president returned to the Oval Office while Winegar and Moretti took a helicopter for the thirty-one-mile flight from the South Lawn to NSA headquarters.

"It's happening," Libby Parra said to Moretti and Winegar upon receiving a call from one of her techs. "He'll call back when he has something."

"Are they trying to penetrate the DOD's servers?" Winegar asked.

"They're beyond the firewalls and into their system," she answered.

"How do you know?"

"He's monitoring the intrusion through a secondary pathway that he created to keep an eye on the file labeled *reactivation code.* We have software that will then enable him to do what we call an IP traceback, which will give him the origin of the breaching computer."

"Does McInnes know what's happening?"

"Not Yet. The same answer as last time."

"I'm curious as to why," the DNI persisted.

"If what we're doing doesn't work and this gets political, I'm giving him plausible deniability. He'll be insulated from the fallout."

"And you'll be throwing your body on the grenade."

"Illustratively speaking."

"Where is McInnes?" Moretti asked.

"In his office with three other intelligence agency directors on a video conference call. When that's over, they'll fly to Prague for the Global Cyber Security Conference," Parra said.

"I've never heard of it?"

"It's an annual forum where nations discuss technological security issues, exchange information, and negotiate cooperative agreements on combating cyber threats and anything else of mutual interest. Most of those in attendance are senior-level government officials, but there are also corporate CEOs and their staff who want to sell hardware, software, programming services, and whatever else their company markets. During conference week, they sponsor cocktail parties, dinners, and other activities to attract attendees so they can make their pitch."

As Moretti was about to ask if she had a list of those attending, Parra received another call from the tech. Seconds into it, he saw a twinge of excitement on her face.

"Meet me there as quickly as possible," she said.

"What?" Moretti asked.

"Our intruder is in this building," she said as she ran from the room.

Moretti and Winegar followed her out the door and down the hall to a stairway, taking it to the second floor. She continued her unbroken pace to a room sixty feet to the right of the stairway door, using her RFID card and an eight-digit PIN to enter the room. Rushing inside, with Moretti and Winegar close behind, they found it was empty, causing Parra to vent her frustration by letting out an expletive.

"Did the hacker get away?" Moretti asked.

"Possibly. But this is the computer they used," she said, pointing to it.

"Are you sure?" Winegar asked. "The sign on the door indicates this office is used by the State Department's Bureau of Intelligence and Research."

"The tech said the computer that accessed the ONR's system was in room 2102. We're here," Parra reaffirmed.

A few seconds later, there was a knock on the door. Opening it, she let a skinny twenty-two-year-old wearing round-rimmed glasses with gold-colored frames into the room. Parra introduced him as the tech who traced the intrusion. "He works in our IT Infrastructure Services System Office," she said, completing the introduction.

"Are you sure this is one?" She asked.

Instead of answering, the skinny tech opened his laptop and pointed to the trail of electronic breadcrumbs on the screen. Neither Winegar nor Moretti understood the displayed data, but Parra did and agreed they were in the right place.

"Who was the last person before me to enter this office?" She asked the tech.

After placing his computer on a nearby counter, he began typing. Ninety seconds later, he gave Parra the name of a State Department intelligence officer who entered the room eight days ago.

"Eight days. How is that possible?" Moretti asked, with the DNI agreeing.

"RDP," the tech answered, confusing Moretti and Winegar.

"Remote Desktop Protocol," Parra volunteered. "It's a real-time, multi-point data delivery system that routes this information to multiple parties. Therefore, it's possible to remotely access this computer to send data to user groups or a specific person."

"It could be anyone in the State Department," Winegar said.

"It could be anyone who knew about this computer and the State Department's RDP procedures. They don't necessarily need to work for State," Parra countered.

"I want to clarify something," the tech said. "This wasn't a hack.

The intruder didn't breach a DOD server. They were already in the system when they accessed this computer."

"How can you be sure?" Winegar asked.

"It's obvious," the tech answered, pointing to the electronic breadcrumbs on his screen.

"Can you locate the computer that accessed this desktop?" Parra asked, pointing to it.

"Technologically, they've covered their tracks. The IP traceback is ineffective."

"But not the electronic trail which led you here," she continued.

"They didn't bother to hide their use of this computer, probably because they knew it wouldn't lead us anywhere."

"But the breach was initiated from the State Department?" Winegar again queried.

The tech wanted to ask if he'd heard a word of what he and Parra said, but given that the question came from the DNI, he formulated a diplomatic response. "Not necessarily," he replied. "With RDP, the NSA, DIA, DLA, and a string of other DOD agencies are already in the system and past the firewalls. If someone understands State's RDP, which isn't rocket science, almost anyone can remotely access one of their terminals."

After fielding a few more questions from Winegar, Parra told the tech he could return to his office and should develop amnesia about everything he saw and was asked to do, which didn't seem unusual to him given that he worked for the most secret agency on the planet. Once he left, the three continued their discussion.

"One thing I've noticed whenever I come to Fort Meade is the enormous number of video cameras that seem to surveil every square inch of NSA property, inside and out," Winegar said. "How is it that there's not a single camera in this wing of the building? Is my eyesight getting bad, or are they hidden?"

"Neither. This area isn't covered by security cameras because the rooms in it are used by outside agencies. There's an inter-agency handshake to not spy on each other's offices."

"Why?" Moretti asked.

"Because no one wants records. If Congress subpoenas our video surveillance of inter-agency offices and sees who enters and leaves, it could appear that we're colluding to orchestrate operations that lack oversight and accountability, which most of the time we are."

"Point taken. Now that the spy has the fake reactivation code and they're in the wind, we've lost our one chance at finding them," Moretti said, his voice heavy with disappointment.

"Our spy will still need to get the code to whoever has Vigilant," Winegar said. "Knowing the NSA's omnipotent communications monitoring and decryption capabilities, they wouldn't want to send them via video or electronic means. With something this critically important, they'll want to deliver them personally."

"Prague," Moretti said.

"Since they can't get on a flight to Moscow, that's what I was thinking. What better place to be inconspicuous, especially with hundreds of people from all over the world in attendance?"

"Those hundreds will make it virtually impossible for us to find them, given we don't know their identity."

"We're not going to find the spy; someone else is," Winegar said.

"Would you like to explain that?

Winegar did.

CHAPTER 8

IT WAS SEVEN IN the evening in Washington when Winegar entered his office and called Iwinski, waking him from a sound sleep at 1:00 am. The ambassador came to life with a grunt, felt for the switch on his nightstand lamp, turned it on, and lifted the handset off the cradle of the encrypted device next to it.

"I'm sorry to interrupt your sleep, Bob," Winegar began, "but I have something extremely urgent to discuss."

"My sleep is always interrupted," Iwinski said as he emerged from his daze. "At seventy-two, my prostrate gets me up every couple of hours for a trip to the bathroom."

Winegar laughed, replying he also had the same affliction.

The two met a decade earlier when the ambassador was an executive at Raytheon, the military's second-largest defense contractor, and the future DNI was a recently retired naval officer who accepted a position at the Defense Intelligence Agency. They interfaced on numerous classified projects and formed a friendship that lasted to the present day.

"If you're calling me in the middle of the night, it must be something neither of us wants to hear. How bad is it?" The ambassador asked.

"Pretty bad. We believe the Russians are behind the theft of ninety-six of our ICBMs, which collectively have four hundred eighty-five warheads and the technology to hide them on the ocean floor," Winegar responded. He went on to explain the Vigilant system, how the theft occurred, and his belief that Moscow had a spy in Washington who gave them the classified information necessary to intercept the *Eagle* and steal the complex system.

"That's a bold move, even for the Kremlin," the ambassador said. "How can I help?"

Winegar explained how they were outsmarted in the trap they'd set to find their spy and now had only one possible way to discover their identity.

"What's that?"

"The consensus is that they're coming to Prague for the Global Cyber Security Conference, using this event as cover to deliver the code."

"Coincidentally, it just might be that the person you're looking for is connected to a triple homicide in a Prague park," he responded, explaining the murders.

"A sniper and an FSB operative working for our side who wanted to defect but was killed along with two CIA agents before he could get on the plane. It sounds like a day taken from the Cold War era. But how do you know there's a connection to my spy?" Winegar asked.

"Because hidden in the FSB operative's clothing was a flash drive and a photo of a person making a dead drop of a drive in a Prague park."

"What was on it?"

"Information on the Vigilant system you mentioned, including the ship's route, where it would lower the capsules, and so forth."

"It sounds like they're my spy. Send me the photo so I can put a name to the face."

"That's going to be a problem because their face has been intentionally blurred," Iwinski said.

"That takes the wind out of my sails. Let's take a step back. Who found these in the Russian's clothing?"

"A local police detective, Juraj Adamik."

"Thank God that ignoring diplomatic immunity didn't bother him. But how do you know the drive he found is the same as the one at the drop? Flash drives are ubiquitous. We and every other country I know use them for drops, and they all look the same."

"Because both had a unique marking," he said, explaining the red circle. "I have to say that you don't seem that disappointed that the face on the photo was blurred."

"I would have liked to have the name of our traitor. However, if I'm going to nail them to the cross, I'll need to catch this person in the act of spying so that I have proof of their betrayal. My problem is that I can't trust anyone in bureaucratic Washington to launch an investigation to find this spy for fear that, intentionally or not, they leak this information," Winegar said. "Therefore, if you have any ideas on how to catch my spy in the act of delivering this code, not knowing when or where the drop will take place, I'd be grateful for the help."

"Work with Adamik," the ambassador said, giving what Laska had told him about the detective.

"I'm not wild about using a foreign police officer for something this sensitive to our national security. How about one of your staff?" Winegar asked.

"The Russians know everyone at our embassy, just as we do with theirs. Adamik's advantage is that, as a local police detective, he won't be linked to working with us because his actions will be perceived as doing his job, which is investigating crimes. I need to mention that not long before you called, he came up with a plan to find the person in the photo."

"It seems like once he's on a case, he won't stop until he solves the crime."

"That's his personality."

"Then it's better that we work together rather than having him as a loose cannon. What's his plan to find the person with the blurred face?"

Iwinski told him.

"That plan is suicide," the DNI emphatically stated.

"He says he's aware of the risks but believes it's the best way to obtain the identity of the person in the photo. His mind is made up. You're not going to stop him, and it will give you the proof needed to show they're working for the Kremlin."

"That's true," Winegar admitted. "Turn him loose and tell him he has our support."

Later that morning, Iwinski summoned to his office two junior attachés who he was pretty sure weren't employed by the CIA. However, he knew he could never be entirely certain because neither the Agency nor the State Department provided him with a list of operatives. The ambassador gave them the bare minimum: he needed their help to expose a spy, what they'd be doing was outside the lines of their diplomatic duties, and the Agency wasn't to be involved. Because being a junior staffer was as exciting as watching paint dry, day in and day out doing the monotonous paperwork the State Department required and which more senior embassy personnel relegated to them, both readily agreed. The ambassador then told them where they were going for lunch, what they needed to talk about, and that their conversation should appear casual and not an information dump. At noon, the pair arrived at the restaurant in Bubeneč, a place Iwinski had previously used to disseminate false information.

Intelligence data collected by the Russians in Prague dated back to 1968 when Soviet-led Warsaw Pact troops invaded Czechoslovakia to clamp down on reformist trends, the Soviets focusing their video and audio monitoring efforts on places where the public gathered, one of which was restaurants. With the passage of time and the Soviet Union's transformation into the Russian Federation, Czechoslovakia split into two countries: the Czech Republic and Slovakia. During the same period, the KGB became the FSB, a change in name rather than substance, continuing their practice of monitoring Prague restaurants and passing the intelligence to Moscow.

Because these surveillance devices required a power source, they were commonly hidden in ceiling fire detectors or overhead lights, transmitting the audio and video feeds through the restaurant's server, in which malware had been installed, to Center 16 in Moscow—the epicenter for Russian communication intercepts, decryption, and data processing, where they were analyzed for context and keywords. If the speaker was deemed important, the audio was sent for human analysis

The two embassy attachés, deemed too low-level to be significant, had only basic information on them stored at the Center, which excluded voiceprints. However, that instantly changed, and they went to the top of the ladder when one of them mentioned Vigilant, Lisov, and the discovery of a flash drive and photo hidden in his boot. This cascade of red flags was enough to put their voiceprints on file and forward the transcript of their conversation to Abrankovich, who received it at 6:00 pm in Moscow, which was one hour ahead of Prague. Upon receiving it, he called Putin and requested a meeting.

The office of the Russian president is located in the northern part of the Kremlin in the Senate Palace, a three-story triangular-shaped yellow building that was constructed in 1787. Because he wasn't the most popular person in the country and lived in fear of assassination, Putin traveled unannounced to offices at his residences in St. Petersburg, Sochi on the Black Sea, and Novo-Ogaryovo on the outskirts of Moscow. To obfuscate his whereabouts, the offices at these residences were identical so that, while on camera, no one would know his location.

When Abrankovich called and asked for a meeting, he was told to come to Novo-Ogaryovo, a government estate nineteen miles west of Moscow. He arrived at the heavily guarded entry gates at 8:00 pm and was directed to leave the vehicle. A member of Putin's security detail then got in and drove it to a parking lot at the perimeter of the property, where it was sniffed by a dog for explosive materials before being visually inspected. While his car was in transit, the general was taken by golf cart to the residence and, after passing through a body scanner and swabbed for explosive materials, he was patted down and escorted to Putin's office. He found the president of Russia seated at a circular conference table to the right as one entered. After a brief exchange of pleasantries and a shot of vodka, Abrankovich pulled a copy of the restaurant transcript from his inside jacket pocket and handed it to him.

"I should have interrogated Lisov the moment we found out he was going to those apartment buildings," the general said in a remorseful voice.

"He was clever, or the Americans were. How did you discover his treason?"

"One of our agents followed him and, once he left, knocked on the apartment door he was seen entering. When a scantily clad Czech woman answered, it didn't take much imagination to determine her occupation, and after asking the going rate for her services, she told our agent. He accepted the invitation, confirming the woman was a prostitute, and planted a passive listening device while inside. Nearly a year later, Lisov returned to this apartment and, to our surprise, was heard speaking with a CIA operative, whose voice was in our database."

"Was the woman in the room when they spoke?"

"That's unknown, but probably not because her voice wasn't detected, and no one acknowledged her presence. More likely, her arrangement with the CIA called for her to leave whenever there was a meeting."

"What did they speak about?"

"The classified affairs of our Prague embassy, including our covert operations."

"What about the other apartments?"

"I'm having them checked, but I assume it's the same setup."

"It was a brilliant deception because Lisov wouldn't have been the first of us who had a mistress or indulged in one of life's pleasures," Putin said, his voice devoid of emotion. "What concerns me is that the assassin you selected failed to adequately search the bodies because, if they had, we wouldn't be in this predicament. Unreliable people can't be in our employ."

"I'll take care of it. We can still correct this because, according to the attaché's conversation, the Prague detective who discovered the drive and photo hasn't turned them over to the American Embassy, or even the police department, for fear the ambassador will preempt his investigation by demanding he stops looking into the murders, allowing their State Department to sweep them under the carpet to avoid a diplomatic embarrassment."

"Why does he want to investigate matters that the police have already ruled accidents?" Putin asked.

"That's unknown."

"This detective concerns me because he's obviously smart to uncover what he has in such a short time. He must know we'll do whatever needs to be done, including killing him, to stop his investigation and to protect what he's uncovered from becoming public. Is this personal?" Putin asked.

"It doesn't appear to be."

"What do we know about him?"

Abrankovich took a paper from his inside jacket pocket and began reading. "Detective Juraj Adamik is a loner who's divorced, has no children, is a borderline alcoholic, lives in a Prague brothel and, according to a past newspaper article, has a phobic determination to solve every case to which he's been assigned, which has led to a one hundred percent success rate."

"Are you saying he's never failed to solve a case?" Putin asked.

"Not according to the article that I read, which was recent."

"I want his investigation to stop while Archangel delivers the reactivation code in Prague. If anything delays its retrieval, that's the same as not receiving them. The Vigilant consoles will self-destruct, and this operation will have been a failure. Take the gloves off. Kidnap and interrogate this detective. I want to know everything about his investigation, including who he's spoken with and what they've told him. Once that's done, kill him and anyone he's spoken with, and get rid of the bodies in such a way that they'll never be found."

Abrankovich acknowledged the order. "There's one more thing," he said, knowing that as others discovered, keeping Putin in the dark was a deadly mistake. "I ordered the *Pantera's* captain to remain submerged in deep water or a thermocline to be undetectable. Therefore, there's no way to contact the boat until it nears the surface and releases an antenna buoy, which allows it to send and receive signals. However, the captain has orders that this can only happen once it reaches Russian waters."

"How are you handling this problem?"

"The *Pantera* is scheduled to surface less than a week after leaving the American ship," he said, recalling the boat's timeline. "I'll have the captain power up the consoles and enter codes then."

"How close are you cutting this, Grigori?" Putin, who wasn't known for taking someone's word on anything, asked.

"We'll have an eight-hour window," the FSB director answered.

"Don't fail."

It was 10:00 pm in Prague when Adamik returned to the brothel. Having had nothing to eat all day except for the protein bar of indeterminate age he found in his jacket pocket, the detective went straight to Madam Irenka's kitchen instead of his room. There, he ladled from the large pot on the stove a bowl of kyselo, a hearty sourdough soup with dried porcini mushrooms, onions, and potatoes, to which a generous amount of caraway seeds was added. As he ate, the detective placed the lab report on the table and laid beside it the crime scene photos, which included four sets of boot prints.

Making a cast of a boot print in the snow takes expertise because putting plaster or a gypsum-based product, which gives off heat during the curing process, on the print would destroy the impression. Therefore, forensics first sprays the imprint with snow impression wax, which provides support and retards melting. Once the wax dries, a casting medium such as plaster can be applied, and the forensic-quality print can be removed as evidence. Because the victims were photographed when they arrived at the morgue, along with each piece of their clothing, Adamik could identify the three sets of boot prints belonging to the victims. That meant the fourth, found near the bodies and on the basilica tower, was from the killer.

To identify a boot, lab techs either consult a law enforcement database, access a fee-based commercial system, or contact the manufacturer and send them a copy of the print. Because the killer wore size thirteen boots with HH on the bottom, which the lab tech knew was the logo for Helly Hansen, an upscale manufacturer, he called the company. After faxing them a photo of the boot print, the company's representative told him they were Garibaldi V3s, easily identifiable because of their unique tread mark. Following their conversation and using the data obtained from the boot imprint, the tech used the standardized forensic method of doubling the shoe size and adding fifty to estimate that the killer was approximately seventy-six inches tall. From the depth of their boot impressions in the snow, the forensics tables showed the assailant weighed approximately two hundred pounds.

Adamik continued looking at the crime scene photos while he finished his soup, afterward cleaning his bowl and returning it to the cupboard. Gathering the report and photos, he started toward his room, passing along the way several of Madam Irenka's ladies, with whom he was more than casually familiar, asking if he wanted a companion for the evening. Burned out from the day's activities, he politely declined and decided he needed a good night's sleep instead.

The three intruders arrived in a windowless van and parked outside Madam Irenka's at four in the morning. Knowing that the house closed for business an hour earlier and that those inside would be asleep, one picked the front door lock and they entered. The location of Adamik's room was discovered when one of the men visited the house earlier in the day and asked the woman entertaining him if it was true that a police detective lived in the brothel. After asking him to keep it secret, she confirmed the rumor and, following a few more questions, provided the room's location and told him about the plague on the door. Subsequently, the three men had no difficulty finding Adamik and, after picking the lock, entered his room.

It was over within seconds. Adamik was in a deep sleep as one person placed duct tape over his mouth while another bound his hands and feet with flex ties, and the third injected him with a Benzodiazepine cocktail—a class of drugs that acted on the central nervous system by instructing the brain to release gamma-aminobutyric acid (GABA). This made the nervous system less active and had a sedative effect on his body that was substantially less dangerous than chloroform which, in contrast to what was seen in movies, could collapse a person's airway and allow it to fill with secretions and choke them.

Once Adamik was sedated, the attackers searched the room, ripping apart everything from the mattress to his clothing to find the flash drive and photo. Coming up empty, they decided to leave, one person grabbing the computer off the desk while another slung the detective across his shoulders in a firefighter carry with the third closing the door behind them.

The three men made it to the van unseen and, after placing

Adamik in the back, drove twenty-five miles to a farmhouse outside the village of Bozkov. They brought the unconscious detective inside to a specially constructed interrogation room—a twenty-by-twenty-foot concrete-floored and walled enclosure with a wooden chair in the center and, beneath it, a metal grate that covered a drainage pipe. Several metal cabinets lined one wall, beside which were a half dozen five-gallon water bottles with a stack of towels on top. A rusting metal desk with two chairs was in the far-right corner. Adamik's flex ties were cut and he was secured to the chair, after which the duct tape was removed from his mouth. The men then waited for the person in charge to arrive, which happened ninety minutes later.

"Get him conscious," the six feet four inches tall man who'd entered the room said in Russian.

One of his captors retrieved a syringe from a pouch and injected Adamik, after which he regained consciousness, looking up at the tall man standing over him who was wearing Helly Hansen winter boots.

"FSB, GRU, or Foreign Intelligence Service?" Adamik groggily asked.

"Major Vitali Orlov of the GRU," the man answered. "However, officially I'm a diplomat at our embassy in Prague."

Familiar with the Kremlin's intelligence apparatus, Adamik didn't need Orlov to explain that the Russian Federation had two primary intelligence agencies—the FSB and the GRU or Main Intelligence Directorate. Each had separate responsibilities, with the FSB focused domestically and the GRU on gathering foreign intelligence and covert operations. However, those geographic lines sometimes blurred, with the FSB allowed to operate on foreign soil to correct a domestic situation.

"You have some things that belong to my government."

"Are you referring to what your spy stole from the Americans?"

"Wrong answer," Orlov said as he quickly thrust his right hand into Adamik's torso, executing the karate movement known as a nukite, breaking two of the detective's ribs and flipping the chair, to which he was tightly attached, onto the floor. Adamik, gasping for breath, was having trouble breathing when Orlov's men lifted the chair and set it upright.

"Irrespective of ownership or origin, tell me where you're keeping what you took from that traitorous bastard Lisov," Orlov said, the calmness in his voice engendering fear because of the violence he'd just inflicted.

"It's in my department's evidence room, as the law requires."

"Why put anything in an evidence room that's not part of an investigation? The murders were ruled accidents."

"Procedure. To the police, it doesn't matter whether it's an accident or homicide because whatever is on a person when they die goes to the evidence room until the case is closed and the paperwork completed, after which the items are disbursed to the next of kin or destroyed if no relatives are found. In a situation involving the death of an embassy official, what's found on them will be turned over to an official from that country."

"Are you telling me that the Russian Embassy will eventually receive what was taken from Lisov and that the United States Embassy will get what was found on the Americans?"

"That's the way it works."

"Who besides you have seen what's on the flash drive or the photo?"

"No one. I just started my investigation."

"If that's true, how did two American Embassy employees know of its existence?"

"You'll have to ask them," Adamik said.

"They're dead."

"Then you have a problem."

Orlov wanted to break more of Adamik's ribs but decided against it because it would interrupt his questioning, and he had something better planned. "Why did the police cover up the murders and turn the deaths into accidents?"

"Because triple murders are bad for tourism, which is the lifeblood of our city."

"Then why the investigation?"

"Someone outside the department," he said, keeping the colonel's name out of it, "ordered it as a CYA in the event one or both governments brought up the deaths in the park at a later date. If they did, the Czech government could say the incident was still under investigation."

"Do you know what I think?"

Adamik didn't answer.

"You're lying," Orlov continued when he didn't receive a response. "I don't believe your government would let you keep it in the evidence room because they're subject to diplomatic immunity and would raise the question of why they were taken off the body and sent there instead of being left at the morgue for my embassy to pick up with the body."

"Let's agree to disagree."

"Let me show you how I'm going to get the truth," Orlov said, before speaking in Russian to those around him. "Have you ever been waterboarded?" he asked.

Adamik didn't answer.

"Let me explain the procedure. One of my men will tilt your chair backward while another places a towel tightly over your breathing passages. Water is then poured over the towel. As your sinus cavities and mouth fill with water, an involuntary gag reflex will cause air to be expelled from the lungs, meaning you can no longer exhale. If you inhale, you'll get water into your lungs, and the brain will suffer from oxygen deprivation. When I stop pouring water and remove the towel, you'll gasp for air and your body will get the oxygen it needs to survive. However, if I misjudge your tolerance and pour water for too long, you'll drown in an enormously painful manner. I can tell you what waterboarding feels like because undergoing the procedure is compulsory for GRU operatives. Let me give you a demonstration," Orlov said, motioning for his men to begin.

The man beside Adamik poured water over the towel covering his face for twenty seconds, stopping only when Orlov raised his hand, after which the towel was removed and the detective was allowed to breathe for ten seconds.

"Again," the GRU operative said twice more, the second and third rounds also of twenty-second duration.

"The average GRU agent lasts fourteen seconds before calling it quits. You've done substantially better. I'm impressed. But here's a dose of reality. There are three outcomes from this torture: you either talk and are given a quick death with a bullet to the brain; you continue being stubborn and suffer permanent brain damage and become a vegetable from a lack of oxygen; or you suffocate. If you're going to die anyway, why not make it painless and leave the game on your terms? Once again, where are the items you took from Lisov?"

"I'm a little parched," Adamik responded. "Let's have another go at it."

"Forty seconds," Orlov said to his men, intending to stop before then but wanting the detective to believe that he was about to die or face permanent brain damage if he didn't tell him the truth.

As a towel was roughly put over the detective's face and his chair reclined, two stun grenades flew into the room. They skidded across the floor near Orlov, exploding in a blinding flash of light that activated every photoreceptor cell in one's eyes, producing five seconds of temporary blindness. At the same time, the accompanying one-hundred-seventy-decibel sound agitated the fluid in the ear, causing a loss of balance and temporary deafness. The Russians fell to the floor, incapacitated.

Six men in combat gear, each carrying Heckler & Koch 416 assault rifles, emerged from the vaporous cloud of smoke produced by the grenades and entered the room, quickly cuffing the Russians with flex ties. Adamik was on his back with a wet towel over his face when Iwinski pulled it off. Standing beside him were Calbot and Laska, who cut him loose with a pocketknife.

"It took you long enough," Adamik, who was wet, shivering, and short of breath, said to Laska. "Where's our men?" He asked after looking around.

"I sent them home."

"Explain that to me," the detective said as Laska found a blanket and put it around his shoulders.

Adamik was referring to the plan which called for the colonel to have two officers in a patrol car watch Madam Irenka's because he didn't believe it would take long for the Russians to come after him once the attaché's restaurant conversation occurred. Knowing he'd be interrogated before they killed him to find out what he knew and get back the drive and photo, and that couldn't happen at the brothel, he was confident that he'd be kidnapped. The lynchpin for surviving that scenario was for the officers to see the bad guys enter the brothel, call Laska, and follow the kidnappers. Laska would deploy the department's hostage rescue team that he'd put on alert, taking direction from the officers as to where Adamik was being taken. Although the plan was solid, executing it didn't go as smoothly as predicted.

"That's because I couldn't call our HRT. Instead, I phoned Ambassador Iwinski, who contacted Calbot and told him of the kidnapping. You and I both know the CIA, even in a foreign country, has the resources and equipment to pull off a hostage rescue," Laska stated.

"But why couldn't you call our HRT and keep this local?"

"Because the officers in the patrol car watching the brothel, who saw you being taken and reported it to me, lost sight of your kidnappers when their vehicle was cut off by a slow-moving car and, by the time they'd passed it, your vehicle was nowhere in sight, probably having taken one of the numerous side roads off that highway. After receiving the call and knowing your life was at stake, I phoned the ambassador and asked for the CIA's help, believing they'd know the location of a Russian safehouse that was in the direction you were traveling. They did and told me—their HRT, the COS, and the ambassador arriving just after I got here."

"That was smart thinking. I'd be dead if you hadn't involved the Americans," Adamik said. "By the way, that's your killer," he said, pointing to Orlov. He was about to say something else, but collapsed on the floor instead.

"Get him to my car," the colonel said to a member of the CIA assault team who, after receiving a nod from Calbot, threw Adamik over his shoulder and brought him to Laska's vehicle with the colonel following.

"My associates and I have diplomatic immunity. Look at our passports," Orlov angrily said to Calbot once Laska and Adamik were gone. "You can't touch us. Cut us free or suffer the consequences."

"Consequences? There won't be any consequences because I don't give a damn about your immunity. You killed two of my agents," he said, giving the Russian a steely look. "You and your men are going to be put on a US aircraft and taken to a rendition site in Jordan where professional interrogators will violate your human rights until you tell us everything you know. After that, depending on your usefulness, I'll decide whether to bury all of you in the desert or let you continue to breathe the stench of prison for the rest of your lives. Either way, your Vodka-drinking days are over. None of you are returning to Russia."

"Despite what happens to us, understand that my government will never stop coming after him," Orlov said, nodding toward the door where Adamik was carried from the room. "They'll send others. He'll eventually tell us what he knows and die because you won't be able to stop every kidnapping or assassin."

"I don't care about Adamik or anyone outside the Agency," Calbot said, drawing a look of confusion.

"Then why did you save him?"

"My goal wasn't to save him but to capture and drain Russian assets of every shred of useful information they possessed. Your embassy couldn't object, other than in private to the ambassador or State Department, because they wouldn't want it to be revealed that you killed two American attachés and were about to murder a local law enforcement officer."

"You're telling me this for a reason. Otherwise, we'd be on our way to the plane."

"Under the right circumstances, I can change your travel plans and give you a way to eventually exit the game with cash and a new identity," Calbot said.

"It didn't work out that way for my FSB counterpart."

"GRU?" Calbot asked.

"GRU," Orlov confirmed.

"In my opinion, a step above the FSB. Your training is substantially more intense. Lisov would have been in the States, and we wouldn't be having this conversation if he'd been more careful. You won't make the same mistakes."

"Two years and I'm out," Orlov said.

"Five," Calbot countered.

"Three," the Russian said.

"Deal. Even if you're transferred, we'll get you out, and I'll be on the plane taking you to the United States with a cold bottle of vodka and a tin of caviar."

"Beluga caviar?"

"Of course."

"I suspect I have a second employer," Orlov said, maintaining eye contact with the Chief of Station.

"I expect you do."

CHAPTER 9

"THIS ISN'T GOING TO work," Parra told Moretti, who remained at NSA headquarters while Winegar returned to Washington. It's a big ocean. The longer we take to find the vessel to which Vigilant was transferred, the larger the search area. There'll soon be hundreds of ships to look at, and even with the second Global Hawk I tasked, there is insufficient time to visually inspect each that's riding low in the water."

"It would have been nice to have a pair of eyes in the sky to observe that transfer and give us the name and sailing direction of the ship the Vigilant system is now on," Moretti said.

"Say that again."

Moretti repeated himself.

"I think you solved our problem."

"I only stated the obvious: the *Resolute Eagle* was in an area not under NSA surveillance, the drone surveilling the ship was shot down, and the *Florida* was entangled in a fishing net. Therefore, we didn't have an asset to follow the trawler and see the transfer."

"That's all true. That leads us to suspect that of the four trawlers we originally looked at, the vessel with the scrape marks along its hull attacked the *Eagle. Even* though its holds were filled with machinery, that cargo was taken onboard from another ship in exchange for Vigilant—the vessel we're currently looking for," Parra stated.

"On that, we're agreed."

"You said it would be nice to have a pair of eyes observe the transfer. But we did."

ALAN REFKIN

Moretti, who was sitting on the couch in Parra's office, sat up
as if doused with a bucket of cold water. "The captain of the trawler
with the scrape marks saw the transfer and knows which ship is
carrying our system," he said, irritated at himself for not thinking
of this earlier. "Do you know where our scraped trawler is now?"

Parra began typing on her keyboard. "As of thirty minutes ago,
it was on a northerly heading three hundred and thirty-six miles
from the *Resolute Eagle*."

"How do you know?"

"The Global Hawk sends the position, course, and speed of
every vessel it looks at with its augmented vision system. Assuming
those metrics haven't changed, I have a program that calculates the
trawler's current position."

"And if the metrics have changed?"

"We'll still find them. I'm diverting a drone to verify their
present location. It's twenty times faster than the trawler and looks
at seventeen hundred square miles each hour. They won't escape."

"Just make sure you keep it far enough away from the trawler,
so it doesn't end up in the ocean like the last RQ-4."

Parra said that was a given, and she'd crank up the magnification
on the drone's camera to compensate for the range differential.

"I'd better call the president and get a ride to that ship. It's time
Nemesis pays the trawler's captain a visit," Moretti said.

Major Mark Watkins and his copilot, Captain Scott Durst,
lived in adjoining rooms at the BOQ, or bachelor officers' quarters,
at Joint Base Andrews. Having never married, they preferred living
on base as the average pilot in their squadron traveled between a
hundred and sixty and two hundred days a year. Therefore, without

a family, they felt an off-base residence made little sense. Their crew chief, Master Sergeant Melvin Skinner, who became divorced when his wife would no longer put up with the constant travel, lived in the senior enlisted barracks five minutes from the BOQ.

Their aircraft was a C-17 Globemaster III, a two hundred million dollar plane that was one hundred seventy-four feet long, fifty-five feet high, and had a wingspan of nearly one hundred seventy feet. Although it could carry up to one hundred seventy-one thousand pounds of cargo, it was the aircraft of choice for special operations teams because, with its air refueling capability, it could quickly transport them and whatever equipment was required anywhere in the world and land on a strip of earth as short as thirty-five hundred feet. It could also open the rear cargo door in flight to allow a team and their equipment to exit the plane.

When the call came from the base command post to preflight their aircraft, the three weren't surprised because being summoned without notice was typical for their squadron, its crews on 24/7 call. To the person, each would have said they preferred being in the air to staying at home or having the day off, even though that lifestyle choice had consequences. As they arrived at the C-17, a forklift was loading pallets from the two trucks beside it onto the plane. Colonel Daniel Del Negro, the base commander, was waiting to greet them near the rear cargo ramp. That he was there and not someone from base ops or intelligence indicated this wasn't a routine mission. This belief was confirmed when a CH-47 Chinook, a tandem-rotor helicopter, set down fifty yards away, and Matt Moretti exited the aircraft followed by Han Li, Bonaquist, McGough, and Alvarez, each with a backpack slung over their shoulder and carrying a deployment bag. The last two times he'd transported Nemesis, he'd had to weave the giant aircraft a gnat's whisker above the Amazon rainforest and down a winding river to rescue the team and later put the Globemaster down on a postage-stamp-sized civilian runway and take off with one of its two engines inoperative. He suspected this assignment wouldn't be any easier.

Moretti grinned when he saw Watkins.

"Your sense of timing is impeccable. Maintenance just returned this aircraft to service yesterday after replacing a ten million dollar engine and repairing half the aluminum panels on the airframe because they had more holes than a slice of Swiss cheese," the major said, returning the Nemesis leader's grin and extending his hand.

Del Negro came forward and shook each team member's hand. "President Ballinger called and gave me a list of the supplies you requested from the base armory," the colonel said to Moretti, pointing to the forklift. "He said you'd tell us where you're going once you arrived at Andrews."

"We're doing a HALO jump onto a trawler in the middle of the Atlantic," Moretti replied, referring to the high altitude, low opening military parachute method of insertion where the team would leave the Globemaster from as high as thirty-five thousand feet before opening their parachutes closer to the ship. "Here are the jump coordinates," he said, handing the aircraft commander a slip of paper on which he'd written them.

"I see you're jumping with a CRCC," Watkins said, seeing the pallet with the Combat Rubber Raiding Craft, the military equivalent of a Zodiac Milpro Futura, being taken up the ramp. The fifteen-and-a-half-foot-long and six-foot-wide craft had an engine on the stern and a self-positioning parachute system attached to the pallet.

"We'll use it to board the ship we're after," Moretti confirmed. "The NSA will provide updates on its position during the flight."

"A drop insertion sounds deceptively easy for one of your missions," the major stated.

"There's a complication," Moretti replied, drawing a look of *here it comes* from Watkins. "This ship is suspected of downing a Global Hawk, but we're not sure how because whatever they employed didn't set off the drone's missile warning indicator."

"That's comforting," Watkins said. "A C-17 looks like a flying house on radar. You can't miss it. A surface-to-air missile, nor any other weapon system, would have a problem locking onto and blowing the Globemaster into scrap metal."

"Because of its size, the bad guys will believe the C-17 is commercial traffic transitioning the area. Notwithstanding that, we're going to HALO far enough away from the ship to be out of range of whatever they could shoot at you. Once we're off the plane, you can return to Andrews. This should be an easy insert."

Five hours and fifteen minutes after taking off from Andrews, the C-17 was twenty miles from the drop zone and at thirty-six thousand feet, the average altitude for commercial traffic. Five minutes earlier, Parra had given Moretti the Global Hawk's last reported position for the trawler, which he passed to Watkins. He would have preferred to do the HALO jump during the day when the team could gauge the waves' height and see the CRRC and trawler in the water rather than use their night vision goggles and the tracking computer attached to their wrists to find them. The HALO also meant they'd need supplemental oxygen, that the outside temperature would be minus sixty-five degrees Fahrenheit, and that they'd freeze their asses off in their government-issued cold weather suit on the way down because it wasn't exactly made by Canada Goose.

Ten minutes prior to their jump, the Nemesis team put on their low-cost government-provider cold weather gear over their wetsuits and checked their oxygen masks and night vision goggles. Moretti then gave Skinner a thumbs up, indicating the team was ready, after which the crew chief told the pilot. Watkins then depressurized the plane so that, when the ramp was extended, there was no pressure differential between the inside and outside of the aircraft, sucking everyone and everything in the cargo compartment that wasn't tied down out of the plane.

Once the Globemaster was depressurized, the crew chief, after donning a parka and strapping on an oxygen mask, sat in his webbed seat, fastened his harness, and extended the cargo ramp. At the same time, the team waited for the red light at the rear of the compartment to change to green, indicating they were over the drop zone. When that happened, Alvarez and McGough would be the first to jump, pushing the CRRC in front of them, with the rest of the team following.

"Twenty seconds," the pilot said into his headset, the crew chief passing on that time by extending the fingers on his gloved hands twice. However, no sooner had he done this than a blinding white light replaced the absolute darkness behind the cargo ramp, temporarily blinding everyone in the compartment. The aircraft, which one instant was flying straight and level and the next was violently trying to shake itself apart, sharply pitched upward before falling off on the starboard wing into a steep descending roll that was about to turn into a spin.

While the pilots fought to regain control of the C-17, the team and their CRCC tumbled out the rear of the Globemaster the instant it pitched up. The crew chief almost joined them, which would have ruined his day because he wasn't wearing a parachute. However, he was saved by the 5-point crew harness, which prevented him from being pulled out of his seat restraint when the aircraft went vertical. The C-17 completed one descending roll and was about to begin a second revolution, which would have put it so close to the water that the aircraft would be unrecoverable before it plummeted into the ocean, when the pilots regained control.

"Skinner! Are you and the team alright?" Watkins yelled into his mic once he started regaining altitude.

"I'm alright, but the team was sucked out of the aircraft after the explosion."

"What explosion?"

"The one which followed a white blinding light that took half the cargo ramp with it. It happened so fast that I couldn't tell if the team was dead or alive when they were blown out the back," he somberly stated.

"That explains some of the red lights on my instrument panel. We might be joining Moretti's team if I can't get this beast under control. The plane wants to yaw hard to port," Watkins said, indicating it wanted to veer left. "It's taking all our strength on the rudder pedals to keep it from inverting. Can you retract what's left of the ramp? That might neutralize the yaw."

Skinner tried, but after several attempts, told the pilot that the ramp wouldn't budge. "But we might have a bigger problem," he continued. "The section that's left is fluttering and wants to break free of the airframe."

"That'll take hydraulic and electrical with it, because the primary and backup lines for those systems transit from one side of the aircraft to the other through a conduit that runs inside the base of the ramp," Watkins said.

"I know," Skinner replied.

"Keep me updated on the ramp," Watkins said before turning his attention to Durst and asking him to look for the nearest patch of concrete, slang pilots sometimes use when referencing a runway.

The copilot scrolled through his electronic charts and saw the nearest airport was Cabo Verde.

"Giving me a heading."

Durst did. "The flight notes say it's an island country in the central Atlantic Ocean with a ten thousand feet runway."

"With a runway that length, they'll have large aircraft landing there and the requisite emergency equipment to handle a plane this size, including firefighting equipment, should we need it. How long will it take us to get there?"

The copilot entered the destination into the flight computer, afterward saying they were two hours and thirty minutes away.

"Let's hope our legs hold out and the back of the plane doesn't tear off. So much for Moretti's easy insert."

"Why isn't that aircraft destroyed?" The admiral asked the technician who'd locked the laser on the C-17 and pressed the button that sent a massive number of photons at it. "Radar shows the plane is still airborne," he added, tapping a finger on the monitor to illustrate his point.

"I know the laser struck the plane because I saw on my screen that two pieces of it fell from the sky," the tech replied.

"But it wasn't destroyed."

The tech wanted to tell the admiral that he'd been thoroughly briefed on the limitations of the laser system, giving the distance at which it was effective. However, not wanting to throw kerosene on the fire, he tried to explain the system's weapons envelope to him for a third time.

"Our targeting system is engineered to detect, track, and lock onto an object below forty thousand feet and no more than twenty miles away. The aircraft our weapon struck was near that altitude limitation and slightly more distant, making a precise lock on it questionable and the strike at less than optimum power," the scientist told the officer.

"Less than optimum?"

"Less powerful because energy dissipates with distance."

"I understand," the admiral irritably responded.

Then what's there left to discuss? The tech wanted to ask but thought better of it and changed the subject. "The plane we targeted may not have been a military aircraft," he offered.

"In this remote area of the ocean in the middle of the night, what else could it be?" the admiral persisted.

"We targeted a large plane, nearly the size of a Boeing 777 or an Airbus A330, and nothing was stealthy about it. It was transitioning the area on a steady course and heading, not emanating any pulses or signals indicating it was targeting us. I'm uncertain it was a military aircraft. Therefore, we may not have been discovered."

"There are no commercial airways over this section of the ocean, which is why I chose this route," the admiral said. "What else could it be but a military plane?"

"It's possible that a commercial or private aircraft deviated from published airways to avoid weather, shorten flight time, or for another logical reason. If the Americans had sent an aircraft to track us, it wouldn't have been a plane twenty-five or more times larger than a drone and, because of this size, would be manned and have significantly less time on station than a UAV."

"Maybe I am getting paranoid," the admiral admitted, "but I don't intend to die on my return to base after successfully pulling off the most successful intelligence operation in the history of the Russian Federation. Therefore, we'll embrace my paranoia and assume that any aircraft flying over or near us is adversarial and shoot it down. Understood?"

"Understood," the tech repeated.

When the leading edge of the cargo door was ripped from the aircraft, the Globemaster III was flying at two hundred and fifty mph. That was forty mph over its stall speed, or the minimum speed at which an aircraft is controllable. Any slower, and it would drop out of the sky. When the team fell out of the plane, they were a mile from their drop point, and because the only metal on them was in their parachutes, they were virtually impossible to detect on radar as they dropped toward the ocean. The Zodiac was another matter. Because of its outboard motor and the stash of weapons, ammo, combat gear, and other useful items inside waterproof bags strapped to the interior of the craft, it appeared on radar as a piece of the aircraft falling alongside the ramp that had been torn from the plane in the explosion.

After descending at one hundred and twenty mph before their chutes deployed, the team hit the water at seventeen mph, thrusting them five feet below the surface where each disengaged from their harness and thermal covering, leaving them wearing a wetsuit. Kicking to the surface, they found the sea was calm, with swells of three to four feet and a light wind. Alvarez and McGough were the closest to the CRCC, having hit the water a quarter mile from it, and although they couldn't see the craft in the darkness, the navigation device on their wrist gave them its position. Putting on flippers and a mask, which were attached by a carabiner to their gear, it took ten minutes to reach it. Bonaquist, who was the furthest away, took eighteen minutes to get there.

"Did anyone see what happened to the plane?" Moretti asked, throwing the question out for comment once everyone was geared up.

Although no one knew its fate, the consensus was that it had at least survived for the moment because they didn't see pieces of the enormous aircraft falling around them. However, everyone understand that was no guarantee it was able to make it to land and not ditch at sea.

It was 4:44 am, one hour and fifteen minutes before sunrise.

Moretti's last update from Parra on the location of the trawler was entered by the team into their tracking computers ten minutes before they tumbled out the back of the plane. The computer took into account their current position and showed the heading they needed to take to intercept the trawler. However, if it increased its speed even slightly, the intercept would be behind the vessel, and as Parra stated, it was a big ocean. Knowing they had one shot at this, Moretti instructed McGough, who would be steering the craft, to set their course to be in front of their projected intercept point. If they had to wait a little longer, so be it, but at least the trawler wouldn't have passed them. That readjustment turned out to be critical because, as their electric engine silently propelled them through the inky darkness, they heard the faint sound of a ship's engine off their port side, meaning the trawler had increased its speed. Five minutes later, as the sound of the ship got increasingly louder, they saw its green outline through their night vision goggles.

McGough adjusted course to intercept the vessel. However, even though the seas were calm, their required heading had them cutting diagonally across the ocean swells, the Zodiac robustly bouncing as it closed on and then paralleled the vessel they were after before matching its twenty mph speed.

While McGough kept the craft as close as possible to the trawler without slamming into it, Moretti took what looked like a bean bag gun on steroids out of its waterproof bag. However, instead of containing a small piece of fabric filled with number nine lead shot, it propelled a steel caving ladder with aluminum rungs and flexible sides made from wire rope. Affixed to the top of the ladder was a grappling hook that would grab onto the ship's railing or anything else it snagged.

The Nemesis team leader took fifteen seconds to get a feel for the bucking rhythm of the CRCC, continually adjusting the angle of his shot so that the grappling hook would travel far enough over the railing so that, with a tug, it would grab onto it, but not so far that it would clank off the steel bulkhead five feet behind it and alert the ship's crew to their presence. At the right moment, he fired the ladder. Propelled by compressed gas which made it virtually silent except for a faint pop, his aim was perfect and the hook cleared the railing by a foot and landed on the deck with a faint thud. After a quick tug, it latched onto the railing. Not wasting any time, Moretti went up the ladder as Alvarez anchored it with his weight. Han Li, Bonaquist, and Alvarez followed in that order, and once he secured the ladder to the CRCC, McGough came on board. It was nineteen minutes until sunrise.

Rear Admiral Tolya Balandin became an insomniac when he was placed in charge of the mission to steal Vigilant. Even though the system was no longer onboard, the Kremlin's plan called for the vessel he was on to act as a decoy, giving him a continual sense of insecurity that the Americans would find the trawler and send a special ops team to board it. After that, he believed it was anyone's guess whether they'd sink the ship, let them go because the system they were after was no longer onboard, which he viewed as the least likely outcome, or take everyone prisoner for their role in the theft. Usually, the Kremin would go crazy with such an act of aggression. However, since his vessel shot down a US drone, disabled an American submarine, and stole ninety-six missiles, hundreds of nuclear warheads, and billions of dollars of technology, what could they say? The evidence, the scrape marks on the side of the trawler containing paint from the *Resolute Eagle*, would be all the Americans would need to prove Moscow's involvement. Therefore, not knowing whether he'd be awoken in the middle of the night by United States special forces, he averaged three to four hours of sleep and came on the bridge at four in the morning rather than stare at the bulkheads in his cabin. This didn't surprise the captain, who also suffered the same insecurity. In addition to the insomniac pair, two crewmembers were also on the bridge.

Balandin poured himself a mug of coffee, which, judging from the dense black color, was made some time ago and had been sitting on the warmer. His first taste confirmed this longevity and produced a grimace, but it had the desired effect when the caffeine entered the body. Keeping to himself, he went to his chair on the starboard side of the bridge and stared through the window at the masthead light on the bow, which brightly illuminated the surrounding deck.

Three cups of coffee later, with sunrise about five minutes away, the admiral decided to go below deck and get something to eat, his stomach protesting the incursion of copious amounts of the strongly acidic coffee. As he stood, he glimpsed Bonaquist, Alvarez, and McGough running across the deck. The captain, who'd also seen this, pressed the collision alarm, following with an announcement over the ship's PA system that intruders were onboard the vessel.

The crew were out of their bunks, in their clothes, and grabbing their weapons within thirty seconds of hearing the warning. However, none were part of the GRU's Spetsnaz team, which had boarded the *Resolute Eagle* and subdued their crew. Instead, the team led by Vetrov, the FSB enforcer who reported directly to Abrankovich, had accompanied Vigilant onto another vessel. Therefore, those who remained on the trawler and responded to the alarm consisted of six men, all great at their shipboard assignments but who couldn't hit a target standing in front of them from ten feet away. They, along with the three techs who operated the laser weapon, Balandin, the captain, and the two other crewmembers on the bridge, were the only ones onboard.

Balandin knew the crew would be as ineffective as mall cops against an American special forces team. Realizing he needed to contact Moscow and inform them of the situation, and that he didn't have much time until the bridge was taken, he ran to the entry hatch to lower the steel batten that would secure it, attempting to keep the intruders away long enough for him to contact the Kremlin. However, as he was closing the hatch, Moretti slammed his body into it, throwing the admiral backward and onto the deck as he and Han Li burst inside.

As they entered, one of the crewmembers attacked Han Li,

believing that he could easily grab the automatic weapon from the hands of someone who was too beautiful to be harmful. That belief changed when the snap kick with the ball of her foot struck him in the face with such force that it sent him flying over Balandin and onto the deck. The crewman was out for the count. She and Moretti then frisked the four, relieving them of personal items before binding their hands and ankles with flex cuffs.

As Moretti and Han Li were going through their motions, the remainder of the team encountered the six crew members on their way to the top deck—all of whom laid down their weapons and raised their hands when they saw three armed men in combat gear approaching them. Each was frisked, marched to the top deck, and bound with flex ties. As Bonaquist watched over them, McGough and Alvarez searched the ship, finding the three techs smashing the console that controlled the laser weapon. Just as with the other crewmembers, they surrendered without incident and were frisked, brought to where Bonaquist was watching the other prisoners, and bound with flex ties. Alvarez and McGough continued their search, thirty minutes later reporting the trawler was secure.

On the bridge, Moretti and Han Li began inspecting everyone's wallets, finding that each had an identification card printed in Cyrillic, which was similar to the US alphabet except for the dozen additional letters invented to represent Slavic sounds.

"I'm surprised they have identification," Han Li said. "The photos look like them, but I don't know if their names, even if I could read them, are real."

"Let's send a copy of these to Libby and see if they're in NSA's database," Moretti offered.

He did, and within thirty minutes, Parra called and said she had background information on Balandin, the captain, and the three techs. "I should tell you," she added, knowing he was concerned about the fate of the C-17, "that Watkins and his crew landed safely at a commercial airport on a small island."

Moretti said that was good to hear, and would pass it on to his team.

"Getting back to your captives, the gray-haired person is Rear Admiral Tolya Balandin, the head of the Russian Foundation for Advanced Research Projects. They're responsible for developing systems that ensure the Russian Federation's defense superiority and analyzing its vulnerability to other nations' technology."

"What about the captain?" Moretti asked.

"Timur Gavrikov is, as far as we know, the current captain of a Russian Navy cruiser assigned to the Zapadnaya Litsa Naval Base in Murmansk Oblast on the Kola Peninsula. That he's in command of the trawler means the Kremlin holds him in very high esteem."

"And the techs?"

"They're associated with developing the Peresvet laser weapon, which explains how they shot down the drone without a missile warning indication and destroyed the cargo door on the C-17."

"I should be surprised at how you know all this, but I'm not," Moretti said, amazed at the amount of information Parra could amass in such a short time. "It's as if the Russians gave you their military personnel records."

"Close, but we didn't ask for them if you get my meaning," she responded and ended the call.

"Anything interesting?" Han Li asked as Moretti approached.

He told her what Parra said after they stepped out of earshot of the others. "Let's have Bonaquist bring his prisoners to the bridge so everyone is in one place. We'll gag them so they don't talk to each other or have the officers threaten the crew if they speak with us."

"That's a good idea," Han Li agreed.

While she ripped the shirt off the unconscious crewman and tore it into strips that would be used as gags, Moretti left the bridge to look for a room where he could speak with the prisoners, finding the ideal space when he opened the hatch to the captain's cabin. He returned to the bridge.

"I'll start with him," Moretti said as he pointed to Balandin. Taking a knife from its sheath, he cut the flex ties from the admiral's ankles. Grabbing his arm tightly and pulling him to his feet, Moretti took him to the cabin and removed the gag.

"Rear Admiral Tolya Balandin. Please have a seat," Moretti began, pointing to a chair.

"Your intelligence is as good as I was led to believe," he responded, not the least bit intimidated by his situation.

"I want the name of the ship transporting Vigilant," Moretti said, getting straight to the point.

"That wouldn't do you any good. It's beyond your reach, and you'll never get it back," the admiral said, not denying that he was responsible for the theft. "Our nations operate similarly. You steal our technology; we steal yours. Ultimately, it's a shell game that gives us technological and military parity. Some would argue this keeps the peace."

"We still want it back."

"You can torture me, but I'm stubborn, and the only result you'll get is giving an old man a heart attack."

"I'm curious as to why you didn't kill the *Resolute Eagle's* crew and scuttle the ship."

"For what purpose? We achieved our objective. Your government isn't going to accuse Russia of taking valuable technology from its military as easily as someone takes candy from a baby. That would result in international embarrassment and ridicule. However, if I killed the crew and sunk the vessel, you'd send one of my country's vessels to the ocean floor in retaliation. Again, for what purpose? We have the technology. Life moves on."

Moretti knew he made sense. After a few more questions, he gagged the admiral and returned him to the bridge, exchanging him for the captain, who refused to admit anything and was silent in response to his questions.

"How's it going?" Han Li asked when he returned the captain.

Moretti gave her a look that said he'd had better days. "No one's talking. Threatening Balandin and the captain is a no-win strategy because they know their government will eventually demand their return, probably exchanging them for one or more of our citizens who'll be accused of spying. The crew also understands that cooperation means that upon their return, instead of being hailed by the Kremlin as heroes and promoted for their participation in the theft of Vigilant, they'll be taken to Lubyanka and receive a bullet to the back of the head."

"Not everyone may think that way," Han Li said, nodding toward their prisoners.

"The techs?" Moretti asked.

"They'll know more than the crew," she replied.

"Get me one who speaks English," he said. "If none do, grab anyone."

Han Li asked if anyone spoke English. When a tech raised his hand, she cut his leg ties, pulled him to his feet, and shoved him toward Moretti, who brought him to the captain's cabin and removed his gag. One look at the tech's disheveled hair and clothing and the anxiety on their face told him this was a geek who was frightened about his future.

"You stole classified United States military hardware and destroyed a two hundred twenty million dollar drone," he began in a forceful voice. "You and everyone who participated in those attacks are on their way to a black site, where you'll spend the rest of your life being questioned and violated. Don't expect help from Moscow, because I'll make sure the Kremlin believes this ship went down with everyone onboard."

"I have a wife," the geek protested.

"She'll get remarried. Do you expect me to pat you on the back and say have a nice day after what you did? You're a terrorist who's trying to destroy our country."

"I didn't have a choice. I was ordered on this ship because I could operate and maintain the laser weapon."

"I don't care. The only thing that will keep you from a black site is if we get back our military hardware. What do you know about the ship that's transporting it?"

"You don't know the FSB. When they find out I helped you, they'll kill me and my wife."

"If you help me, I'll help you. I'll make it look like what I learned came from another source."

"How?"

"You'll see. I always keep my word. Do you have a choice?"

After pausing for several seconds to consider his options, which were none, the geek told him that almost everything was transferred to the Russian ship *Antias*.

ALAN REFKIN

"Is that a military vessel?"

"I don't know. It didn't have military markings, but it did fly the flag of the Russian Federation from its stern."

"You said almost everything. What does that mean?"

The tech told him.

"You've got to be kidding me," Moretti replied.

"Will you still keep your word that no one will know I cooperated with you?"

"I always keep my word."

"Then I should also mention that the controls to Peresvet are in the ship's communications room. That's where I was when your men found us."

"Is Peresvet a laser weapon?"

"Yes."

"Why is this important?"

"Because I sent a message to Moscow that the American military had boarded the ship."

"How did you know we were American if you didn't hear us speak?"

"The American flag on your shoulder," the geek said, pointing to it on Moretti's gear. "I saw it on your men when they walked past the weapon's security camera."

"Did Moscow respond to your message?"

"Immediately. I was told to activate the homing beacon and stall your departure until help arrives, which they said would be in six to seven hours."

"Does the admiral or captain know this?"

"I was captured before I had time to tell them."

"Let's keep them in the dark."

Moretti brought the geek back. Displaying the same *I've had better days* look that he's given after interrogating Balandin, he told Han Li in a voice that everyone could hear that he wasn't getting anywhere. He then questioned the rest of the crew which, since none spoke English, didn't go anywhere.

"I couldn't verify what the admiral said because no one else gave me anything," Moretti stated after returning the last crewman he'd questioned to the bridge. "The question is: do we take his unconfirmed information at face value and give him the asylum, money, and protection he demands, or leave him here with the others?"

"His team understood what he was up to and added their agreement that they should trust the admiral since he asked to come with them, making it unlikely that he would lie. Upon hearing this, Balandin tried to protest. However, with the gag inside his mouth, no one understood a word and didn't know if he was protesting what was said or demanding that he come with them.

"Then we'll give him the benefit of the doubt," Moretti stated. "I'll explain to Washington what he told us and request the State Department put him in the witness relocation program on our return to the States." Moretti then left the bridge to the sounds of Balandin's grunted screams, calling Parra and giving her the information provided by the tech.

"I'll find the *Antias* and put a Global Hawk over it," Parra said. "But I'm not optimistic you'll retrieve or destroy the command and control consoles. Some would call that impossible."

"At first blush, so do I, but I have to figure out a way. In the meantime, we have to get off this ship before the Russians arrive."

"About that. Keeping abreast of what's in the area, the nearest

Russian-flagged vessel that's even remotely heading in your direction is two hundred and twenty miles away, meaning it would take more than seven hours to reach you. I believe they have something else planned."

"What are you thinking, Libby?"

"If I was in charge of this operation, here's what I'd do," she said, telling him what she believed would happen.

"If we remain on this ship for any length of time, that's going to ruin our day. We need to get off the trawler ASAP."

"That's especially important because you and your team need to stay alive at least long enough to commandeer the *Antias*, which is getting further away every second."

"As touching as your concern is, I have my own idea of how my team and I can extend our lifespans if you'll pass it along to Cray and have him speak with the president," Moretti said, telling her what was needed.

"You're amazingly consistent."

"Thanks."

"That wasn't a compliment. I meant that your plans consistently lack finesse and get you into situations where you're likely to get yourself and everyone with you killed."

"Oh."

CHAPTER 10

ONE OF THE SIDE effects of waterboarding is that it triggers the release of catecholamines, or stress hormones, causing a rapid increase in heart rate and blood pressure, which sometimes results in a heart attack. The large influx of these hormones into the bloodstream also incites the heart to beat abnormally or causes its muscle cells to contract uncontrollably. Adamik wasn't over the edge, meaning his heart wasn't about to call it a day, but he was close when he was carried to the colonel's Škoda Kodiaq, a mid-size crossover SUV similar to the Volkswagen Tiguan Allspace, and laid in the back as flat as anyone five feet eleven inches tall could be. With his friend breathing erratically, shivering uncontrollably, and his teeth chattering, Laska cranked the car's heater to its maximum setting, which took a while to get going because it was cold and the vehicle wasn't moving. He got Adamik out of his soaked clothes, replacing them with his cashmere overcoat, scarf, and knit cap, which soon became wet from absorbing the water still clinging to the detective's body.

"This isn't going to work. The heater is not kicking out enough warm air. I'm going to find you dry clothing," the colonel said as he got out of the car without waiting for an acknowledgment from Adamik and began retracing his steps to the farmhouse, hoping to find clothing from one of the assailants inside. Failing that, he intended to strip one of them and bring their clothing back to the car. However, another thought occurred when he passed the two Lenco BearCat Tactical SUVs that were used by the Agency's hostage rescue team, seeing three of their members securing their weapons and equipment in preparation for returning their vehicles to wherever they kept them. Laska approached one of them and asked if he had spare clothing, telling them who it was for.

"I heard he was waterboarded twice and didn't give the Russians the time of day," the man said. "He's a badass. Let him know we could use someone like him if he wants to come over to the dark side."

"I'll tell him."

"From what I saw, we're about the same size," the team member said, handing Laska his team bag. "There's a clean set of what I'm wearing, plus some other stuff he might find useful."

Laska thanked him.

"What's his name?" The man asked as the colonel turned to leave.

"Adamik," he answered. "Juraj Adamik."

He returned to his car, finding the detective sitting up with his hands almost touching the rear heater vent. Laska told him about the encounter with the HRT member and his invitation to join the team.

"I heard the CIA has a good pension," Adamik said.

"Czech police officers don't get waterboarded."

Adamik gave him a questioning shrug.

Laska realized what he'd said. "Most of the time. Let's see what's in the bag."

As Adamik continued to warm his hands, the colonel began removing its contents, handing the detective a towel, thermal underwear, a tactical jumpsuit, boots, socks, and a jacket, but only showing him the bottle of Red River Texas Bourbon he'd taken from the bottom of the bag. "That's for later," Laska said.

"My heart no longer feels like it's going to explode. But I do have a headache, although not as bad as when I self-medicated with the Slivovitz."

"A valuable health tip which I'll pass onto the force," the colonel quipped.

The ambassador knocked on the window, and Laska got out of the car.

"How is he?" Iwinski asked.

"He's getting back to being Adamik."

The detective, dressed in a tactical jumpsuit and jacket with CIA stenciled on the front and back, stepped out of the vehicle and approached them. "We need to get back to the farmhouse, or we'll never know what Orlov is telling Calbot because the CIA has a reputation for not sharing information," Adamik said.

"You know that Calbot will insist on taking over the investigation to find our spy and won't want local law enforcement involved?" Iwinski said.

"What do you want to do?" Adamik asked, looking at the ambassador and Laska.

"What we said earlier," Iwinski answered. "We still need to protect ourselves because, if something goes wrong, the CIA will have a dozen people at Langley working on how to spin what happened to their benefit, portraying us as the ones who screwed up."

"Therefore, whatever factual information we discover will be our only defense. Since we're in agreement, let's get back in the game and join the party inside the farmhouse to see what the CIA is up to," Adamik said, receiving nods from Laska and the ambassador.

When they returned to the interrogation room, Calbot abruptly stopped speaking with Orlov and frowned when he saw Adamik wearing the HRT gear, although he didn't want to take the time to get into a conversation about how he got it. From the look of irritation on his face, he wanted to tell the three to get out because they were interrupting his conversation with the Russian assassin. However, he knew he couldn't because Laska was the senior police officer in Prague, and Iwinski was the American ambassador and a close friend of the president. Calbot also understood that the colonel could arrest Orlov and throw him in a cell, making the assassin the problem of the Russian Embassy, who'd immediately get him released from jail and flown to Russia, guaranteeing that the CIA wouldn't get another shot at speaking with him.

"What are you going to do with him?" Iwinski asked Calbot, pointing to Orlov.

"I learned that he knows has information that's of critical intelligence value to the Agency. However, if he's arrested, this useful information depletes rapidly. For your purposes," he said, looking at Iwinski, "he's not at a level where he knows the identity of our spy. For the benefit of both our countries," he said, switching his focus to Laska, "letting the CIA speak with him seems to be the logical choice."

"Why is it logical?"

"Because he's a diplomat, and you don't need the criticism you'll receive from those above you for arresting him. It's not a good career move."

"Therefore, he's going with you?" Iwinski asked.

"He's not going with me. I only want to speak with him before he returns to the embassy."

"As a guess, that would mean he escaped Adamik's rescue by the CIA and Prague police and was lucky to make it back to the embassy alive," Iwinski predicted. "How is it credible that he survived that confrontation?"

"Because he'll be nursing a nasty flesh wound for a couple of days," Calbot said, taking his gun from his shoulder holster and sending a round that creased the soft tissue of Orlov's left arm, drawing blood and shocking the assassin and everyone else in the room. "The wound and accompanying infection will give credibility to his story. An inspection of this place will show shell casings and bullet holes reflecting a gunfight took place, once again giving credence to his explanation of events and putting him above suspicion."

"He needs a doctor," Iwinski said.

"It can't appear that he received medical help in the two days he avoided our efforts to capture him and eventually made it back to Prague."

"There seems to be a lack of bullet holes in this place to corroborate your story," Laska said, looking around the room.

"There won't be once you're gone. The Russians are very good at forensic science. I need to be precise at where the shots came from, and that where the weapons are found is consistent with Orlov's story."

"You've obviously done this before," Laska commented.

"Once or twice."

"What about his men?" the ambassador asked. "They saw what happened and watched the both of you carrying on a conversation."

"They'll be taken to another country and debriefed, although the story will be that they defected and requested asylum in exchange for what they know. Depending on what that is, they'll either go into a protection program or spend the rest of their lives somewhere they don't want to be. Therefore, what occurred here will correspond with Orlov's explanation of events, giving no one a reason not to trust him in the future."

"The disposition of him and his men is not your decision; it's mine, and I prefer that they occupy our jail cells. Thinking on it, repercussions or not, they kidnapped and tortured one of my men, and Orlov is responsible for a triple homicide. Technically, the Czech Republic has the sole right to arrest and detain them. No one will sympathize with a murderer," Laska said, interjecting himself into the conversation. "Remember that the United States is a guest in our country."

"Normally, you'd be correct about your jurisdiction," Calbot responded, his voice unexpectedly confident. "However, thanks to your efforts, there was no triple homicide. As for kidnapping your detective, as we discussed, do you want to open Pandora's Box by arresting Russian diplomats? That will expose your coverup of the murders. If you give them to me, everyone wins in the end."

"My staff will still need to question Orlov because, even though he might not know the identity of our spy, he could have information that will lead us to him," Iwinski said.

"With all due respect, you're an ambassador in charge of a diplomatic mission and not an investigative arm of the United States government. The Central Intelligence Agency has the authority in a foreign country to investigate and question anyone who represents a clear and present danger to the United States or knows someone who is," Calbot clarified. "Regarding espionage, we're technically obligated to coordinate with Czech intelligence and not the police. However, I can tell you from experience that they'd say this investigation belongs solely to us because they'd rather not stir up a hornet's nest with the Russians over something that only affects the United States and not their sovereignty."

"If I was a suspicious person, and given the CIA's reputation, I'd say you and the HRT didn't come here to rescue Adamik, but had another agenda," the ambassador said.

"Which is?"

"To turn the Russian into your agent. What better way to spy on Moscow and feed them disinformation at the same time? It would be a significant feather in your cap."

"You'll have to trust that the CIA is here because it acted in everyone's best interest," Calbot said, ignoring Iwinski's remarks.

"That's an oxymoron," the ambassador responded.

"What does that mean?"

"Look it up in the dictionary," he said, storming from the room.

"Can I get a ride back to Prague?" Iwinski asked. "Calbot's not returning to the embassy anytime soon, and after what I said, he'll probably tell me that he doesn't have room in one of the team vehicles."

Laska told him to get in. The ambassador sat in the back to keep an eye on Adamik.

"I'm sorry I wasted your time with this investigation. You did everything I asked for and more. I owe you," Iwinski said to Laska.

"What Calbot said hasn't changed anything."

"On the contrary, everything's changed now that he's taking charge of the investigation," the ambassador countered.

"What does taking charge really mean?" Adamik interjected. "He doesn't know anything of substance other than a high-level American spy is feeding the Russians valuable intelligence. As far as the photo is concerned, although someone whose face has been blurred is making a drop, that person may or may not be your spy. That's a supposition we made because of the flash drive. However, an intermediary could have made the drop for them. As I said, the Agency knows next to nothing. However, that could change if they learn when and where Archangel is to drop the reactivation code."

"I don't disagree. But most of what Calbot said also rings true. Therefore, how do we keep ourselves in the game without him having the State Department or the Agency clip our wings?" Iwinski asked.

"By taking a different approach. How long do you think this spy has worked for the Russians?" Adamik asked.

"I can't answer that because we know next to nothing about them. But let's suppose they're a senior-level official and not a political appointee, which I don't believe because they couldn't transition from one administration to the next. In that case, they've worked their way to a position of trust and authority. In my experience, it usually takes a couple of decades to get to the top, whether in government or industry. I also don't believe this person is a politician, meaning a member of Congress, because that's a group of narcissists and not idealogues. They've figured out how to become rich by catering to lobbyists and special interest groups, and using inside information for stock market transactions. Therefore, spying is too risky and not as profitable," Iwinski stated.

"Politicians are no different here," Adamik admitted.

"Getting back to what you said, what's your different approach?" Iwinski asked.

"I believe the spy and their handler, to keep their identities a secret to all but a few, have worked together for some time and that if we identify the handler, we'll identify the spy," Adamik said.

"It makes sense that he'd have the same handler the entire time because Moscow would want as few people as possible to know about him. But won't identifying the handler be as difficult as finding the spy?" Iwinski asked.

"If done individually, yes. But not together."

"Is he always this confusing?" Iwinski asked Laska.

"Most of the time," he replied to the ambassador before turning to Adamik. "Juraj," the colonel said, addressing the detective by his first name. "For those of us who are less gifted than you, explain what you're thinking in more detail."

"From what we know, it appears the Russian embassy has been the conduit for the transfer of information with their spy. That's important because, in my experience, it's a protocol for embassies to keep a record of those who are assigned there or enter the premises, such as visiting State Department and DOD officials, government contractors, officials from alphabet agencies, ordinary civilians, etc.," Adamik stated.

Iwinski confirmed this recordkeeping was standard practice for diplomatic missions.

"If we compare the names of those who worked at or visited a Russian embassy or consulate with the records from American diplomatic missions in those same cities and at the same time, the names that match will be our spy and their handler."

"There will be hundreds of thousands of records to compare, half of which we can't access because that information resides in the Russian Federation's databases," Laska responded.

"Nevertheless, this information exists, and I'm confident that, because of the ambassador's relationship with the president, we can get this comparative analysis," Adamik said.

"It's a stretch to presume we have Russian embassy visitor logs and staff records," Iwinski said.

"From what I hear, your National Security Agency has records for how much caviar the Russian Embassy orders for its parties. I don't believe the issue will be whether the data exists, but if they release it by presidential order and do not say that the records don't exist because they wish to hide their monitoring capabilities and fear that politicians and those associated with them will reveal this sensitive information."

"I'll ask the president. He'll convey the importance of obtaining this information and that the existence of this spy impacts the entire intelligence community, including the NSA," the ambassador said. "Assume we identify this person. How do we prove they're our traitor?"

"By setting a trap," Adamik answered.

It was 6:45 am local time and forty-five minutes past midnight in Washington when Iwinski returned to his office and called POTUS, waking him from a sound sleep. The ambassador apologized for calling at this hour, which Ballinger quickly brushed aside by saying that, as the Chief Executive of the United States, he was always on call. Iwinski then told him about Adamik's kidnapping, the CIA's intervention, and the detective's idea on how to identify their spy.

"That's very clever," the president conceded.

"The detective believes the NSA has this information, but that's speculation," the ambassador said.

"I recall from the capabilities briefings I received when I first came into office that, if this data exists, although the NSA may have it in its entirety, the composite of this information is more likely to reside in the databases of several alphabet agencies and government entities. Although I don't know with ones, I'll find out," the president responded.

"The downside, of course, is that if what we believe is correct, the spy may be in one of these agencies or entities and take steps to cover their tracks."

"I have a way to retrieve the data and keep this search quiet."

"How?"

"Leave that to me."

Once the call ended, Ballinger phoned Angela Johnson at Nemesis, updated her on what happened, and put the ball in her lap. Because she, along with ex-NSA techs Alexson and Connelly, lived in base quarters at Site R, she got the techies out of bed and to the team office in less than twenty minutes. When they arrived, she held a mug of strong black coffee in one hand and pointed to two Red Bulls in front of their computers with the other. The techs, who thrived on the one hundred and eleven mg of caffeine in each can, made a beeline for them. As they were getting fully caffeinated, she explained what was needed.

"Since the Nemesis computer system pulls data from every government database, we don't need to hack into them because we're already connected. However, you should know there are approximately one hundred fifty thousand servers across the federal government in over fifty-nine hundred data centers. Once we write the algorithm to pull the required information, it'll take time to access them and perform the permutations necessary to get the list of names," Connelly explained.

"The president said he recalls that the information is contained in the databases of a few alphabet agencies and government entities. However, he can't recall which ones. He also says the NSA may have it all."

"Which is why we need to access the databases for the entire federal government, including the NSA," Connelly continued. "Our search will range from embassy employees to civilians appearing on an embassy's visitors log. If there's a link between two individuals, we'll find it. However, performing comparative analysis on decades of data in multiple databases involving many people and multiple cities will take a while," Alexson stated, with Connelly agreeing.

"Define a while," Johnson said.

"If everything goes perfectly, approximately twelve hours."

"And if things don't go our way?"

"If we have to strong-arm the information, meaning going outside government databases to civilian systems, eighteen to twenty-four hours. That's as close an estimate as I can give because we've never done this broad a comparative search."

"What can I do to help?" Johnson asked.

"Get us more of these from the commissary," Alexson said, holding up his can of Red Bull, after which he and Connelly turned away from Johnson and began discussing what their algorithm should look like. It was 1:30 am.

As the Nemesis techs began writing their algorithm, Parra was wide awake and staring at the photo of the person suspected of being the mole. What troubled her was that she knew the face was pixelated rather than blurred for a reason. Knowing she was getting into an area beyond her technical expertise, she phoned the skinny twenty-two-year-old kid with round-rimmed glasses who'd previously helped her, waking him up and telling the techie to get to the office because he was coming to work six hours earlier than usual. Although there were other geeks she could have called, some of whom were working the night shift in the building, she didn't want to widen the circle of those involved in finding the spy.

The skinny tech, who didn't live close to NSA headquarters, arrived at her office at 2:30 am. Parra didn't waste any time, showing him the pixelated photo and asking if he could reveal the face.

"That depends on whether the process to obscure it involves an encryption key. Let me take this to my lab. I should be able to unblur it with one of the programs in my computer," the tech said, hoping he could keep that promise.

Visual cryptography uses an encryption algorithm to obscure visual information, such as photos. Various off-the-shelf products do this, all of which the NSA can break instantaneously, something that software companies know but will never admit because it would be bad for sales.

However, an hour after he began his attempt to unblur the face, which involved the use of numerous proprietary programs and every cryptographic tool in the NSA's arsenal, the skinny tech discovered that none worked, leading him to the only possible explanation: that whoever blurred this image used a one-time pad, or OTP, knowing it was the only encryption method the NSA couldn't break because it required the unique single-use key.

The reason for this unbreakability was that the OTP used a random series of characters for encryption. For example, while the first * might encrypt to the letter A, the next * might encrypt to an X, and the third to a symbol, such as an @ or %. Conversely, a V could encrypt to a C, and a # to an A. This randomness made decryption impossible without the key.

Before giving Parra the bad news that there was no way the

underlying face could be revealed without the key, he wanted to show her that he'd tried everything, and that his analysis was systematic and thorough. Therefore, to cross every t and dot every i, he decided to impress her by adding to his report that he'd examined the photo with a digital microscope. Not expecting anything to come from this analysis because he viewed what he was doing as window dressing, he nearly fell out of his chair twenty minutes later when he looked at the microscope's LED display screen.

CHAPTER 11

WHEN ABRANKOVICH LEARNED THAT an American military team was onboard the trawler, he phoned Putin and briefed him on the situation. "We have to assume that someone on the crew will talk," the general stated.

"Do you understand the implications of that statement?"

"That everyone takes what they know to their graves."

"We haven't much time."

"I'll arrange it," Abrankovich responded.

"And take the same precaution once the *Antias* completes its mission."

The general said he'd make the necessary calls at the appropriate time.

"What's the fastest way to destroy the trawler?" Putin asked.

Abrankovich, accessing the military database, took a moment to find the answer. "Because none of our naval assets are close, and the ship is beyond the range of a cruise missile, I'll need to dispatch an aircraft."

"From which base?"

"Our nearest foreign installation is in the Central African Republic, approximately three thousand miles from the ship. The Tupolev Tu-95 aircraft there carry Storm missiles capable of destroying the vessel."

"How long will the aircraft take to get to its target?"

"Six or seven hours."

"Give the order. Afterward, tell the person you spoke with on the ship that help is on the way and to do whatever it takes to keep the intruders onboard."

"We'll be killing Americans."

"The stakes are too high to let them live. I can't chance that Balandin, the captain, or anyone else tell them what we've done. A secret is only a secret if no one knows."

Commander William Quinn of the *USS Florida* was in his cabin contemplating whether he should retire to Wyoming because he enjoyed the outdoors and it was the least populous state which, after being inside submarines for most of his career was a plus, or whether he should grow old in a slightly more populated one like Montana. The reason for this sudden interest in where to retire was his belief that when he returned to port and filed his report detailing the sequence of flawed assumptions he'd made, assuming command didn't put together his litany of mistakes beforehand, that he'd be relieved of command and forced to retire, hopefully at his current rank. However, unknown to him, two happenstances were in process that would negate his screwup and save his career. The first was that naval operations determined that, since *Florida* had over five months left on its one-hundred-eighty-day deployment and was already in the Atlantic, it was the perfect submarine to patrol the Arabian Sea, a current naval priority. Not knowing of the *Resolute Eagle* fiasco, orders were issued.

Because time is money to everyone but the government, commercial vessels transitioned from the Atlantic Ocean to the Arabian Sea using the Suez Canal, which was the shortest sea route between Asia and Europe, and then proceeded across the Red Sea and Gulf of Aden to the Arabian Sea. However, because of the numerous undersea listening devices placed by foreign governments on the relatively shallow ocean floor along that route, the United States Navy had a standing order that its submarines would take the longer Cape Route, which skirted the Cape of Good Hope in southern Africa, where the ocean was significantly deeper. Subsequently, the *USS Florida* was on this route when the captain's second career-saving moment came in response to Moretti's call to POTUS requesting his team and their prisoners be evacuated from the trawler. During their conversation, and unknown to Quinn, he also asked the president to arrange for another group to accompany Nemesis in boarding *Antias* and for the secure transport of Vigilant once it was secured.

"It looks like we're back in the game," Quinn told his XO after handing him their new orders.

"This is from the National Command Authority, which usually means the White House," the XO said, surprised it came from the highest military authority and not the Chief of Naval Operations. "Could this be the same trawler that dropped its net on us?"

"If it is, I'm only sorry the NCA didn't say to put a torpedo into it," Quinn said, wanting to even the score with the captain of that ship.

"Our orders specify that we proceed to the listed coordinates at our fastest possible speed, using the provided homing beacon frequency to establish the ship's precise location. We're then to come alongside and bring onboard a special operations team and their prisoners, taking direction from the team's leader as to where *Florida* will sail following the rendezvous."

"Bring the boat to flank speed and set course for the given coordinates," Quinn said, flank speed for *Florida* being forty mph. "Once we're underway, have the comms officer monitor for the homing frequency and, once we're in range and he's locked onto it, provide course adjustments to the bridge," the captain ordered. Five hours later, the *USS Florida* surfaced abeam of the trawler and, after taking everyone onboard, left the ship adrift with its homing beacon still active.

The flagship for the United States Second Fleet was the aircraft carrier *USS Dwight D. Eisenhower*, under the command of Captain Charles Ruebensaal. Nicknamed *Ike* by the Navy, some crew referred to it as *Ikeatraz* because every Navy ship had a derogatory nickname attached to it, as that was the nature of life at sea.

The Second Fleet's mission was to project US naval power from the North Pole to the Caribbean Sea, and from the eastern shore of the United States to the middle of the Atlantic Ocean—an area of six million, seven hundred thousand square miles. The *Eisenhower* was in the mid-Atlantic when the ship's comms officer arrived on the bridge and handed Ruebensaal an envelope with *a Top* Secret stamp on it. Inside were orders from the National Command Authority ordering the ship to send a helicopter to the *USS Florida*, providing its position and contact frequency, and bring onboard a special operations team and their prisoners. The team was to be given tactical command in the field and unrestricted assistance to support its intercept and boarding of the Russian-flagged factory fishing vessel *Antias*, whose current position, course, and speed were provided. Once the vessel was secured, the *Eisenhower* was to bring the fishing vessel's cargo onboard, using the captured ship's cranes to make the transfer. Afterward, they were to leave the *Antias* intact and set course for their home port of Naval Station Norfolk, placing the cargo under heavy security while en route.

"It doesn't look like we're bringing frozen fish onboard if we're putting it under guard and returning to port," Kullman remarked after the captain showed him the orders. "Prisoners?"

"That could be interesting. Also, supporting a special ops team boarding a Russian vessel could put us and our support group in the middle of an armed conflict. Give the other ships our projected course change to *Florida,* and I'll brief their captains. Afterward, get two Black Hawks on the flight deck and prepped. Also, make sure their crews are briefed that the team they're carrying may be doing a hot insertion onto the *Antias*," the captain said.

"To confirm, you want to prep two Black Hawks. One will accommodate the team," Kullman volunteered.

"If this mission is as important as it appears, I want a backup aircraft."

"Understood."

Ruebensaal and Kullman worked well as a team, having served together onboard the amphibious assault ship *USS Marco Island*, with Ruebensaal requesting him as his XO when given command of the giant carrier.

"The *Antias* is currently under power at twenty-eight mph," the XO said, moving to the electronic chart on the bridge and bringing up the factory ship's current position. "At full speed," which he knew was forty mph, "this would be our intercept," he said, putting his finger on a spot on the map. As he was doing this, the comms officer returned to the bridge and handed Ruebensaal another Top Secret envelope.

"It looks like we have more good news," the captain remarked after reading what was in the envelope. "This came directly from the president, identifying one group of special operators we're bringing on board as Moretti's team."

"If Moretti's involved, this might not be any less dangerous than when he and his team were rescuing a hostage from a ship, and we protected it from two missile-carrying Mi-24 Hind helicopters that were streaking towards the vessel," Kullman said.

"I remember—the good old days on *Marco Island*," the captain remarked. "It also looks like we're getting the same players together because this message goes on to say that Hunter and his squad from SEAL Team 4, the same squad that fought alongside Moretti during the hostage rescue, are in transit. This is their arrival time," he said, showing the last part of the message to the XO.

"There are eight operational SEAL teams, each with two eight-person squads. If Hunter and his men are on their way here, the odds are that it's because Moretti requested them. It's a good thing you prepped a second Black Hawk," Kullman stated.

"Moretti must think the Russians won't voluntarily give up whatever cargo is on the *Antias*, and they will have to take it by force. That's why he requested Hunter's team. Whatever cargo they're after, it must be pretty important to place it under heavy guard on an aircraft carrier surrounded by its support group," Ruebensaal said.

"Securing this cargo may drag *Ike* into a combat situation."

"Maybe. This means that we need to get any complacency out of our crew and be razor-sharp if the shit hits the fan. Hold at least two combat drills and have the support ships do the same to ensure we're at the top of our game and ready for armed conflict," Ruebensaal said.

The UH-60A Black Hawk helicopter was a fifty-foot-long, fourteen-foot-wide, and twelve-foot-high aircraft that could reach a speed of two hundred twenty mph. Although it had a combat radius of approximately three hundred and seventy miles, meaning the operational distance it could carry men and equipment and then patrol the area for a fixed amount of time and return with a safe fuel load, its maximum one-way distance with a full load of fuel was thirteen hundred and eighty-one miles.

After lifting off from the *Eisenhower*, one of the carrier's Black Hawks rendezvoused with the *USS Florida* and, hovering over the boat, lifted Moretti's team and their prisoners onboard the aircraft. Two hours later, when it returned to the carrier, the trawler's crew was taken to the brig while Moretti and his team were escorted to their quarters—two-person rooms located, according to the sign on the entry hatch, in officer country. Moretti and Han Li and McGough and Alvarez were paired in two-person accommodations, while Bonaquist had a cabin to himself.

"The captain wants to see you and your team in the ready room in fifteen minutes," their escort said, unable to take his eyes off Han Li.

"What's a ready room, and where is it?" Moretti asked.

"It's where aircrews have their pre- and post-flight briefings. We're on deck 02; the ready room is on 03, one deck below," he said, afterward explaining which direction they should turn once they left their cabin, the ladder they had to take to get there, and the several other twists and turns that needed to be made to end up at their destination.

"Just remember the bullseye is 3-95-2-P."

"Bullseye?"

"They're throughout the ship—yellow squares painted on the wall which contain codes that act as maps, each giving your location. The ready room code of 3-95-2-P means it's on the third deck, at the ninety-fifth frame, and the second compartment outboard from the ship's centerline on the starboard side. The P is the code for a ready room. Since there are several of them on board, if you get lost, find a crewmember and give them the code instead of saying you're going to the ready room. They'll point you in the right direction."

"Got it," Moretti said, repeating the code.

The Nemesis team left their cabins five minutes after their escort departed and took the down ladder to deck 03, finding themselves at the intersection of four passageways and uncertain which to take. Complicating the situation was that, although *Eisenhower* had a crew of five thousand sailors, the nearest ones to them were some distance away. Therefore, there was no one to point them in the right direction.

"Any suggestions?" Moretti asked, throwing the problem to the team.

"This bullseye shows we're on the correct deck and at the ninety-fifth frame," Han Li said, pointing to it, "so we have a starting point. Where it gets fuzzy is finding the second compartment outboard from the ship's centerline on the starboard side because we don't know the location of the centerline or which direction is starboard."

"McGough," Bonaquist said. "The Corps is part of the Navy. Didn't they teach you this stuff?"

"I spent most of my career flown into action by an Air Force aircraft or taken there by helicopter. I never spent much time on Navy ships, and when onboard, I followed the herd to one of the food service areas or briefing rooms. I know that the ship's starboard is to the right as you face the bow, and port is to the left. Beyond that, I have no clue."

"And the centerline?"

"On this floating city, your guess is as good as mine."

Moretti suggested they pick a direction to see if the numbers increased or decreased, and they could adjust to find their destination. While that logic seemed sound, ten minutes later, they still couldn't find the ready room. Their salvation came when they encountered a crewmember who escorted them to the ready room after hearing the bullseye address.

As they entered, they were greeted by Ruebensaal and Kullman, Lieutenant Eric Hunter, squad commander of Seal Team 4, nicknamed LT by the team, who pronounced each letter separately; Petty Officer First Class Nate Frye, their squad leader; Petty Officer Third Class Steve Kirk, and the five other squad members.

Once Moretti and his team had a chance to get a cup of coffee, Ruebensaal told everyone to take a seat in one of the thickly cushioned armchairs, after which he read the orders that he received from the NCA.

"They don't indicate the nature of the cargo. Does anyone know what we're after?" Hunter asked.

"Moretti, can you fill in the blanks?" The captain said.

"Four days ago on February sixteenth, in an area of the Atlantic Ocean north of Bermuda," Moretti began, "a Russian-flagged trawler pulled alongside the unmarked Navy vessel *Resolute Eagle*, and an assault team of approximately forty boarded it and stole Vigilant, our nation's newest and most technologically advanced weapon system."

"It sounds as if the Navy was going to drop it onto the ocean floor," Ruebensaal said. "If I'm not mistaken, the seabed in that area is several miles deep. Only a DSV wouldn't be crushed at that depth. But, you said Vigilant was a weapon's system."

"The system consists of ninety-seven missiles with MIRVs

housing four hundred eighty-five nuclear warheads," Moretti said, explaining UFPs and the crushproof capsules in which the missiles resided. "Setup and activation of the system are handled by two command and control consoles, which were also stolen. This means whoever has this package can launch one or more of these missiles and decimate nearly five hundred targets. In naval terms, think of one Vigilant system as having the nuclear firepower of five missile submarines," Moretti explained, drawing looks of astonishment from everyone but his team, who already knew what they were up against.

"How did you get involved?" Kullman asked.

"Not going into specifics, my team was tasked with retrieving what was stolen. We found the trawler, paid it a visit, and discovered that the missiles and warheads had been transferred to the fishing factory *Antias*, which is the target of our mission."

"Let's go back. I've always believed that launching one of our nuclear missiles would be impossible without a code from the NCA," Ruebensaal said, trying to confirm what he'd been taught.

"That's how I understood the system worked," Moretti agreed. "However, because Vigilant wasn't activated, the NCA doesn't have control over its missiles. Whoever has the consoles can create a launch code and select the impact points. In other words, if we don't get our weapon system back, we're going to be subjected to nuclear blackmail for decades because, at the depths these sit, they're undetectable and indestructible. And, even if one was discovered, any explosive device we try to launch at it will implode long before reaching its target."

"Our backs are to the wall. We need to retrieve this system," Ruebensaal said.

"I'm all for that. Getting back to the *Antias*, we should expect forty tangos who won't willingly hand over the system," Hunter said, using the special ops term for a terrorist or enemy combatant.

"Forty is the number I was given, and I don't expect they'll give up the missiles without a significant fight," Moretti confirmed.

"Taking a look at the logistics," Ruebensaal said, "at our present speed, we're only gaining twelve miles every hour on the *Antias*, which means it'll take more than a day to intercept it. Has the president considered sending one of our aircraft armed with a Harpoon antiship missile, or *Eisenhower* launching a cruise missile, to sink the ship? That vessel would be on the ocean floor within the hour."

"President Ballinger made it clear he doesn't want to blow up the ship because the explosions might damage one or more of the crush-proof containers that encapsulate the missiles. If that happens, when it sinks and reaches crush depth, the nuclear warheads will implode, and radioactive waste will be released and spread worldwide because of the ocean's currents. Economic and environmental catastrophes will ensue. Shorelines will become radioactive; ships will become contaminated; economies dependent on fishing will suffer because of the radiation levels in marine life; and the United States will become a pariah because, once the radiation contaminants are analyzed, the fission materials will be verified of United States origin."

"Whenever you're ready, we'll use Black Hawks to transport your teams to the ship," Ruebensaal said to Moretti.

"What are your thoughts?" Hunter asked the Nemesis team leader.

"Your team will disable the vessel while mine neutralizes their communication capabilities so they can't summon help," Moretti answered.

"That works. Forty tangos. This will be messy," Hunter said.

"The only easy day was yesterday," Moretti told him, repeating the Navy SEALs motto.

"We'll make that happen," he said, the rest of his team agreeing. "When is wheels up?"

Moretti looked at Ruebensaal.

"Again, it's at your command," the captain said. "The Black Hawks are ready, and the crews are waiting by their aircraft."

"Give us thirty minutes to coordinate our functions and give you a list of the equipment and munitions we'll need onboard the helicopters," Moretti said, drawing a nod from Hunter and Frye that this would be enough time. "Once our supplies are on the aircraft, it's wheels," Moretti said.

"Given the *Antias'* distance from the carrier, the Black Hawks will need to return for fuel not long after you're inserted. If the shit hits the fan, don't expect cover fire from them."

"The only easy day was yesterday," Moretti and Hunter simultaneously replied.

The Tupolev Tu-95, which took off from the Central African Republic seven hours earlier, was a four-engine turboprop strategic bomber, around the size of an American B-52, with a range of seven thousand eight hundred miles. Within its bomb bay, it carried Kh-22 Storm missiles. Designed for use against aircraft carriers and their battle groups, the Storm was overkill against the unarmored and much smaller trawler.

The plane's pilot used the ship's homing beacon signal, relayed via satellite, to get the trawler's position. Although he could have launched the Storm from as far away as three hundred seventy miles and used the sudden loss of the homing beacon signal to verify its destruction, his orders were to film the ship's destruction.

Prior to launch, he had a choice of selecting either the high-altitude or low-altitude mode. The latter meant the missile's liquid-fueled rocket engine would ignite, take it to thirty-nine thousand feet and, guided by a gyroscope-stabilized autopilot, send it into a dive toward the ship where it would impact the vessel at a speed of Mach 3.5. However, because he was filming the trawler's demise for the brass in Moscow, he selected the high-altitude mode, which he knew would be a Hollywood-worthy event, the missile rapidly climbing to eighty-seven thousand feet before diving toward the trawler and impacting it at Mach 4.6.

The pilot released the Storm from the aircraft ten miles from the trawler and, as scripted, it rapidly climbed to an altitude of sixteen and a half miles before descending at more than thirty-five hundred mph and obliterating the ship on impact.

CHAPTER 12

IT WAS 6:30 AM when Adamik, accompanied by Laska, returned to Madam Irenka's, where he took a shower, changed clothes, and went to the kitchen. A pot of Bohemian beef soup with noodles was on the stove, and both ladled a generous amount into their bowls before sitting at the communal table. Neither spoke for five minutes, preferring instead to focus on eating the flavorful soup.

"Do you think Calbot's story of just wanting to speak with Orlov is true, or do you think he wants to turn him into a CIA spy?" Laska asked after returning the spoon to his empty bowl.

"Definitely, a spy," Adamik said. "Lisov was their spy at the embassy, and now that he's gone, Orlov is the perfect person to replace that hole in their intelligence gathering."

"That makes sense," Laska agreed. "But why would Orlov cooperate? He has diplomatic immunity and Calbot would have to let him go."

"When we interrupted his conversation with Calbot, Orlov wasn't protesting about his diplomatic rights, nor about the disposition of his men. That would indicate that he's already onboard with working for the CIA."

"As long as we're speaking about spies, let's talk about the American spy," Adamik segued.

"You came up with an ingenious way to uncover them. The ambassador was impressed."

"It has its flaws, but the list of names we get will include them."

"What flaws?" Laska questioned.

"I'll get to that later. First, consider that the most common motivators for turning against one's country are a femme fatale, money, and ideology."

"That seems right."

"I'm not certain this spy would do what they've done for money because senior US government officials are paid well and usually receive more than their salaries in speaking engagements and honorariums. Besides, they couldn't showcase their wealth by displays of extravagance, which would bring about questions about how they got so rich. A beautiful woman is always possible, but the honey trap usually doesn't last for decades."

"That leaves ideology," Laska said.

"This is equally puzzling because someone in a senior government position, especially at an intelligence agency, is generally very patriotic and has drunk the Kool-Aid, so to speak. Yet, that seems to be the most logical explanation."

"Why does the reason they became another country's asset matter? When the computer search produces a match, the Americans will have their spy—unless you'd like to explain the flaw you mentioned."

"The flaw is that senior officials frequently take their staff with them when they change positions. They work as a team."

"The flaw is the list itself," Laska said, now understanding the problem. "The spy may not be a high-ranking official, but someone on their staff. That significantly complicates your investigation."

"Given our time constraints, more than you know," Adamik admitted.

When the skinny tech examined under the digital microscope

the photo that Parra gave him, he cranked the magnification to ten thousand, which produced a larger blurred image on the LED screen. He then looked at the non-encrypted portion of the photo so that he could include in his report that he'd inspected the entire image, knowing that meticulousness was considered a religion at the NSA. As expected, nothing was found. Lastly, the tech worked his way outward toward the edge of the paper and the black specks along one border, which he assumed were made by a leaky cartridge depositing toner onto the paper outside the copied image—referred to by copier techs as black spots.

Intending to impress those who read his report with his thoroughness, he decided to examine each speck and note the number inspected. However, when putting them under a microscope, he discovered that the orderly row of specks wasn't cartridge residue but a series of letters, numbers, and symbols that were too small to be seen with the naked eye or under low magnification. "That's very clever," he said to himself, knowing immediately that he was looking at the one-time pad key that would unlock the pixelation.

He photographed the row of specks and digitally transferred them to a deciphering program, doing the same with the pixelated image. Moments later, the face unblurred. He didn't need to put the person he saw through the Agency's facial recognition database because everyone in Washington knew and respected him. He called Parra.

"Are you sure his face hasn't been superimposed over someone else?" she asked after arriving at the lab and seeing the image.

"The deciphering program confirms the image has a singular digital platform."

"In English."

"It confirms the decrypted image is the base layer and that it's composed of only one sequential series of digits."

Parra, who didn't understand the second explanation any more than the first, but knew she was in verbiage quicksand with the skinny tech and that he believed he was already at a kindergarten level explaining what he discovered, decided to skip over the technobabble and trusted his expertise and belief that the face wasn't superimposed.

"Print me a copy of what's on your screen and erase everything relating to this from the database. Your conversation with me and everything you saw and did never happened."

The skinny tech cleared his throat and sheepishly looked at Parra as he returned the paper with the pixelated face and the one he'd printed with it unblurred. "I'm not able to erase anything from the database," he said.

Parra, who'd forgotten that only she and several others had this God-like power, logged into his system and erased the data.

It was 4:00 am when she returned to her office and downloaded to a digital file everything the NSA had on the person she suspected was a Russian spy, including their work calendar, afterward calling the president.

"We unblurred the face in Lisov's photo," she said after apologizing for phoning at this hour.

"No apology is necessary; I'm used to it. Who's our spy?" Ballinger asked.

She told him.

"That's someone I would never have suspected. Are you positive this image hasn't been altered, and his face photoshopped over that of another person?" POTUS asked as he walked past several surprised Secret Service agents and into the kitchen with his phone to his ear.

"We have software that indicates there's been no substitution or altering of the face," she answered as he made himself a cup of Intenso from the Nespresso machine on the counter.

"Do we know where our suspected spy is now?"

"According to his calendar, at a conference in Prague."

The president didn't ask how she accessed his calendar, knowing that if the information was on a database, the NSA could get it. "The Russians have a large embassy in Prague. That would be a convenient place to make the drop."

"I would caution, sir, that even though this photo clearly shows this person is making a drop of the flash drive Lisov carried, which is distinctive because of the red circle drawn on it, it's not proof that he's our spy. It's only an assumption."

"But a pretty good one since the Vigilant system was confirmed to be on that drive," Ballinger responded.

Parra knew he was right.

"I understand we'll need more proof than a photo from our spy at the Russian Embassy to confirm he's our guy, which is why I have someone working on another way to reveal their identity," POTUS said, electing not to tell her about the search being conducted by Alexson and Connelly.

"How long will that take?"

"I'm told I'll have the answer by this afternoon. Until then, keep what you know to yourself, and we'll soon see if our suspects align," Ballinger said before ending the call.

It was 2:30 pm, and Alexson and Connelly, who were steadily depleting Site R's inventory of Red Bull while waiting for the data that was extracted from the various databases to be compiled and compared, were debating with one another as to who would have the tuna sandwich on wheat, both preferring it to the egg salad on white bread that Johnson had also brought back from the commissary with their liquid stimulant. Deciding that a flip of the coin would determine the outcome, Connelly reached into his pocket and removed a quarter.

"Call it," he said to Alexson.

"Heads."

As Connelly flipped the coin high above their heads, neither saw it land because, at that moment, the data they'd been expecting appeared on the computer screen. Johnson, who was at a desk in the corner watching the playful interaction between the techies with amusement and drinking one of the Red Bulls she'd poached, saw their screen come to life and came closer so she could see what was on it.

Five names were on the screen. Three of them worked in United States government agencies, and one was a retired government employee. The fifth name was a Russian diplomat. She called the president.

At the same time as Alexson, Connelly, and Johnson were looking at the computer screen, Iwinski was entering Madam Irenka's brothel. Because the early evening was when it started to get busy, the lobby was filled with girls looking for a hookup. As a result, it took the ambassador ten minutes to talk his way past the not unsubtle solicitations that were thrown his way. Madam

169

Irenka, who was watching from a distance and expected her girls to be flirtatious, wondered why Iwinski hadn't picked someone and if, instead of a customer, she had a voyeur on her hands because people only entered the brothel for one reason. Having no idea of his identity, she told him that house rules dictated he had two choices: pick a lady and have a good time or get out. When he said he was there to see Adamik, she sighed and, after telling him how to get to the detective's room, made one last stab at getting his business by saying that the detective's friends received a twenty percent discount.

"As tempting as that is, the detective and I have much to discuss and a different agenda this evening," the ambassador replied.

He found the room without trouble and knocked on the door. When Adamik opened it, his eyes widened in surprise at seeing that the ambassador had come to the brothel to see him and invited him inside. Laska was also astonished when he saw the strait-laced diplomat.

"What are you doing here?" The colonel asked. "This isn't the best place for an ambassador to be seen. One click of a cellphone camera and a social media post, and you'll be the featured headline for every news outlet worldwide."

"I know that, but this couldn't wait. Also, I didn't think any brothel would let their customers take photos of the girls, nor that most people here would want anyone to know about their extracurricular activity."

"Those are good assumptions because the rules are that everyone leaves their phone in their vehicle and, since most who come here are married, that your secret is also their secret. The better question is: how did you get past the girls and Madam Irenka? With few exceptions, she throws out anyone who doesn't want to make use of her establishment," Adamik said.

"Apparently, you're one of those exceptions, although the girls didn't like taking no for an answer, and neither did Madam Irenka. She only let me in because I said I was here to see you. To your comment," he said, switching his gaze to Laska, "I needed to meet with either you or Adamik and, since your office said you were gone for the day, I decided to leave you alone and bother him," Iwinski said, nodding toward the detective.

"I could have come to see you," Adamik said.

"That wouldn't have worked because Calbot is at the embassy. He'd have inserted himself into our conversation, so I came here. I'm surprised to see you," he said to Laska. "You must have an understanding wife if you and Adamik meet here instead of at your office."

"The definition of understanding is subject to interpretation," Laska replied, causing Iwinski to change the subject.

"Don't you find this environment distracting?" He asked Adamik.

"When you live here, you get used to it. The ladies are nice, there's always food on the stove, and as for what you call the extracurricular activities, they're a slice of life that one can either participate in or ignore."

"Are these temporary or permanent accommodations?"

"I haven't decided," he confessed. "We'll see where life takes me. What brings you here?" He asked.

"I have your list of suspects," Iwinski stated, removing a folded piece of paper from his pocket and handing it to him.

Adamik unfolded it and saw the names. "Four Americans and one Russian," he said as Laska looked over his shoulder at the list.

"There's a retired government official and his three assistants, who are still in government service, the four transferring together as a team between embassy assignments. Also, as you predicted, the handler is a Russian Embassy official who, for two decades, was assigned to embassy duties in the same cities and at the same times as the four Americans. He's currently a diplomat at the Russian Embassy in Washington and, interestingly, is listed as an attendee at the cyber conference," the ambassador said, summarizing what the president told him.

"Are any of the Americans attending the conference?" Adamik asked.

"All are," Iwinski replied.

"What do you know about the retired government official?"

"When in government, he was one of Washington's most powerful and respected persons and had considerable sway in shaping the decisions made by the last administration. His retirement didn't last long. He's now the head of a Washington mega-company with extensive government contracts. Google him, and you'll find reams of information about this person," Iwinski said.

"What about his former assistants?" Adamik asked.

"As I said, they're still employed by the government. One works at the CIA, another at the NSA, and the third is on the DNI's staff."

"Do all three work in Washington?"

"In the area," Iwinski replied.

"Can I get their photos and that of the Russian?" Adamik asked.

"I can get all but the Russian in minutes. The handler's photo will take a little longer because I need to get it from State or Customs and Border Protection. However, your government will have their photo on file since he will have used his diplomatic passport to enter the country to attend the conference," the ambassador told Laska.

"I'll get it," the colonel stated.

"Earlier, when I asked you how we get the proof necessary to catch the spy, you said you'd do that by setting a trap," Iwinski reminded the detective. "Now that we've narrowed the spy to four people, how do you intend to set that trap without them becoming suspicious?"

"Because I won't be focusing on them. It's all about the handler," Adamik said, explaining what he meant.

Ilya Glazkov was, at least on paper, a professional diplomat with twenty years of foreign service experience who held the title of Senior Counselor at the Russian Embassy in Washington, DC. Although his job description dictated several duties assigned to that position, he only had one, which was to act as an intermediary between the Kremlin and Archangel. He'd been the American's handler from the day he recruited him and one of only three people who knew his identity. Even though they hadn't seen one another for more than a decade, a precaution to protect the spy's anonymity in case either was followed to their meet or a colleague saw them together, they'd worked out a system of communicating with one another, incorporating safeguards that would verify the authenticity of the contact.

Caution dictated that they use a variety of dead drops, such as a loose brick in a wall, a hole in a tree, and even the uneaten half of a peanut butter sandwich, in which the spy would place a flash drive. Once the drop was made, that party would put a chalk mark on a bus bench or other innocuous location to signal the drop was ready to be retrieved.

Glazkov never made nor retrieved a drop while in Washington because, as a senior counselor, he assumed that he and every other official of relevance at the Russian Embassy was being followed. However, *of relevance* was an ambiguous and subjective term. The embassy had one hundred eighty-four diplomats and employees, making it impossible for the FBI, even in conjunction with other government agencies, to watch everyone 24/7. As a result, he tasked lower-level staff to retrieve and make the drops.

When Abrankovich was notified that Archangel had obtained the codes necessary to protect the command and control consoles from self-destructing, it was directed, because of their critical nature, that the drop be made in Prague which, because of the cyber conference, provided the perfect cover. The FSB, along with the spy agencies of many other countries, had long ago established a significant presence in the City of a Hundred Spires due to its proximity to Europe and the former satellite states of the Soviet Union, using the city as a launching pad for their illicit activities.

Retrieving the drop required planning because, just as their government followed senior embassy officials in Prague, so did other countries. That problem could have been solved by having a junior embassy official retrieve the flash drive. However, because of the sensitivity of Archangel's information and Lisov's treachery, Abrankovich only trusted Glazkov.

To leave and return to the embassy unseen, the FSB used tunnels that the Nazis constructed after they invaded Czechoslovakia in 1939 and confiscated the building the Russian Embassy now occupied. The tunnels were never discovered during Prague's building boom because no drawings of them existed beyond the one at the embassy, and they were so deep underground that they ran far below current utility, sewer, and water lines. To Moscow, this was the ideal way for Glazkov to get into the park, extract the drop from the nearby bench, and return to the embassy without being noticed, a plan that Abrankovich wholeheartedly approved.

CHAPTER 13

UNDER COVER OF DARKNESS and flying just above the water, the two Black Hawks approached the *Antias* from the stern with the Nemesis team in one aircraft and the SEALs in the other. The ocean-skimming approach was necessitated because the helicopters, even under minimal power, each produced a sound of eighty-five decibels, which at night could be heard from a distance of five miles. To overcome this problem, the pilots used night vision goggles to fly a dozen feet above the waves, putting their aircraft's noise at ocean level and allowing the combat aircraft to approach unheard and unseen on the ship's radar.

The attack began when Hunter's squad lowered an inflatable craft into the water and rappelled onto it. Afterward, using a caving ladder that they attached to the ship's starboard side, two team members climbed onboard and positioned themselves to provide cover fire for the four who would follow. The remaining two SEALs, charged with stopping the vessel, stayed in the inflatable to prepare the explosive device that would disable the ship's propulsion system. At the same time, the helicopter carrying Moretti's team approached the *Antias* from the port side and, duplicating the SEAL's boarding procedure, came onboard.

Disabling a moving vessel the size of a factory ship without its sinking required specialized know-how, which Moretti acknowledged was squarely in the SEAL's wheelhouse. The Nemesis team, primarily ground-pounders, would be focused on disabling the *Antias'* communications. During their short planning session onboard the *Eisenhower*, Hunter and his team knew they couldn't stop the ship by destroying its rudders, something they'd done on previous operations, because the *Antias* had twin propellers. That meant if the rudders became inoperative there was a high probability, given the importance of the cargo, that the captain would steer the vessel by varying the power to each prop and limp along until he reached his objective. Therefore, the only sure way to stop the ship without sinking it was to shut down its propulsion system. Typically, this was done by commandeering the bridge and engineering. However, with an estimated forty combatants on board, that approach was dicey because a firefight, especially in the ship's confined spaces, could prevent them from achieving either objective. Therefore, he and his team believed the only way to disable the propulsion system was by blowing apart one of the propellers. They knew this risked the explosion tearing one or more holes in the hull because of the proximity of the propeller blades, but there was no other way.

Propellers, also called screws, create thrust by pulling water in and pushing it out at a higher speed, making it an extremely bad idea for anyone to get near them. Therefore, the plan was to put the device in the water and let the screw suck the explosives into it. Hunter had a choice of using either primary or secondary explosives. The difference was that secondary explosives required detonators. But, since the explosive device would be moving toward the propellers, they'd have no way of knowing the exact moment it reached the blades. Exploding it too soon or too late meant the screws would be unharmed. Subsequently, they decided to use a primary explosive which, although it also had its challenges, detonated on impact.

The average fully loaded cargo and container vessel sits

two-thirds underwater. Given the tonnage of the missile containers and the size of the ship, Hunter felt the same ratio would apply to *Antias*. Using the factory ship's publicly available maritime data, he calculated that with this weight, its hull would extend twenty-seven feet below the surface—a critical calculation if they were to deliver the explosive charge to the propeller blades because the device needed to be weighted so that its buoyancy would keep it slightly below the hull so that it could be drawn into the screws, but not so deep that it passed beneath the targeted propeller.

In constructing the device, the housing was the first issue that Hunter's team addressed because it had to be sturdy enough to hold both the explosives and weights but not so strong that it was only dented and expelled by the propeller blades rather than pierced by them, which was necessary to trigger the explosion. Frye came up with the solution, suggesting they use a large cooler chest like the one he saw in the galley to hold the explosives and weights, certain the propeller could easily pierce its plastic and polyurethane shell. With the team agreeing that would work, Frye confiscated it from the galley.

The explosive device was assembled on the Black Hawk, Frye consulting a buoyancy table to determine the right amount of weight to add to the chest so that it'd sink to twenty-nine feet. The quantity of explosives placed into the chest, however, was a guesstimate based on the team's experience. It needed to be sufficient to destroy the screw on impact, but not powerful enough for the shock wave to rip a hole in the ship.

Lifting the chest out of the inflatable craft, the two SEALs carefully placed it on the water and watched it sink from view, targeting the ninety-ton starboard propeller. Moments later, there was a muffled explosion.

The captain felt the ship vibrate sharply, turn to starboard despite a lack of input from the bridge, and then begin to slow. He called engineering.

"The starboard propeller might have struck a submerged shipping container," the chief engineer surmised, having been on a ship that had struck one of the thousands of containers that fell into the sea each year and became maritime hazards.

"Did the impact activate the safety shut off?" The captain asked, hoping for the best.

"The damage is uncertain, but I believe it's serious because I've lost starboard thrust. Also, whatever struck that propeller impacted the other because it vibrated so badly that I had to shut it down. But that's not the worst of it. The debris from whatever we hit breached the hull, and engineering is taking on water," the chief engineer said.

"Can you control the flooding?"

"That's unknown until I get a diver in the water to inspect the damage. The pumps are running off the emergency generators, but they're not keeping up. The water in engineering is continuing to rise." Their conversation abruptly ended at that moment as two explosions rocked the bridge.

The Captain didn't need to guess what was happening because immediately afterward, the ship's satcom and VHF communications loss-of-signal fault lights illuminated, making it clear they had intruders. Given his cargo, he had no doubt they were American special forces.

Removing the satellite phone from his pocket, which was direct-to-satellite and didn't go through the ship's telecommunications system, he called the captain of the Russian Navy's cargo vessel *Leonov,* giving him the *Antias'* situation and the vessel's coordinates.

"I have eighty-five naval infantry onboard," the *Leonov's* captain said, referring to the Russian Navy's equivalent of United States Marines. "If your Spetsnaz soldiers don't kill them, my men will."

"How long until you arrive?"

"Less than three hours. Hold firm. We'll be there and kill your intruders."

Once Moretti set off the charge that destroyed the ship's communications systems, he activated a battery-powered jammer that prevented the use of individual satellite phones. However, by then, the captain had already spoken to the *Leonov*, whose captain alerted Moscow to the situation and was pushing his ship's engines to the breaking point to get to the factory ship.

Following the call, the *Antias'* captain grabbed the intraship phone, which was hardwired throughout the vessel, to alert those onboard that they had intruders, although most came to that conclusion after hearing the explosions and feeling the ship coming to a stop. However, Kirk and Frye stormed onto the bridge before he could make that announcement. Dressed in combat gear and brandishing automatic weapons, they ordered everyone to lie flat on the deck. While this happened, the two SEALS who'd destroyed the ship's propulsion system came onboard and joined their teammates.

Upon hearing the explosions, the Spetsnaz team jumped out of their bunks and were in their combat gear and on their way topside thirty seconds later. However, when they attempted to step onto the dimly lit main deck, they were met with a withering barrage of gunfire that inflicted ten casualties, showing the GRU soldiers that they faced an equally elite force and that getting past them and retaking the ship wasn't going to be easy.

For their part, Moretti and Hunter knew, from the fierceness of their enemy's focused and unhurried return gunfire, that they faced skilled professionals who didn't panic in tense situations. They also understood they couldn't maintain their intensity of firepower because they were rapidly depleting their ammunition. Therefore, after the initial barrage that killed ten Spetsnaz, they became more judicious when expending rounds. The remaining GRU soldiers took advantage of this and charged on deck. Although they lost another ten men, the remaining nineteen entrenched themselves behind equipment and other barriers on the main deck and began peppering Hunter and Moretti's teams with intense gunfire, creating a stalemate.

"I'd like to ask *Eisenhower* to send a couple of Black Hawks. With their mini-guns, it wouldn't take long to get us out of this mess, but...," Moretti said to Hunter as they hunkered down behind a bulkhead off which numerous bullets were ricocheting.

"But we can't because of the jammer."

"You have it."

"How long is its battery life?" Hunter asked.

"Longer than we have."

"I was afraid you'd say that. If we're conservative with our rounds, we can hold out for another forty-five minutes. After that, we're lobbing spitballs," Hunter said as two bullets narrowly missed his and Moretti's heads.

The exchange of gunfire continued for forty minutes with the GRU soldiers, because of their aggressiveness, losing another seven men while Moretti and Hunter's teams, who used steel bulkheads and other hardened barriers for cover, didn't suffer a fatality. However, five SEALs and Bonaquist suffered non-life-threatening wounds. Realizing they were almost out of ammunition, Moretti considered giving the order to leap into the water, knowing an inflatable was tied to each side of the vessel and, in the darkness surrounding the ship, they'd be difficult to see. Out of range of the jammer, they could also summon help. However, he couldn't give that order because some of the wounded weren't mobile, and once they were gone, he believed that anyone who was left behind would be killed.

As he desperately tried to think of an alternative, because their chances of survival if they remained onboard were zero, a series of airborne explosions rocked the sky overhead and the deck of the *Antias* became as bright as if it was daylight. Looking up, both groups of combatants saw the aerial flares and two Black Hawk helicopters coming toward the ship, the aircraft drawing a barrage of gunfire from the GRU soldiers. However, with their fuselage able to withstand hits from 23 mm shells, the small arms fire was utterly ineffective against the aircraft.

The helicopter's pilots didn't have a problem separating Moretti and Hunter's teams from the bad guys, even though the combat gear each wore was nearly identical, because only the bad guys were shooting at them. Each aircraft wasted no time in unleashing its two 7.62 mm mini-guns, each capable of firing six thousand rounds per minute. It didn't take more than a couple of seconds for the gunfire to cease, five Spetsnaz surviving only because they threw down their weapons and laid flat on the deck.

Once the gunfire stopped, Moretti and Hunter stood, turned around, and saw the enormous profile of the *USS Eisenhower* in the distance.

"How far away is the *Leonov*?" Ruebensaal asked Kullman, who was in the carrier's Combat Information Center, or CIC, the ship's tactical center and radar tracking room.

"Three hours," the XO replied, the CIC earlier giving him the vessel's course and speed when it came within range of the carrier's detection systems, learning the identity of the Russian naval vessel from the *Leonov's* Automatic Identification System, or AIS. "Our database shows it's a cargo ship based at the Zapadnaya Litsa Naval Base, which is twenty-seven miles from the Norwegian border and seventy-five miles from Murmansk. If they didn't switch off the AIS, they must want someone to know they're coming."

"It's a warning. The Russian Navy doesn't enter this area of the Atlantic, because there's nothing of strategic value, without a reason. It's not a stretch to believe they're here to take the missiles onboard, knowing we'd never attack a Russian military vessel. That's smart," Ruebensaal conceded. "This could turn into a political nightmare and military conflict if they send men onto the *Antias*, a Russian-flagged vessel, and attempt to retake it by force before we've finished offloading the containers. If that happens, look for both sides to accuse the other of aggression."

"Then we'll complete the transfer before then. But there are technical problems to overcome since the *Antias'* angle of loll is nearly ten degrees," Kullman said, referring to the angle from upright at which the ship was floating, "and it was already low in the water before then because of the massive weight of the missile containers."

"And as the water continues to enter the ship, its weight will only increase, making it a ticking time bomb that could send it to the bottom at any minute," Ruebensaal added. "The more it lists, the harder and slower it will be to extract the containers. I don't know the maximum angle for this vessel before it sinks, but at this weight, I'd estimate it might take only five or ten degrees more of loll to have it sucked under the waves."

Kullman agreed with that assessment.

"Alert our escort vessels to the *Leonov's* estimated arrival time, although I assume they're already tracking it, and have a team of boatswains flown onto the factory ship to receive our mooring lines," he said, referring to docking ropes.

As the boatswains were being taken to the *Antias*, Ruebensaal explained to those on the bridge how he planned to bring the missile containers onboard, drawing an outward gasp from the helmsman, who had responsibility for steering the ship.

Once the boatswains were on *Antias* and verified the location of the factory ship's cleats, which are mounted fixtures designed to secure a line, the helmsman began maneuvering *Ike* to come alongside. This procedure required a high degree of seamanship, not only because it was nearly midnight and pitch black outside, but also because the carrier had an empty weight of seventy-nine thousand tons, adding twenty-three thousand tons for crew, cargo, ballast, and so forth. The *Antias* was also no Skinny Minnie, having an empty weight of eleven thousand tons, but added to that was a monstrous cargo of ninety-six containers weighing sixty-five tons apiece. Given the massive weight of both ships, even the most minor maneuvering error would result in the sinking of the *Antias* which, on maritime life support, wouldn't take more than a nudge to send it to the bottom.

Ruebensaal's maneuver required *Eisenhower's* starboard side to come alongside the *Antias* because three of the four aircraft elevators onto which the missiles would be placed and brought into the carrier's cavernous aircraft bay were on that side of the ship. However, because of the *Antias'* angle of loll, the extraction of the containers needed to begin from the starboard side of the factory ship, in which it was listing, to lessen the weight and keep it afloat longer. This required the helmsman to steer the carrier's bow toward the bow of the factory ship as if they were on a collision course.

To help the helmsman position the ships beside each other with a gap between them, and in addition to the distance readings received by two-way radio from the boatswains, Ruebensaal ordered that the carrier's deck lighting be pointed at the factory ship and all portable illumination equipment be brought to the starboard side of the flight deck and aimed between the vessels. Once those were in place, the helmsman positioned *Eisenhower's* bow at a slight angle to the *Antias'* starboard side, keeping the carrier's speed to a crawl.

As it got closer, the helmsman changed course slightly so that *Ike* became parallel to the factory vessel, using the carrier's rudders to bring it closer as the *Antias'* boatswain gave constant distance readings until the vessels *kissed*, resulting in a loud scrapping sound that resonated through both ships. When that occurred the hawsers, the nautical term for thick ropes used for mooring, were shot onto the *Antias*, where they were secured to the cleats fore and aft. Ruebensaal and a group of engineers then came onboard the factory ship. As the engineers raced below to determine how to extend the life expectancy of the vessel, Ruebensaal walked the main deck, finding Moretti and Hunter standing beside one of the cranes. From the expressions on their faces, they had a serious problem.

"What is it?" The captain asked, getting straight to the point.

"Other than the fact this ship could sink and take everyone onboard with it at any time?" Moretti answered.

"I already know it'll be a future fish sanctuary. Tell me something I don't know."

"We need this ship's cranes to transfer the missile containers because the carrier's cranes aren't long enough to extend onto this vessel," Moretti continued.

"Again, I know that," Ruebensaal replied.

"But what you may not know is that the ship's generator power, which we're on because the propulsion system is down, isn't wired to these cranes."

"That's something I didn't know. If we need power, I'll have one of the electrical engineers I brought on board get it for you, one way or another. Is the jammer is off?"

When Moretti said he'd turned off the device, Ruebensaal called on his two-way radio for one of the engineers to return to the main deck. She arrived minutes later and, after looking at the crane's motors, said matter-of-factly that each required four thousand volts to become operational. While that sounded like a lot to Moretti, it wasn't a big deal to the engineer who called the carrier and had two power cables with the necessary voltage dropped onto the *Antias'* deck.

"Who's going to operate these?" Ruebensaal asked.

"Two members of my team, McGough and Alvarez, have construction experience and said they've operated cranes, although nothing this big," Moretti said.

"The only cranes we have onboard the carrier are for moving disabled aircraft, so I don't know if any of my crew has experience with large cranes, but I'll ask."

"That's appreciated," Moretti responded, Hunter shaking his head in agreement.

Ruebensaal made another call, discovering that the Navy sent his small crane operators to a manufacturer's school for certification. Since the other attendees were from civilian companies, where different types of the manufacturer's cranes were used, but all had standard features, the course was taught using their most sophisticated equipment, not only to preclude having a class for each type of crane but also in the hope that the operators would eventually get their employers to upgrade to the one on which they were instructed. Ten minutes later the two operators arrived, accompanied by Frye and Kirk, who'd accompanied the wounded to sick bay.

At midnight local time, which didn't mean much in the middle of the Atlantic, the first two containers were brought onboard the carrier and taken two decks below the flight deck to the hangar bay.

A typical commercial crane operator can lift and load twenty-five containers per hour. However, because the *Antias'* list was now at twelve degrees and steadily worsening, each operator could only transfer fifteen containers per hour. Therefore, at 2:30 am, with the *Leonov* nine miles away, only sixty-two of the missile containers had been taken onboard the *Eisenhower*.

The *Leonov's* captain ordered the eighty-five naval infantry to assemble on the ship's main deck, along with their inflatables, in preparation for leaving the ship. The major in charge of the group, along with the other infantry members, had been individually selected for this operation. Each had spent years onboard various naval vessels—all bored with their monotonous tours of duty, in which their primary activity was constantly cleaning their weapons to counter the salty ocean air. Yet to engage in a conflict, they viewed this assignment as a chance to free themselves from the shackles of boredom and do what they were trained for: engage and defeat an enemy force. However, most realized there was no guarantee that whoever attacked the trawler would also attack the *Antias*, and that they may be back to cleaning their weapons tomorrow because their assignment was to provide security to prevent anyone from interfering with the transfer of containers between ships. When the major, wanting to know when to deploy his group, walked onto the bridge to get the estimated disembarkation time, he saw *Leonov's* captain and several crewmembers bent over the radar screen and went to see what they were looking at.

"We have company," the captain said, seeing him approach and pointing to the five images on the screen.

"What am I looking at?" The major asked.

"We're here," the captain answered, pointing to the center of the screen. "This is the *Antias*, which is nine miles away," he said, putting a finger on it. "The other four blips are ships six miles behind the factory ship. As the limit of our surface radar is fifteen miles, they just came into view."

"Americans?"

"That's unknown because their AIS systems are off, although they know who we are because ours is active so that the *Antias* could follow our arrival. Nothing's changed," the captain said, seeing the major was apprehensive because of the additional vessels. "You'll still follow your orders and secure and protect the factory ship during the transfer of containers."

"I'd like to know if my men are going into a conflict with the US Navy or their special operators. That would significantly change our tactics," he said. "The *Antias* must see the same ships. What do they say?"

"We haven't been able to contact them."

"That seems suspicious."

"We'll know more in fifteen minutes when we have a visual on the ship with our night vision equipment."

Five minutes later, they saw the *Antias* through their night vision goggles and, towering over it, a giant aircraft carrier transferring missile containers onto its aircraft elevators.

"Conflict with an aircraft carrier, even with as large a team as mine, will be suicidal, especially since the other four contacts will be their support vessels."

"Moscow demands that we bring those containers onboard *Leonov* at any cost," the captain said in a forceful voice. "The Americans are on our vessel in violation of international law. Get onboard *Antias*, order them off the ship, and say we'll create an international incident if they don't."

The major wanted to ask the captain if he had taken and passed a stupidity test with flying colors. He equated his group's interaction with the US Navy as equivalent to threatening the school bully with tattling on him to the principal, and a visit to the nurse following that one-way discussion. "That may not work since they're taking back what we stole from them," he said, trying to reason with the captain.

"I'm not going to tell Moscow we failed without trying. If the Americans don't listen to reason, you'll take possession of the containers by force and transfer them to our ship before they can react. Once they're onboard, they wouldn't dare attack a Russian naval vessel."

Summa cum laude on the stupidity test, the major thought to himself. "They and their support ships have enormous firepower."

"They're not going to attack a Russian naval vessel," the captain repeated. "Think about this logically. The carrier can't harm us because it's unable to launch aircraft unless it's moving. You have more infantry than that ship has special forces or marines. You're the predominant military force. You're the apex predator."

The major, who believed the ship's captain was like other hardliners he'd met who, as long as their life wasn't at risk, had no problem sending others to their deaths as long as they could tell Moscow they followed orders. "All US carriers have attack helicopters. If they don't blow up my inflatables on the way to the *Antias,* they'll fire on my men as soon as we start a conflict; that's if one of the carrier's support vessels doesn't dial up a missile and put it into the hull of this ship. Respectfully, I believe you should put the decision in Moscow's lap and ask if they want an armed conflict with the US Navy or if we should walk away and deny we had any involvement in whatever the Americans might claim."

The captain, seeing a chance to move the expected failure of the mission to Abrankovich and avoid being held responsible for the ensuing conflict or loss of the containers, liked the suggestion and phoned Moscow under the guise of giving the general an update.

"The missiles and warheads are gone and of little importance compared to the command and control consoles, which are technological gold. Don't provoke a conflict. Get our people, living and dead, off the factory ship before it sinks," Putin stated after Abrankovich gave him the current situation.

"The Iranians will be angry we lost the UFPs," the general said, knowing they agreed to pay billions in US dollars for them, money the Russian Federation desperately needed to keep its economy afloat.

"They're always angry at someone, and no operation is without risk," Putin countered. "Our sole focus is to get the command and control consoles onto Russian soil, where we'll replicate Vigilant."

"Should I order a naval and air escort for the *Pantera*?" Abrankovich asked.

"I don't want to reveal its position because, if I were the American Navy, I'd do anything to prevent my enemy from obtaining this technology. That includes putting a torpedo into the *Pantera* before it reaches our waters. Besides, at one thousand feet below the surface and following the thermoclines, even we can't find our submarine," Putin confidently stated.

CHAPTER 14

ILYA GLAZKOV HAD AN uneasy feeling in the pit of his stomach. As Archangel's handler, he'd been effective at keeping his decades-old involvement with the spy a secret by having intermediaries make and retrieve his drops, which he considered a bulletproof system since it stood the test of time. However, because of Lisov's betrayal, he was the only one Putin trusted to interact with his top spy. Subsequently, he was ordered to fly to Prague, retrieve Archangel's drop, and put it in a diplomatic pouch to Moscow.

Following Lisov's betrayal, he'd expected Putin to significantly decrease the number of intermediaries, which currently stood at ten members of their diplomatic mission in Washington, to reduce the possibility of exposing their premier American spy. However, he didn't expect the president to declare he would be the only person who could make or retrieve Archangel's drops. Despite the FSB colonel's treachery, Glazkov didn't consider that a prudent move. Foreign intelligence agencies routinely followed senior members of their diplomatic corps, leaving junior diplomats unwatched because of a lack of manpower to keep every employee at the embassy under 24/7 surveillance. Therefore, since his position marked him as a senior diplomat, he was always under human or drone surveillance when he left the embassy, making interacting with their nation's top spy impossible. However, since he knew convincing Putin to change his mind would be fruitless, he needed to find a way to make being the sole contact work. As it turned out, the solution was given to him and came from World War II.

Sitting in a conference room at their Prague embassy, Glazkov glanced at his watch, which he'd done every couple of minutes for the past hour, waiting for the appropriate time to leave. Getting to the drop site early wasn't an option because it was a given that he and Archangel couldn't be seen in close proximity, especially with the possibility that an attendee from the cyber conference might want to decompress and stroll through the park, which was a short distance from the conference.

When it came time to leave, he felt exhausted from the stress, although he'd done nothing but sit and drink coffee while waiting. The embassy official who came to get him escorted Glazkov to the elevator and pressed the button for the basement, the massive level running under half the embassy grounds. Extending from it were four World War II tunnels constructed by the Nazis, entry beyond the thick steel doors requiring an embassy access card and retinal scan. His escort took him to the furthest tunnel, which was well-lit and had a dry concrete interior. Because it was his first time in one of these tunnels, he was surprised at the clean air and the lack of water seepage. Most of those he'd entered over the years had a rank smell, and stagnant water pooled on the floor. When he looked closely, the reasons for this became apparent when he saw the thick cream-colored waterproof coating on the walls and the numerous vents along the ceiling.

"The tunnel ends several miles ahead," the embassy official stated. "To exit, climb the ladder, unbolt the metal cover above it, and push it open. It's attached to two hydraulic cylinders, so it will take minimal effort. No one will see you step out because you'll be in the middle of a dense stand of twelve-foot-high Prague Viburnum— an evergreen that retains its foliage in the winter. Afterward, push the steel plate down. The park bench will be north of you. When you return, ensure you re-bolt the metal plate. We don't want uninvited visitors to enter and post the tunnel on social media."

"Understood."

"If you hear or see anyone around the Viburnum when you're about to step into the open, wait them out. The same applies to your return."

"I'm assuming this metal door locks when I leave. How do I open it on my return?" Glazkov asked. "I don't see a keypad."

"We have cameras," he said, pointing to one. "When you reach this door, security will buzz you in. Udachi," the official said, the Russian word meaning good luck, afterward slamming the door shut and leaving Glazkov alone in the tunnel.

"That's Archangel," Iwinski whispered to Adamik as he put his finger on one of the photos he received, pointing to the unblurred face the president got from Libby Parra and sent to him.

They were hiding in shrubs fifty yards from their suspect and looking through spotting scopes, which had greater magnification and clarity than binoculars. Using adapters, they'd attached their iPhones to the scopes and watched the spy sitting on the same bench that was in Lisov's photo, recording him dropping a flash drive into the recess below the right support arm. Although a six-person security team surrounded their suspect, creating a protective security bubble around their protectee, each looked away from him for threats. Therefore, no one noticed what he was doing.

Once the drop was made, the spy remained on the bench for another fifteen minutes and read the *Financial Times* before getting up to return to the conference, giving anyone who saw him the impression he came here for a brief respite from the pressures of the day.

"He was the last person I would have suspected," Iwinski confessed.

"Do you know him?"

"Not personally, but anyone who has worked in Washington would recognize him. What makes his being our spy astonishing is that he's filthy rich, so he doesn't need money, and has a history of taking a tough stand on Russia, including advocating technological embargoes and financial sanctions."

"An effective smoke screen, which is why he's remained above suspicion," Adamik said. "Now that we have a video of him making the drop, all we need to remove all doubt that he's communicating with the Russians is for Glazkov, who arrived early this morning from Washington, to get the drive. If Vigilant is as game-changing as everyone has led us to believe, he won't let it sit there long."

Forty minutes after the spy left, they saw Glazkov poke his head out of the dense growth of evergreens south of the bench and, with no one in sight, quickly step out of the Viburnum.

"We have company," Adamik whispered to Iwinski, who was surveilling a different section of the park when the diplomat appeared. The ambassador repositioned his scope and turned on his cell phone video.

Glazkov sat on the bench and, seeing no one was in the area, retrieved the flash drive, afterward briskly walking to the thicket of Viburnum and disappearing within them. Iwinski and Adamik left their hiding place and followed, pushing their way into the dense evergreen shrubs until they reached the metal plate that covered the tunnel access. Iwinski pulled on it but got nowhere.

"This must be the entrance to an abandoned utility tunnel, sewer line, or other underground passage, which is why they used this particular park bench for their drop," the ambassador said.

"But it doesn't explain why Colonel Laska, who's staking out the Russian Embassy, didn't see Glazkov leave and follow him to the entrance for this passageway."

"We agreed he'd call you if Glazkov left," Iwinski reminded him.

"Unless he didn't see him leave."

"The colonel impresses me as being very organized. It doesn't seem like anything escapes him," the ambassador said.

"Nothing does. That's why I believe this leads to the Russian Embassy," Adamik volunteered.

"That's quite a distance."

"It's the only explanation that makes sense. It also explains why we have no record of Lisov or a vehicle leaving the embassy the night of the triple homicide, especially since we have two patrol cars stationed outside their gates 24/7 for diplomatic security."

"Now that we have the spy's identity, what next?" Iwinski asked as he and Adamik climbed out of the evergreens.

"I have a suggestion," a familiar voice said. Startled, they turned and saw Mark Calbot and three of his agents. The COS walked to Iwinski, took the two pieces of paper from his hand, and looked at the unblurred photo and the other pictures.

"Is that the spy?" Calbot asked, returning the unblurred photo without betraying that he knew the person in it. "And this is Ilya Glazkov, who's probably their handler," he stated, pointing to the Russian diplomat whose picture was on the second paper, also returning it. "I thought we had an understanding that anything of foreign intelligence value fell within the CIA's purview and that you'd promptly give it to the Agency. I don't recall a sharing arrangement with the Czech government," Calbot told the ambassador.

"That depends on the circumstances."

"Which are?"

"Whether you're overstepping your authority and have a parallel agenda."

"I don't like those accusations. Why the sudden doubt?"

Iwinski removed a piece of paper from his pocket and handed it to the COS. "I find it remarkable that you don't know the person in the first photo. This is their bio. Read it."

"I know who he is."

"He was once Chief of Station at this embassy," Iwinski continued.

"I'm well aware of their background. Are you saying he made the drop I saw Glazkov retrieve and that he's a Russian asset?"

"We have videos to prove it," the ambassador answered.

"No wonder the Russians wanted to interrogate Adamik."

"What's your agenda?" Iwinski asked.

"You already know the Agency's agenda," Calbot replied, ignoring the question. "We gather and analyze foreign intelligence, conduct covert operations outside the US, and stop threats before implementation. In other words, we keep our nation safe."

"A word salad. You said a lot but told me nothing."

"Tell me what you know, and maybe I can help."

"It's too highly classified. You're not cleared to be inside the tent," Iwinski said.

"I can get inside with one phone call," Calbot threatened.

"Not this tent."

"The president?"

Iwinski shrugged,

"Alright, I'll play nice. How do I get inside?"

"You don't. I don't trust you."

"I've proved the Agency is the only organization in Prague that's strong enough to keep this detective alive. Without my support, he dies."

"Let the police worry about Adamik. Worry about yourself," Iwinski said, Adamik remaining silent during their exchange.

"I don't have to because the Russians won't target someone from another intelligence agency unless their backs are to the wall. Otherwise, there'd be a reciprocation," Calbot stated.

"Shepherd and Miller worked for you. Did they put the Russian's backs to the wall?" Adamik asked, entering the conversation.

"Orlov told me his target was Lisov and anyone who met with him. He didn't know they were embassy employees. On the other hand, you're just a police detective and not an intelligence agent or someone with diplomatic credentials. You're subject to a different set of rules."

"Which are?"

"Don't get caught. Do you understand the Russians are the predator, and you're the prey? They'll keep coming after you or anyone else they feel is a threat because there won't be any consequences. Your colonel is hardly going to go hunting Russian diplomats, and you can't take them to court because they have immunity. However, kill someone in the CIA or US government, and we'll give you a body in return or obtain a concession that's painfully to our advantage."

"I have the advantage on my home turf."

"How did that work out for you last time?" Calbot asked.

"Not as well as I would have liked. It could've gone better," Adamik admitted.

Iwinski intervened. "Get to the point and tell us what you want," he abruptly stated, knowing that Calbot had something in mind.

"The CIA will protect your detective while this plays out."

"That's uncharacteristically generous and a good way for you to keep tabs on us while covering up this incident and treating it as if it never happened. As I said, I don't trust you," the ambassador said.

"If I wanted Adamik dead, I'd have dragged my feet getting to the farmhouse outside Bozkov, or told you the Agency couldn't get involved in a local matter."

"That makes sense," Adamik admitted.

Iwinski, having dealt with the CIA in the past, didn't buy the Chief of Station's newfound benevolence. "I have another theory," he said.

"What's that?"

"That you weren't there to save Adamik since, by your admission, he's of no tangible value to the Agency in the future. Instead, you wanted to capture, interrogate, and turn a Russian assassin. You may also want to turn this Russian spy."

The smile on Calbot's face confirmed Iwinski's intuition. "Turning Orlov was a priority, and I wasn't going to waste that opportunity. The decision whether to turn this spy will be made at a higher level."

"A group you hope to join."

"We all have aspirations."

"To achieve that, you need the proof that's on our videos," Iwinski said.

"That's precisely what I want. This person is known to everyone in power at Langley. He has unique and nearly unfettered access to the highest levels of the DOD and knowledge of the defense programs they're developing because he's retained his security clearance. Needless to say, because he's passing information beyond our borders, the CIA is statutorily involved. However, I'm willing to partner on this."

"The word partner is not in the Agency's lexicon. As I said, I don't trust you."

"I get that. I have a proposition."

"You want sole credit for identifying and arresting the spy whose name we handed you on a silver platter," Iwinski said.

"As I said, we all have aspirations, and it would get me promoted. Going with your idea, I'll need your cellphone videos to get me there."

"And in return?"

"The Agency protects Adamik from the Russians who, I believe, still want an up close and personal conversation with him."

"What do you think?" the ambassador asked Adamik.

"Colonel Laska will need to approve this because my phone and its contents belong to the Czech police. He'll have conditions."

"Which are?"

"As a guess, since the United States has no authority to arrest someone on our soil, the Czech police, in cooperation with the ambassador, will arrest and hold this person until he can be extradited to the United States."

"I can go along with that as long as the arrest and extradition aren't made public, he's released to us within a day, and this is kept between our governments."

Adamik responded that, although the average extradition took three to six months, the government had the authority to expedite and keep the proceedings secret for national security reasons, adding that he believed Colonel Laska would accept those terms. "Once the arrest happens, you'll get the videos," the detective concluded.

"I want them once Laska agrees to our terms."

"As the ambassador said, it's a matter of trust. Once you have the videos, there's no incentive for you to keep your end of the bargain," the detective countered.

"These videos are too important to be held by local law enforcement, especially if the Russians get wind of their existence. The CIA is better able to protect them."

"They're not the property of the CIA," Adamik said.

"You don't understand. I'm taking the videos with me. I can't chance that anything will happen to them," he said, pointing to the three agents behind him, who opened their suit jackets to reveal their handguns. "Don't force me to be unsociable."

"How will you explain to Langley, your State Department, and the Czech government that you attacked a US ambassador and a local police detective to steal our cellphones so that you could take credit for catching a spy that we identified? Not only wouldn't you get credit for uncovering them, but at the insistence of my government, at the very least, you'd be demoted and given a desk job."

Calbot cleared his throat, knowing his bluff didn't work. "I may have been hasty and misjudged the capabilities of local law enforcement. Your proposal stands. I'll protect Adamik, and you'll give me the videos once the police arrest our spy. However, as discussed, the arrest and extradition can't be made public; he's released to us within a day, and this is kept between our governments."

"I think Colonel Laska would accept those terms. Are you okay with this?" The detective asked Iwinski.

The ambassador said it worked for him.

"I have one last question," Adamik said, looking at Calbot. "What happens to my protection once the spy is arrested and you're handed the videos? I only ask because the Russians are big on revenge."

"The CIA isn't providing a lifetime protective detail. We're just giving you time to figure out how you'll stay alive once we're out of the picture."

"Won't my death reflect badly on you at the Agency?"

"You mean, will the death of the detective I saved from Orlov, who probably had numerous local enemies, affect the career of the brilliant and courageous Chief of Station who discovered and arrested a deeply embedded spy who eluded the CIA and the rest of the intelligence community for decades? What do you think?" Calbot asked.

"That's what I thought."

When Glazkov returned to the embassy, he phoned Abrankovich and confirmed he had the flash drive. Following the call, he put it in a diplomatic pouch, completed the customs exemption documents that allowed it to bypass inspection, and summoned an embassy driver to take him to the VIP terminal at Václav Havel Airport, Prague's primary air transport hub, where a courier was waiting onboard an Aeroflot A320 Airbus that Putin sent from Moscow.

When street traffic cooperated, the drive to the airport took twenty-five minutes. However, today it was uncooperative because of a string of accidents, the journey to the VIP terminal taking an hour. The facility, built to accommodate private aircraft and get their passengers into and out of Prague with the least amount of hassle, had its own customs and immigration office. Therefore, when Glazkov showed the diplomatic tag on the pouch and presented the required documentation, the official stamped the forms without hesitation and cleared him to take the pouch onto the Aeroflot plane, where he handed it to the courier. Two hours and forty-one minutes later, the aircraft arrived at the Chkalovsky Air Base, where Abrankovich took the pouch from the courier the moment he stepped off the aircraft.

Following their encounter with Calbot, Adamik and Iwinski drove to the brothel. On the way, they noticed an SUV was following them; the detective confirmed this by varying his speed several times and, pulling to the side of the road, watched the SUV do the same. When both vehicles entered the brothel's parking lot, the SUV pulled into a space thirty feet from the detective's car.

Adamik quickly got out of the car, drew his gun, and approached the SUV from the front so he could see the driver, the other windows on the vehicle being heavily tinted. As he got closer, the driver put his right hand inside his jacket, causing the detective to zero his weapon in on the man's chest and rest his finger on the trigger. However, instead of a gun, the driver pulled out a plastic card and pressed his diplomatic credential to the front window for Adamik to see. Removing his finger from the trigger and holstering his weapon, the detective looked down and saw that the car had US diplomatic plates. After nodding to the driver, he joined Iwinski at the front door.

"His creds say he's a US diplomat. He works for you," Adamik said.

"Only technically because my diplomats don't follow people. Only their ambassador violates that diplomatic norm. They're CIA."

"It looks like Calbot is keeping his word," Adamik said.

"For the moment," Iwinski replied.

As they entered the lobby they saw Laska, who for the last thirty minutes had been politely turning down offers from several of the ladies for what they called a stress relief treatment.

"Let's get something to eat," Adamik said as he led Laska and Iwinski to the kitchen where a large pot of bramboračka, potato soup with mushroom and root vegetables, was on the stove. Each ladled the hearty meal into a bowl and had just brought it to the kitchen table when Madam Irenka approached carrying a cardboard box.

"Adamik. I thought I saw you and your friends sneaking into the kitchen," she said, moving his bowl aside and putting the box in front of him.

"We weren't sneaking," he said with a grin, knowing that being slightly abusive was her way of showing she liked someone.

Opening the box, he saw a court order, below which was a stack of parking tickets. The order directed Irenka Kallis to let a city building inspector into the brothel to verify that the half-century-old structure complied with the city's current building codes. Until now, Adamik had never known Irenka's last name, with everyone always referring to her as Madam Irenka.

"Why the need for a court order? Hasn't the city previously contacted you or tried to inspect the property?" He asked, handing the document to Laska.

"They sent me several letters and, a month ago, an inspector came inside my house and said he wanted to look around."

"What happened?" Adamik asked.

"I said whether you look or require a more physical interaction, you still must pay—in cash because I don't accept credit cards."

"That's not the type of look he had in mind."

"I know, but he was dráždivý," she said, using the Czech word for irritating.

"When he said he wasn't going to pay, I told him to leave, or I'd send him home with his equipment in his pocket."

"Threatening a city official. That was tactful. Is the house code compliant?" Adamik asked.

"A hundred percent, yes. One of my clients is a general contractor and does me the occasional favor of making any changes necessary to comply with new city codes."

"Then what's the problem?"

"I can't let them inspect the house."

"Why?"

Irenka hesitated before deciding she had no choice but to confide her secret if she wanted the court order to go away.

"I have several large stills in the basement that have been here since I bought the house."

"You bought this place from a bootlegger?" Adamik asked.

"From his widow. She wasn't into the family business."

"You're bootlegging moonshine from your basement?" Laska interjected.

"I make a superior alcohol product that I sell in my house, and distribute at a fair price to others who want high-quality alcohol."

"You wouldn't happen to put this superior alcohol in name-brand bottles such as Slivovitz?" Adamik asked, recalling his recent hangover.

"Of course I do. It sells better in brand bottles," she admitted, "and mine tastes the same as the original, or close to it. But if the inspector sees the stills, he'll close down my house, put me in jail, and require I pay the back alcohol excise taxes on what I've sold."

"Plus levy a hefty fine and tell the branded liquor manufacturers," Iwinski added.

"I need your help, Adamik. Remember our accommodation."

In the past, the detective had taken care of Irenka's numerous parking tickets by having a friend in the IT department erase them from the system. However, overriding a court order was beyond their capabilities. Wondering if he was going to have to find another place to live because he couldn't help Irenka, Laska came to his rescue by saying that if her client-contractor wrote a letter on his company's letterhead that the house was compliant with city engineering codes, and used the right technical buzzwords, as the city's chief law enforcement officer he'd take it to the court clerk and ask them to certify that the brothel had been properly inspected.

"You can do that?"

"In the past, the court has always accepted documented verifications from the city's senior law enforcement officer."

"Do that for me, and I'll let you have a stress relief treatment whenever you like," she said.

"I'll settle for a seat at your kitchen table," Laska said, not wanting to get into a discussion that he was married and faithful to his wife, which wouldn't make sense to her because most of her clients were married.

"Getting back to business," Iwinski said to Laska once Madam Irenka left, "how do you plan to arrest this spy, get your government's approval for expedited extradition, and keep it out of the papers?"

"Every one of those conditions is going to be a problem. I know the deal you and Adamik made pending my approval, but we can't arrest him, even in secret," Laska replied, "because he hasn't broken any laws within the Czech Republic. Therefore, the arrest would need to be on behalf of the United States, who will request an expedited extradition for laws he's broken in your country. Given this person's notoriety, that he hasn't been indicted nor convicted of a crime, and that what he's accused of doesn't involve the Czech Republic's national security, I can't see the government accelerating his transfer between countries. Doing so would make it appear we're a puppet of the US government."

"What if we dispensed with the diplomatic process and got him to the United States by another means? I'm sure that Calbot could arrange for such an extraction," Adamik said. "He'd probably prefer it."

"He may want that, but someone of this stature going missing in Prague is as bad for tourism and my city's economy as a triple homicide and would generate headlines globally. We need another approach," Laska replied.

"I don't disagree," Iwinski said, "but how do we protect Adamik? The moment Calbot finds out he doesn't need us, he'll take matters into his own hands and throw him to the wolves, meaning the Russians."

"I have an idea," Adamik said, interjecting himself into the conversation. "We're not going to arrest, deport, or secretly fly the spy to the United States or a rendition site. Nor will we walk away. Remember, the only reason we wanted to find them was to protect ourselves from being sacrificed by the CIA, who we believed would do anything to protect themselves if something went wrong and they needed a scapegoat. Based on our discussion with Calbot, that was a well-founded assumption. Nothing has changed. We're still their lightning rod. We just need to resolve this matter differently than anticipated to keep our promise to Calbot, yet not arrest the American spy."

"How is that possible?" Iwinski asked.

"We kill them," Adamik calmly replied.

CHAPTER 15

THE CAPTAIN OF THE *USS Florida* looked at his orders from the National Command Authority as a career-saver, believing that another operational assignment from the highest source of military orders meant that he and his boat were still trusted with sensitive missions, which were the only ones assigned by the NCA. However, he knew that trust existed only because he hadn't filed his mission report on *Florida's* surveillance of the *Resolute Eagle*, which would happen when he returned to base. Therefore, he hoped a perfect performance on this assignment would cancel out his screwup on the other. He handed the orders to his XO, who was standing beside him.

"Moretti and his team," he remarked, reading that he would give *Florida* its mission once he came on board.

"I wonder what they're up to this time?" Quinn asked.

"I'm unsure of who they are. They're not SEALs, Rangers, Delta, or any other special ops group with which I'm familiar, particularly because an Asian woman is a member of their team. They're off-the-books for sure," the XO answered.

"It doesn't matter. We're going to excel at whatever we're given," the captain stated, he and the XO understanding this was their chance at redemption.

"It'll be a challenge getting to the rendezvous site at the GIUK gap in the timeframe given," the XO said, looking at their orders that referenced the naval choke point in the North Atlantic, GIUK being an acronym for Greenland, Iceland, and the United Kingdom. The gap, which separated the Norwegian Sea and the North Sea from the open Atlantic Ocean, was the point where Russian submarines and naval vessels had to transit when leaving their bases on the Kola Peninsula for patrols in the Mediterranean, off the eastern seaboard of the United States, and the southern Atlantic Ocean. Transitioning it was also a necessity for returning home.

"I know. Go to one hundred ten percent on the reactor," the captain ordered.

The XO, who looked nervously at Quinn, acknowledged the order but knew that, although the design safety margins for *Florida* were between one hundred ten and one hundred fifteen percent, stressing the reactor's core for an extended period could lead to a meltdown.

"We'll be noisy," the XO advised. "Every sub within a hundred miles will be able to hear and track us."

"It can't be helped. *Florida* isn't going to be late for this rendezvous."

The XO understood that the captain gave this order knowing the colder water into which they were sailing had a higher density that created more resistance on the screw. While requiring more power to maintain speed, the water density also produced more distance per revolution of the screw, making *Florida* very fast.

"After we're underway, conduct a series of operational readiness drills to ensure the crew is sharp by the time we reach the gap. Judging from what we've seen from our previous encounter with Moretti and the area into which we're sailing, I don't think he's done with the Russians."

"That's what I was afraid of," the XO replied.

"The last of the containers are onboard," Ruebensaal said to Moretti as the Nemesis team leader came on the bridge of the *Eisenhower*. "My orders are to bring them to Norfolk, after which they'll be sent to the defense contracting company for inspection."

"What about your prisoners?" Moretti asked, referring to the crews of the trawler and *Antias*."

"We'll transport them and the bodies of those who were killed to the *Leonov*. My engineers tell me the *Antias* can't be saved and will sink within the next two hours. What about you and your team? Are you hitching a ride with us back to Norfolk?"

"The president has something else planned for us," Moretti said. "What's the chance of getting an aircraft to transport us to the Amílcar Cabral International Airport in Cabo Verde?"

"XO, what's the distance to Cabo Verde?" Ruebensaal asked Kullman, who quickly looked it up and said it was nine hundred miles and well within the operational range of a Black Hawk.

"Spin one up to take Moretti and his team there. Then ensure our course to Norfolk keeps us within range of the Black Hawk until it comes back onboard."

Kullman relayed the first part of his orders to the Air Boss.

"I wish I could say I'm sorry you're leaving," Ruebensaal told Moretti, "but every time you come onboard, I have to pull your cookies out of the fire and restock my armory."

That drew a laugh from the Nemesis team leader.

"I won't ask why you're going to the island of Cabo Verde, but my guess is that it won't be relaxing."

"Our next ride is waiting for us there." Moretti said. "However, I expect what follows will be similar to what we encountered on the *Antias*."

"That bad?"

"Maybe worse."

Watkins and his crew watched from the maintenance hangar as the C-17 landed smoothly at the Amílcar Cabral International Airport, having received a message several hours earlier that this was their replacement aircraft and that a repair team and the parts necessary to get their damaged Globemaster airborne were onboard. However, it was the second part of the message that caused concern, ordering Watkins to take Moretti and his team, who would be landing at Amílcar Cabral shortly, on the arriving Globemaster to wherever they directed and then afterward follow their orders.

"We're the replacement crew for this aircraft, and we're transporting Moretti and his team?" Skinner asked, looking at the orders that Watkins handed him but living in denial about what he read.

"That's what it says," Watkins answered.

"We've never flown Moretti anywhere where we haven't either been shot at or had extensive aircraft damage," Skinner said.

"It doesn't look like this mission is going to be different," Watkins said, looking at a second message that gave the arriving Globemaster's cargo manifest. "LALO jump equipment, a weapons pod, etcetera. Because they're making a low altitude insertion, we're to drop them from six hundred feet."

As Watkins was saying this, their replacement aircraft pulled in front of the hangar in which the crippled C-17 was sheltered, the pilot shutting down the four powerful Pratt & Whitney turbofan engines and turning on the auxiliary power unit, or APU—a small internal engine that provided autonomous electrical and mechanical power when the turbofans weren't operating. Moments later, as the cargo ramp lowered and everyone began stepping off the plane, a Black Hawk set down fifty yards from the Globemaster, and Moretti and his team disembarked.

"How do you plan to kill us today?" Watkins asked Moretti as he shook his hand, Skinner and Durst having broken off—the crew chief waving forward the two fuel trucks standing by for the plane's arrival and Durst to preflight the aircraft, leaving Watkins and Moretti alone.

"I was glad to hear you and the crew survived. I had my doubts that your plane was still airworthy following the explosion."

"It was a close call, but The Moose got us here."

"Is that the plane's nickname?"

Watkins confirmed it was. "Listen," he said.

As the Globemaster began taking fuel from the trucks and venting air during the process, a bellowing sound similar to that made by a moose could be heard. Moretti, who grew up in Alaska, was familiar with the sound.

"From the manifest, I saw you're making a LALO jump. Where are we dropping you?"

As was his habit when giving drop coordinates to the aircraft commander, Moretti wrote them on a piece of paper and handed it to the pilot. "These coordinates will be updated during our flight, but the drop point will be close to that spot," he said.

"Another ocean insertion?" Watkins asked after looking at what he'd been handed.

"It's the stretch of water between Greenland and Iceland," Moretti confirmed.

"I understand the need for every item on your manifest list

except for one. In all the time I've flown The Moose and transported numerous special operations teams with every imaginable type of arms, explosives, and support equipment, I've never had one bring this last item," Watkins said, pointing to the manifest list. "What's it for?"

"Insurance."

As Russian submarine K-317 began its transition of the GIUK gap, the Navy's seafloor monitors detected the faint noise that emitted from its screws, relaying the information along a series of nodes to an analytical station in Iceland, which ran it through its comparative database and determined the contact to be the *Pantera*. The boat's identity, position, course, and speed were then relayed by satellite to the Department of Defense and disseminated to specific organizations within it. Two of those were the ONR and the NSA.

The United States was far from the only country that saturated this area with undersea sensors. Great Britain and other European nations also had extensive monitoring equipment along the gap's ocean floor because it was the sea portal for Russia's northern fleet to approach continental Europe. Due to the strategic importance of the GIUK gap, the Russian Federation also had sensors within it, knowing foreign navies needed to take this route to get to the Arctic and spy on their country's naval and air facilities on the Kola Peninsula. Therefore, with hundreds of technologically sophisticated sensors from various countries spread throughout this narrow space, some might believe it would be impossible for a submarine to transition the gap unnoticed. However, these technologically sophisticated devices could be negated by a phenomenon of nature known as a thermocline.

A thermocline is the transition layer between warmer surface water and the colder layer beneath. Its depth and strength vary from season to season and year to year, tending to be deeper in the summer when the surface temperature is the highest, and shallower in the winter. Submarines sail in this transition layer to evade detection, the physics of sound waves dictating that they travel faster in warm water and bend toward colder layers of the ocean. This means that sonar transmissions are reflected and return at different angles when striking this temperature differential, rendering the submarine silent because whatever noise it makes won't penetrate the thermocline, making it undetectable to sonar receptors.

Because the captain of the *Pantera,* Vitya Yerzov, had been a submariner for two decades and spent two-thirds of that time stationed at the Gadzhiyevo submarine base and the Okolnaya submarine support base in the Kola Peninsula, he had an intimate knowledge of the GIUK gap and the seasonal variations of its thermocline layers because he'd sailed through it over a dozen times. Although he didn't know the locations of the foreign sensors because they were deep, passive, and had hydrophones that listened for sounds rather than sending out pulses of energy that reflected off an object, he did know the twists and turns of the thermoclines, which enabled his boat to stay invisible as it wove through the gap and northward into the Norwegian Sea.

For decades, the Russian Navy accumulated data on the correlation between the air temperature above the ocean's surface and water temperatures at various depths and locations throughout the gap. It used this to produce submarine charts, which showed the location and depths of the thermoclines that weaved through the underwater mountain ranges. Following these charted routes made

Pantera undetectable to the vast array of undersea sensors—most of the time. The chink in the armor was that there were pockets of temperature inversions known as haloclines, caused by areas of high water salinity, which made a submarine detectable to undersea sensors for the short period in which it passed through them. Because these inversions occurred sporadically, they were impossible to chart.

When the *Pantera* entered a halocline, its passage was detected by an undersea sensor, and the data was forwarded to various functions within the Department of Defense, where it was analyzed, evaluated for relevance and, if determined to be a routine sailing, flagged as read and sent to an archival database for storage. All but one analyst concluded the *Pantera* was coming off a routine patrol and returning to its home port. The one who didn't make that erroneous assumption was Libby Parra, who immediately called Moretti.

The Globemaster had just completed an aerial refueling with a KC-135 Stratotanker, enabling it to remain airborne for approximately nine hours, when Moretti walked into the cockpit. "There's a slight adjustment to our drop point," he said, handing Watkins a slip of paper with the new coordinates. "Once we're gone, stay in the area. I may need your help."

The aircraft commander handed the paper to Durst, who entered the revised coordinates in the navigational computer.

"By help, you mean dropping your insurance policy?" Watkins asked.

"I'll only use it as a last resort if there's no other way to accomplish my team's mission."

"By last resort, you mean people will be shooting at you, your team, and the unarmed aircraft flying support?"

"That's probably the interpretation I'd go with," Moretti admitted, "because the people who have what we want and won't willingly give it up. Just remember that our insurance can't be dropped above five thousand feet or more than three miles from where it's impacting."

"That puts us within range of a shoulder-fired missile, which is deadly accurate against an airborne target within five miles."

"I know the risks to you and your crew, but I needed a weapon with a very specific amount of explosive power that could be deployed from a cargo plane, and those are its operational parameters. Using anything larger would run the risk of killing us."

"If I don't bring this aircraft back in one piece, my chief of maintenance might have the same mindset."

"Any idea when this sub of yours is going to surface?" Watkins asked Moretti when they reached their coordinates ninety minutes later and all they could see is ocean.

The Nemesis team leader shook his head, indicating he had no clue. "The captain has my satphone number. We'll have to circle the area and wait because this mission is scrubbed without the sub."

"You should understand that after being tagged by a laser weapon that almost brought down my aircraft during your last drop, I'd like to get you and your team off this plane as soon as possible."

"I'm sure you would," Moretti replied, as he stood behind Watkins and looked out the cockpit window for their next ride.

After thirty minutes of circling, the submarine breached the surface of the water. Moments later, Moretti's satellite phone rang, Quinn telling him that *Florida* was ready to take the team onboard.

"It looks like we'll be leaving you," Moretti told Watkins. "Thanks for the ride."

"This may be the only time I'll return with my aircraft intact after transporting you and your team," Watkins said as he pulled back on the throttles and began gradually descending to six hundred feet.

"The day is still young. Stay close," Moretti said before going to the rear of the plane and joining his team, who were attaching their parachute ripcords to an overhead cable and checking each other's equipment. After hooking up to the cable, he took the lead position just ahead of Han Li, who assumed Bonaquist's position because Moretti's number two was recovering on the *Eisenhower*.

The advantage of a LALO jump is that it gets you on the ground, or wherever you're landing, quickly. Therefore, there's less opportunity to be seen and shot at. The flip side is that there's no reserve chute. Therefore, if your primary fails, you're screwed.

Skinner made a final review of each person's cable connection and re-checked their equipment before strapping himself into his webbed seat and lowering the ramp. Once it was down and locked, the pilot turned on the red light at the rear of the cargo compartment, indicating the aircraft hadn't yet reached the drop zone or DZ. A minute later, Skinner heard Durst in his headset saying they were ten seconds away, after which he held up the ten fingers on his gloved hands for the jumpers to see.

When the green light replaced the red, Moretti leaped out of the aircraft, followed by the other members of his team. As each jumped, their weight yanked the static line and pulled the parachute from the deployment bag, breaking the line once it opened. The descent from six hundred feet to sea level happened quickly, and with only a slight wind, the team had no difficulty stepping onto the forty-foot-wide deck of *Florida* seconds later. Alvarez and McGough were the last to arrive, landing with a loud thud because each had strapped to them a heavy equipment pod containing the group's weapons and other essentials.

After they discarded their parachutes and harnesses, the XO escorted the team below deck. The *Florida* then submerged to one thousand feet and remained stationary at that depth by adjusting the water in its ballast tanks until it achieved neutral buoyancy. The captain then joined the team and his XO in the wardroom and, following some niceties, told Moretti that he'd been ordered by the NCA to follow his directives.

"What are my orders?" Quinn asked.

"As before, *Florida's* crew will forget every facet of their participation in this mission. It didn't take place, and we were never here because we don't exist."

"Just like last time, the crew has been briefed. My logs will only reflect the NCA reference number. Additionally, as before, we've turned off the ship's communication with the outside world, using only my encrypted satellite phone when a call is necessitated, and scrubbing the navigational computer of where we've been and the route to get there."

Moretti complimented the captain on his thoroughness.

"What's our mission?" Quinn asked.

"We're chasing the Russian submarine *Pantera*, which will transition the GIUK gap with two stolen US command and control consoles."

"Can you provide more detail?"

Moretti thought for a moment before deciding that the captain and XO had to know what was at stake for the mission to go smoothly. "The consoles contain extensive technological details on a Top Secret weapons system called Vigilant. With this data, I'm told the Russians can replicate our system very quickly."

"What's Vigilant?"

"It's a system whereby an ICBM with multiple warheads is put inside a crushproof capsule and, with a self-leveling weight, lowered to the seabed in the deepest part of any ocean. Once there, it sits like any missile, waiting for an authenticated launch command."

The two naval officers were momentarily speechless before Quinn broke the silence. "They'd be undetectable and, therefore, impossible to target," he said.

"That's the idea. This technology cost billions to develop and puts us a decade ahead of the Russians, which is why we can't let the consoles make it to shore."

"Are we going to sink the *Pantera*?"

"Not if we can help it. Our goal is to destroy the consoles while doing everything we can to avoid killing the crew."

"Do you intend to find the boat by relying on the undersea sensors in the gap?" The captain asked.

"I've been told that Washington will track the *Pantera* and provide its location."

"Speaking from experience, submarine commanders are a slippery bunch. If I were the captain of this boat and had the cargo you mentioned, I'd be in the thermoclines, making me undetectable unless the submarine passes through a halocline."

"I received this before my jump," the Nemesis team leader said, handing him a piece of paper that gave the Russian sub's course, speed, and location.

Quinn looked at what he'd been given, then handed it to his XO.

"Looking at their depth, speed, and last coordinates, they won't pass through this section of the gap for almost six hours," the captain explained.

"That gives us time," Moretti said.

Quinn wanted to ask *time for what?* But he needed another question answered first. "If you don't intend to sink *Pantera*, how will you get it to surface?"

"That's where I need your expertise. At what distance will the Russian sub detect *Florida?*"

"If we do this right, they may not know we're here, and if they do, it won't be until they're virtually on top of us because the Russians aren't the only ones who have the location of the thermoclines in the gap," Quinn stated. "Knowing *Pantera's* course, depth, and speed, we'll position ourselves in the same thermocline and parallel to where they'll pass. Not to sound like a broken record, but how will you force it to the surface?"

Moretti told him.

"I'm sorry I asked."

CHAPTER 16

MORETTI'S PLAN TO GET the *Pantera* from its thousand-foot cruising depth to the surface was to have one of the Razorbacks, referred to as uncrewed underwater vehicles or UUVs, strike the Russian sub's giant seven-bladed propeller, believing the impact would cause the sub to surface and inspect the damage. However, as he learned from Quinn, the problem in making this happen was that *Pantera* was speeding along at thirty-seven mph, and a Razorback had a max speed of around six mph. Therefore, there was no way the impact could occur once the sub passed them because the Russian boat was six times faster than the UUVs and would leave them in the dust, so to speak.

"What about a head-on impact?" Moretti asked.

"It's hard to tell. The Razorback could break apart without causing any damage, cause enough damage for the boat to surface, or sink it. But I believe there's a better way," Quinn said.

"You've got my attention."

"Striking the propeller is a good idea, but not from behind. Instead, we hit it from the side. Unlike the *Florida*, the Russian boat doesn't have a shroud around its screw. We launch the Razorback, have it silently wait for the *Pantera* to arrive, and send it into the screw. The timing would have to be perfect, but it can be done. However, there's a risk."

"Which is?"

"Depending on the angle of impact, it's possible that the *Pantera's* giant screw chops up the Razorback without it incurring enough damage to force the boat to surface. However, we can mitigate that risk by launching our second Razorback. The twin strike should cause enough damage to send the sub to the force to see what happened."

"What type of damage are we looking at?"

"Putting the screw out of alignment, bending the propulsion shaft, or damaging the waterproof seal around the propeller shaft, which will cause water to enter the sub. Any one of these problems would necessitate that *Pantera* surface to inspect the damage, after which you and your team could execute the next part of your plan."

Six hours after the *Florida* inserted itself into the thermocline and waited a thousand feet below the surface for the *Pantera* to arrive, its passive sonar detected the submarine at the same depth and with the heading and speed that Moretti had received from Libby Parra and passed to Quinn.

"It looks like your Washington source was spot-on," the captain said, standing beside the Nemesis team leader and looking at the *Pantera* on two LED screens. The twin video feeds came from the pair of Razorbacks the sub previously launched out its torpedo tubes. Stationary in the water, they were now providing a head-on view of the approaching Russian sub.

"Time to get the *Pantera* topside," Quinn said to his XO.

The *Pantera's* first indication that they'd been unmasked came when the sonar operator detected the noise emanating from the Razorback's propulsion screw. "Torpedoes in the water," the operator said loud enough to be heard by everyone on the bridge, afterward providing the bearings of the two UUVs. Yerzov, his experience and training kicking in, rapidly gave a series of commands that began by launching countermeasures, afterward increasing the boat's speed to flank while turning thirty degrees to starboard and ordering a rapid ascent. He gave this last command knowing that most present-day torpedoes could descend below sixteen hundred feet, which was the crush depth for K-317. Because *Pantera* was an older submarine, he couldn't evade what he believed to be torpedoes by leading them to their implosion depth, which was generally nineteen hundred feet, below which newer Russian submarines could operate. Instead, Yerzov understood the only way his boat could survive this encounter was to confuse the weapon's tracking systems.

Evading a torpedo isn't easy. Most submarine captains agree that the possibility of avoiding or escaping it is minuscule once it locks onto its target. This is because most are wire-guided, meaning a thin spool of wire links it to the submarine's fire control computer, which unerringly steers the explosive device until impact. Therefore, a target's destruction is inevitable under normal circumstances. However, Yerzov believed he could confuse the other submarine's computer and break its guidance lock by leaving the thermocline and then reentering it at a different point, breaking the other boat's fix on *Pantera* before allowing it to again sail in the thermocline unseen. Technically, that assessment was correct because, as the *Pantera* ascended at flank speed, *Florida's* electronic lock on the Russian submarine was broken, and K-317 electronically disappeared off the sonar operator's screen. That should have been the end of it; however, because the Razorbacks were positioned in front and on either side of it, and under visual as well as computer guidance, Yerzov's actions didn't fool the two members of *Florida's* crew who were watching the *Pantera* approach the Razorbacks and using their joysticks to maneuver the UUVs into position. Subsequently, as the boat turned hard to starboard, they visually guided the Razorbacks into its massive propeller, one striking it from the port side and the other from starboard. Although the seven-bladed screw chopped each UUV into pieces, the impacts bent the propeller blades. This disrupted the balance and rotation of the screw, causing significant vibrations throughout the boat which triggered sensors that automatically shut down the propulsion system.

Yerzov didn't know what struck *Pantera*, although he was sure they weren't torpedoes or he'd be dead. Deciding it was too dangerous to remain a thousand feet below the surface where the water pressure was four hundred forty-one psi or thirty atmospheres when he didn't know the extent of damage to his boat, he ordered an emergency ballast tank blow. This forced high-pressure air into the main ballast tanks, causing *Pantera* to rise to the surface rapidly. Once there, Yerzov broke radio silence and contacted Abrankovich.

"Are you sure it was an American submarine?" the general asked. "Perhaps you hit an uncharted undersea obstacle. If two torpedoes struck your boat, you and your crew would be dead."

Yerzov wanted to reply that undersea obstacles don't have propulsion systems, nor do they generate screw noise. He also wanted to add that because *Pantera* was a thousand feet below the surface with stolen American property, and the United States was one of the few technologically advanced nations that could have mapped the gap's thermoclines, allowing one of its submarines to stealthily wait for *Pantera's* approach, there was no doubt in his mind that they were behind the attack on his boat. However, since irritating the head of the FSB wasn't good for one's longevity, he diplomatically replied that only the Americans would have the ability to disable and not sink his boat at that depth.

After a few seconds pause, the general agreed with that assessment. "Going along with the assumption it was the Americans, that would mean they didn't sink you because they want to get back their equipment rather than destroy it. Which means it's prudent to assume that the sub that attacked you has a special forces team onboard prepared to take over your boat."

"They can try, but they'll be unsuccessful," the captain replied. "I have crewmembers on deck who are armed with automatic weapons, RPGs, and an Igla," he said, referring to the portable infrared homing surface-to-air missile. "I'll kill anyone or anything approaching my boat, including aircraft."

The general liked what he heard and told Yerzov that he'd personally greet *Pantera* when it docked and pin medals on him and his crew. "Hold firm," he said. "I'm sending naval vessels to escort you and your crew home to a hero's welcome."

"When will they arrive?" Yerzov asked.

Abrankovich put him on hold while he checked. Several minutes later, he returned to their conversation. "Naval warships will be there in six hours. In the meantime, I've ordered two Tupolev Tu-142 anti-submarine aircraft from Rogachevo Air Base to provide air cover. Expect them in four hours. Until then, the success or failure of this operation is entirely in your hands," he said, ending the call.

Yerzov had been to Rogachevo and knew it was the closest base with aircraft capable of flying the eighteen hundred-plus miles to get to him and remain overhead for an extended period. He would have felt better if Abrankovich had sent fighter aircraft, which would have arrived in half the time. However, he understood that wouldn't have worked because, although they'd arrive sooner, their fuel consumption made it impossible for that type of aircraft to stay in the area for long. Therefore, for the next four hours, he and the crew were all that were standing between the Americans and whatever they had planned.

"They're on the surface," the XO said to Moretti before adding that *Florida* was sixty feet below and a three hundred astern of *Pantera*.

"Can they detect us?"

"Not a chance; we're in their baffles," he replied, referring to the blind spot behind a sub, through which its hull-mounted sonar couldn't hear because the area was insulated so that the noise from the boat's machinery wouldn't interfere with its sonar array.

"It's time to take a swim," the Nemesis team leader replied as he left the bridge.

Dressed in scuba gear, Moretti joined his team in the lockout trunk, which was similar to an airlock in that it allowed people to transition between two areas of different pressure. Although the compartment was designed for the crew to escape the submarine in an emergency, it was also used by special forces to leave and return to the sub undetected. Once inside the compartment, the hatch was secured, and the seawater valve opened to flood the chamber while the air was compressed until it equaled the pressure of the sea outside.

Moretti's goal was for the *Pantera* to remain on the surface long enough for the crew to escape into life rafts, after which he and his team would destroy the consoles and accelerate the boat's demise. Initially, the plan was to attach a small charge to its hull, the explosion creating a hole too large to be repaired at sea but small enough so it would give the crew enough time to abandon the sub before it sank. However, the details of that plan changed during a session with the captain, XO, and the boat's engineering officer, which he called to get their opinions on where his team should plant the hull charge.

"There are a few things I need to explain about submarines," Quinn told Moretti. "The *Pantera*, like all subs, has diving planes, which assist in submerging or surfacing the boat by pitching its bow and stern up or down. Ballast tanks control buoyancy. Pumping water into them submerges the sub, and the reverse causes it to rise, making the submarine more or less dense than the surrounding water. If I were in your position, I'd forget just punching a hole in the hull."

"Why?" Moretti asked, the rest of his team just as curious.

"Because the best way to ensure your explosion sinks *Pantera*, at a rate which lets everyone escape and doesn't allow the crew to patch the damage or isolate the inflow of the sea within a watertight compartment, is to puncture one or more of the ballast tanks. Ballast tank damage can't be repaired outside of a dry dock, meaning it's only a matter of time until it fills with water and the boat sinks. How long that takes is a function of the damage."

"You're saying that placing a charge on the hull is imprecise because I'd have no way of knowing if the hole that I create could be repaired or would sink the boat too soon. Whereas, breaching a ballast tank would doom the boat, but at a rate that would allow everyone to escape," Moretti summarized.

"You have the essence of it," Quinn said. "However, since the hull encompasses the entire boat, it will need to be breached in the area where one of the ballast tanks is behind it, creating a breach in the hull and the tank beneath."

"You'd be taking a surgical approach rather than using blunt force trauma," the engineering officer added, drawing a laugh from everyone in the wardroom. "Because breaching a ballast tank assures the sub will sink, and the water in this area of the gap is deep, when *Pantera* reaches its crush depth it'll implode with the equivalent force of three tons of dynamite, causing the air within that space to become superheated to thousands of degrees and combusting everything within the imploded hull."

"Shredding and incinerating whatever the *Pantera* is transporting," Quinn added, drawing a nod from the engineering officer. "Therefore, precision is everything. Too large a hole in the hull or a ballast tank, and the sub sinks before the crew can escape. Conversely, if it's too small, the sub may make it to Russian waters and transfer its cargo."

"Understood," Moretti said.

"Remember, you just have to punch a hole in the ballast tank. Don't use too much explosive," the engineering officer said, drawing inquisitive looks from Moretti and his team.

"For the benefit of an ex-Army Ranger and the other ground-pounders on my team, define what you mean by too much explosive."

Given the same size explosive, an underwater detonation produces far more damage than one on the surface. This is because water is denser than air, harder to move and compress, and an excellent shock wave conductor. Therefore, the primary blast, sometimes called the overpressure, is considerably more lethal than its surface counterpart.

The approach recommended by the engineering officer was to place two explosive charges, one on each main ballast tank, in case one, for whatever reason, didn't do the job. After calculating how much explosive was required, he told Moretti to remove two-thirds of the amount in the limpet mines the team brought with them from the *Eisenhower*, or they'd break the *Pantera* in half. He also emphasized that his team needed to be out of the water and back onboard before setting off the explosion, or they'd become part of the ocean's food chain. An hour later, Nemesis left *Florida* and swam to the Russian submarine.

Two limpet mines were attached to the *Pantera's* hull at the locations given by the engineering officer. Each would be detonated automatically by a time delay device called a fuze, activated by the person planting the charge. Because sound waves move four times faster in water than in air, the effects of an underwater blast travel a substantial distance and can harm or kill anyone in the water, even though they may not be near the explosion. Therefore, after placing the charges, the Nemesis team didn't waste any time returning to the submarine. Ten minutes later, the shock waves from the twin explosions rocked *Florida*.

Prior to the explosions, Yerzov was listening to the preliminary damage assessment from his XO, who said that whatever struck them, which he and the captain agreed weren't torpedoes or they'd be dead, damaged the giant seven-bladed propeller, bent the shaft that connected the steam turbine machinery to it, and compromised the propeller shaft seal, which prevented water from entering the sub from the opening where the propeller shaft exited the hull.

"Can we get underway and remain submerged until the aircraft from Rogachevo arrive?" Yerzov asked.

"Yes, captain. We'll be substantially slower because of the damage but can remain in the thermocline. At half speed, we can pump out the water faster than it breaches the shaft seal."

"Then get underway immediately because I expect the American submarine to make another attempt to get us to surface so that special forces, which I assume are on their boat, can board us and reclaim their technology."

"How will they get us to surface?" The XO asked.

"I don't know, but however they intend to do it, we'll make it more difficult by getting underway. Because they're undetectable on sonar, I expect the American submarine is in our baffles, where I'd be if I were their captain. We'll use that to our advantage. Load tubes one and two and open the outer doors," Yerzov said. "Be ready. Once we're underway, I'll turn hard to port. When I do, get a lock on the Americans, and we'll send both torpedoes into their hull before they can react. Once they're on their way to the bottom of the ocean, the success of our mission is assured." However, just as he finished his sentence, a pair of explosions rocked the submarine, throwing the captain and XO onto the deck. Moments later, engineering called and said that both main ballast tanks were taking on water.

The *Pantera*, like all submarines, had two hulls—a light and pressure hull. The light hull is the outer non-watertight shell that gives the boat its cigar shape, referred to as a teardrop hull, and its hydrodynamic characteristics—the efficiency of its shape affecting how much power is required to propel it through the water. In contrast, the pressure hull is constructed to withstand the massive outside ocean pressure while providing normal atmospheric pressure within. The space between them is used for ballast tanks, which control the boat's buoyancy, and fuel tanks and equipment that can operate outside the pressure hull.

The combined thickness of both hulls can be up to ten inches of steel. On *Pantera*, it was eight, the light hull being two inches thick, one more than US submarines. Therefore, while the engineering officer was correct in his assessment that the amount of explosive in the limpet mines that Moretti had initially planned to use would break a submarine in half, he was thinking of those manufactured in American boatyards. He didn't know that *Pantera*, commissioned in late 1990, had a much thicker skin than its successors and the hulls of US submarines, which were constructed from thin, high-tensile, high-yield, and low alloy steel. As a result, while the twin explosions put a hole in both ballast tanks, which would eventually put the submarine on the sea floor, the *Pantera* wasn't getting there anytime soon.

"How much water are we taking on?" The *Pantera's* captain asked engineering, receiving an answer that the pumps could handle most of it but that the boat would sink in approximately eight hours.

"Attaching explosives to our hull to breach the ballast tanks was a brilliant move," Yerzov conceded to his XO. "If not for the thick skin on this aging boat, we'd be forced to surface and abandon it—which is what the Americans are expecting."

"Your orders?"

"Surface so we can lessen the pressure on the hull and lessen the inflow of water into the breaches. After that, the same as before: to repel boarders until our Air Force and Navy arrive. If we do, we'll be the victors."

"They could easily sink us."

"As I said, if they wanted to do that, we'd be dead already. They want to destroy the equipment we're carrying and spare the crew. That sentimentality will be their downfall."

Two hours after the explosions, with *Florida's* sonar unable to detect the splash of life rafts in the water, Quinn became tired of waiting for the *Pantera's* captain to order his crew off the boat, after which he'd put a torpedo into K-317 to expedite its arrival on the ocean floor. Feeling he'd have a better grasp of the situation by putting eyes on *Pantera*, he extended a photonic mast, knowing it'd make his boat visible to those onboard the Russian submarine. Conversely, he reasoned, there was no way their captain would believe he'd left the area, given the minimal damage he'd caused when he could have just as easily sunk their boat—the implication being that he wanted what they were transporting.

Expecting to see the *Pantera* low in the water and on the brink of sinking from the flooding of its ballast tanks, Quinn instead saw that it was riding high, indicating the explosive charges didn't have the impact they expected. "Look at this," he said to Moretti, pointing to the LED screen on which the feed from the mast appeared.

"The only effect those charges had was to alert them to our presence. I count twenty armed crew on deck and not a life raft in sight," Moretti responded.

"That's because the sub isn't sinking, at least not appreciably."

"Any idea why?"

"The only explanation that makes sense is that the outer hull was substantially thicker than we believed," Quinn answered.

"We don't know the thickness of a Russian submarine hull?"

"There was no standard thickness on the older Soviet subs, and the Russians don't provide the Navy with their hull specs. In my chief engineer's defense, if you'd planted your original charge, you would have broken the Russian submarine in half, causing it to sink immediately and taking the crew with it."

"Point taken," Moretti replied.

"Do you have another idea of how to destroy those consoles without me putting a torpedo into *Pantera?*" Quinn asked.

"Yes, but it's not going to be well received by the person who needs to implement it."

"What the hell does that mean?"

Before Moretti could answer, the communications officer came on the bridge and handed him a manilla envelope with *Top Secret* stamped in the center. Opening it, he read the message from Libby Parra. The expression of concern on his face wasn't lost on Quinn as Moretti handed him the message.

"A pair of Tupolev Tu-142 anti-submarine aircraft, which routinely carry sonar detection buoys and APR-3M ASW acoustic homing torpedoes, will be here in less than four hours. Two hours later, four Russian naval vessels—a cruiser, two destroyers, and a frigate, each having SS-N-14 Silex homing torpedoes, will arrive," Quinn said, reading the message aloud. "It's signed Libby but doesn't give the organization to which she's affiliated. This is good intel. CIA?"

"NSA," Moretti countered.

"From my experience, that means the information is more reliable. Given what the Russians are sending, I don't believe they plan to give us the deference we gave *Pantera's* crew. Whatever your non-well-received plan is, make it fast."

Moretti called Watkins.

The insurance policy that Moretti brought onboard the C-17 was called Viper Strike, although in military parlance it was referred to as a GBU-44/B—the letters standing for guided bomb unit, sometimes called a smart bomb. The GPS-aided laser-guided glide bomb was intended to be an anti-tank weapon, with its two-pound shaped-charge warhead designed to penetrate a tank's thick steel armor. It was five and a half inches in diameter, weighed forty-two pounds, and had a length and wingspan of three feet.

"I take it, as usual, everything is not going according to plan," Watkins said after Moretti told him he needed to deploy Viper Strike.

"I've had better days, which is why I need you to drop the Viper and target the submarine at these coordinates," Moretti said, having gotten them from *Florida's* XO.

Durst input the *Pantera's* position into the navigation computer as Moretti gave it.

"Target the center of the submarine, slightly below the waterline. I'm hoping the Viper will only pierce the outer hull and tear open the ballast tank beneath, creating a small hole that will gradually sink the sub and allow the crew enough time to abandon the boat."

"Hoping?"

"I know the reality of what happens may be different, but I'm out of options because too many people are on the sub's deck for us to make another swim and place charges."

"As long as you're hoping, you realize my crew and I have no training on how to use the guidance computer you gave Durst?" Watkins said, referring to the laptop, which used a GPS link to an orbiting DOD satellite to guide the weapon to the electronic bullseye his copilot would put on the target.

"One of my team, who's used Viper, told me the computer interface is intuitive and that, like a glide bomb, it's gravity-activated. All Skinner needs to do is push it out of the back of the plane. Just make sure you're no more than three miles away or higher than five thousand feet when he does. The weapon system can't lock onto its target beyond those distances."

"We have you covered," Watkins said as he looked down at the spec on the ocean that he knew was the surfaced Russian sub.

Following Watkins' conversation with Moretti, Durst turned on the laptop. Seconds later, the screen came to life. "Moretti was right about this being an intuitive weapon," Durst said. "The screen checklist has two action items: put the electronic bullseye on whatever you want to hit and press the enter key for target lock."

"The government never makes anything that's this simple to use. A civilian contractor developed this," Watkins stated. "If the government designed this weapon, we'd be on page twelve of our checklist," he added, pulling back the throttles and starting the Globemaster into a spiraling descent that would rapidly take it below five thousand feet and within three miles of *Pantera*.

Yerzov was standing on the sail, the portion of the sub that rises above the main body of the boat, looking through his binoculars at *Florida's* photonic mast five hundred yards directly astern of him when the sound of the C-17's engines caught his attention. Like all submarine commanders, he had no way of knowing an aircraft was in the area because hearing and seeing a plane were the only two ways anyone on a submarine could detect it. The reason was that submarines were designed to be on the surface only when entering or leaving port, marine engineers thereby believing that installing radar on undersea boats was unnecessary.

The captain lifted his binoculars skyward toward the sound of the approaching plane, seeing the sun reflect off the cockpit windows before it came into view. From its size, he believed it to be a C-17, the aircraft of choice for inserting Navy SEALs. Therefore, he felt he had only one option: destroy the approaching aircraft before it could deploy the team. Looking at the armed crewmembers on the deck, he focused on one as he left the sail and approached the person holding the Igla surface-to-air missile.

"Is that plane within range of your weapon?" Yerzov asked, pointing to the aircraft.

Gauging the distance, the crewmember didn't need to look at the digital readout from the weapon's sighting system to know it was, confirming to the captain that it was within the missile's weapons envelope.

"Destroy it," the Yerzov ordered without hesitation.

Skinner positioned the Viper Strike at the edge of the open cargo ramp, after which he strapped himself into his webbed seat. "The GBU is ready to deploy," he told the cockpit.

"Strap yourself in tight. I'll be making a rapid ascent after Viper leaves the aircraft. Get ready for release."

"Roger that."

Watkins then simultaneously increased his rate of descent and pulled the throttles back to the stops, the reduced power preventing the plane from exceeding its maximum speed and ripping it apart as gravity and the plane's momentum accelerated it toward the ocean. Upon reaching five thousand feet, he told Skinner to release the Viper.

Once Moretti's insurance left the aircraft, Watkins leveled the aircraft, pushed the throttles forward, and pulled back on the yoke to gain altitude as he began to distance the plane from his target. While he was doing this, Durst used the laptop's built-in trackball to guide the smart bomb, making minor adjustments to keep it aimed at the center of *Pantera* and just below the waterline.

Following Yerzov's order to destroy the aircraft, the crewmember removed the protective cap on the Igla's missile tube and placed the five-foot-long cylinder on his shoulder, methodically going through the launch procedures he'd been taught. Because he'd never fired a missile, only simulating a launch in class because the weapon was too expensive to have every student launch one, his deliberateness in trying not to screw up while carrying out the captain's orders consumed an excessive amount of time. His target was now rapidly ascending, necessitating a constant readjustment of the crosshairs on his scope to get the green light, indicating a missile lock—a necessity for the Igla to activate and leave the launch tube. When the indicator light finally turned green, the digital readout on the display screen in his eyepiece showed the aircraft was only two-tenths of a mile within the weapon's distance parameters and at ten thousand feet, just one-thousand below the missile's altitude limit. This meant that, although he had a green light, the plane would quickly be outside the optimum kill zone. Rather than face the captain's anger by telling him the aircraft was almost out of range and might escape or suffer less than catastrophic damage, he pulled the trigger, figuring that he could blame the weapon if the aircraft wasn't destroyed. Once activated, the Igla's solid-fuel rocket motor ignited, producing a flame and blast of charcoal-colored smoke as it quickly accelerated to Mach 1.9.

Once the Viper left the C-17, Durst's laptop received a continuous video stream from its camera, a red dot showing the weapon's projected impact point as he made minor adjustments to keep it on target. However, his attention shifted when he saw a yellow flame followed by a trail of smoke coming from the sub's deck.

"Missile in the air," Durst exclaimed, causing Watkins to look out the large side window at the missile streaking toward the plane.

There weren't any written procedures on how a C-17 was to evade missiles. The plane's pilots, aircraft manufacturer, and the Pentagon considered it something better left unaddressed because they knew, but didn't want to document, the outcome of such an encounter. Instead, the Air Force left any mention of this out of the Globemaster's pilot manual rather than tabbing it with a blank page because there were no procedures, leaving evasive maneuvers to the discretion of the pilot. Therefore, when Watkins saw the missile trail, he abruptly banked the aircraft forty-five degrees to the right because it was the only thing he could think of to narrow The Moose's profile from a target the size of a house to a single-car garage. That move saved the aircraft, but not the left engines, the missile striking the outboard number one, which sent shrapnel into the adjacent number two. Although they remained attached, the massive three-and-a-half-ton power plants suffered extensive damage, sending pieces of them through the fuselage and into the cavernous cargo compartment, a large piece missing decapitating Skinner by less than a foot. As the Globemaster shuttered, receiving lift from the right wing because it still had both engines, the drag from the plane's left side pulled the plane sharply to the left and down toward the ocean.

With both of the left engines on fire, Watkins flew the plane while Durst went through their engine loss procedures, the military having a checklist for almost any eventuality. After retarding the thrust levers and pulling the fire switches, which closed the engine and spar shutoff values to prevent fuel from further feeding the fire and engulfing the wing, the extinguishers discharged.

When the plane banked steeply to the right, followed by a sharp descending drop to the left after losing both port engines, Durst's laptop dropped onto the flight deck and bounced around the cockpit, cracking the screen before finally ending up behind the captain's seat. Neither pilot thought about the computer because they were focused on saving the aircraft. However, at this point it didn't matter because, illustrating the pilot's statements that the Viper was easy to use because the government wasn't involved in its development, thereby making the system user-friendly, the software continued to extrapolate Durst's last adjustments and maintained the point of impact, guiding the Viper into the center of *Pantera's* starboard side two feet below waterline. The explosion created a two-foot-wide hole in the light hull and a second hole in the starboard ballast tank, giving *Pantera* thirty minutes before the weight of the incoming water pulled it below the surface. Upon receiving this timeline from his chief engineer, Yerzov ordered the crew to abandon the boat and called Moscow.

The C-17 was in serious trouble. Looking at the left wing, the pilots saw that the surface was deformed, indicating its structural integrity and airworthiness were in question, and it could break away from the airframe at any moment. Although they'd reestablished control of the aircraft, stopping its rapid descent two thousand feet from the water before regaining lift and slowly increasing altitude, the left wing was vibrating badly. They didn't know if the stress they were now placing on the aircraft to gain altitude, and after that to maintain flight, would snap it loose.

"Skinner, are you alright?" Watkins asked as the aircraft continued to climb.

"I'm fine. What happened?"

"A missile took out our port engines," Watkins said.

"That explains the shaking."

"Put on your chute; we may lose all or part of our port wing," Watkins said before turning his attention to Durst. "What's the nearest airfield?" He asked his copilot.

Durst looked at his navigation system, afterward shaking his head. "You won't believe this," he said.

"Cabo Verde," Watkins guessed.

Durst confirmed it was the closest point of land.

"Will we need to refuel to get there?"

"It looks like we'll have enough," he answered once he completed the calculation. "The port wing looks like it's ready to go. I don't know if it'll last until Cabo Verde."

"It's vibrating badly, which would indicate some of its points of attachment to the fuselage have been broken or significantly weakened. If it continues at this level, there's no way the port wing will stay attached to the airframe. But maybe we can buy some time by cutting our airspeed. That should reduce the vibration and wing stress. Redo the fuel calculation and see how slow we can go and still have enough fuel to reach Cabo Verde."

Durst did the calculation, telling Watkins that reducing their airspeed to fifty percent power was the slowest they could go and still reach the Amílcar Cabral International Airport. Both pilots previously agreed that the added weight from an air-to-air refueling and the turbulence that sometimes occurred during such a maneuver might be enough to snap the port wing.

Watkins pulled back on the throttles to fifty percent power.

"You don't seem worried," Durst said, noticing Watkins' calm demeanor.

"I won't say I'm not worried, just confident that we'll make it safely back to Cabo Verde, just as we did before."

"Why?"

"Because Moretti isn't onboard or asking for our help," Watkins replied, drawing a laugh from his copilot.

Florida's photonic masts caught the dramatics of the Igla's launch, the Globemaster's apparent escape, the Viper's explosion as it struck *Pantera*, and its crew getting into life rafts.

"It won't be long now," Quinn said to Moretti, who, along with his team and the XO, was looking at the mast's feeds. "Seeing how it's settling in the water, I'd say it has no more than half an hour before it goes under."

That prediction turned out to be uncannily accurate. Thirty-one minutes later, and with the crew safe in life rafts, *Pantera* sank stern-first into the GIUK gap. As it reached crush depth, *Florida's* sonar operator and every undersea listening device in the gap recorded a loud hissing sound, indicating that *Pantera* had imploded.

CHAPTER 17

TRAVIS SULLIVAN, WHOSE CODE name was Archangel, stood six feet three inches tall and had a medium build, gray hair, and hazel eyes. He was seventy-four years old and, although never married, came close a couple of times until he realized his profession, which was being a spy, would get in the way.

Born in Austin, Texas, the only child of a middle-income family, he graduated from the University of Texas with honors, obtaining a degree in business administration. His career path came by accident when, five months before graduation, the school held a job fair for students seeking employment or an internship. One of the companies soliciting applicants was the CIA, which because the Vietnam war was raging and they were deemed part of the government that got us into that quicksand, had only a few students looking into the opportunities they offered. Sullivan intended to pass their booth because government employment didn't pay as well as the private sector. However, as he increased his stride to pass it quickly, he realized that joining the Agency might be the perfect way to avoid being drafted, making the assumption that, as part of the government, they had enough influence to keep their employees from being conscripted into military service.

Deciding he had nothing to lose because he didn't have a job, he filled out an employment application and, five months after passing a series of interviews and background checks, joined the other twenty-one thousand employees at CIA headquarters in Langley, Virginia. Seven months later, his assumption about the Agency's power to exempt their employees from the draft proved correct when he received a notice to report to Army boot camp and, after bringing it to his supervisor, was told to ignore the letter and that it'd be sent to administration for, what he called, rectification. A week later, he received a telegram from the draft board changing his status from 1-A, which indicated he was available for unrestricted military service, to 2-A—a deferral based on the government's assessment that he was in an essential occupation.

His first position within the CIA was that of a Collection Management Officer, which provided data and assessments to other intelligence organizations. Liking the challenge and discipline of the Agency and the job security it offered because, as the war ended, the national unemployment rate surged to eight and a half percent, he decided to make a career of it. Because the best opportunities for advancement were given to those with field experience, he applied for and was accepted into the Field Tradecraft course, spending six months at The Farm, the CIA covert training facility within Camp Peary, a nine thousand-acre military base in Virginia, where he became expert in dead drops, brush passes, and surveillance detection, taught in conjunction with weapons and parachute training, and other skills essential for survival in the field.

His first assignment was to operate undercover as a diplomat at the US Embassy in Belgrade, Yugoslavia, recruiting local assets and gathering intelligence data. However, a year after his arrival, and with no intelligence or recruiting successes, he knew it was only a matter of time until he was brought back to Langley and relegated for the remainder of his career to a desk job as a low or mid-level agent. However, that all but certain future radically changed the night he attended a cocktail party at the Soviet Embassy, social functions at foreign embassies being common because they all had the same objective: recruitment and gathering intelligence from diplomats, or those masquerading as such, especially when they had too much to drink. For those with other frailties, honey traps using stunningly beautiful women or attractive men, depending on one's persuasion, were employed to charm and entice them into a sexual entanglement, after which they were blackmailed into providing classified information.

"You don't drink or take advantage of the recreational drugs or beautiful and willing women we provide," Ilya Glazkov, a Soviet diplomat with whom he got along well, but had unsuccessfully tried to recruit, said as he walked up to Sullivan, who was standing alone on the embassy's balcony. "You're making it difficult for me to extort or recruit you," he added, surprising him with his honesty.

"Strange talk for a diplomat."

"Let's respect each other's intelligence. We know neither of us are diplomats. We're operatives. I'm with the KGB, and you're with the CIA."

"How do you know I'm with the Agency?" Sullivan asked.

"The type of questions you've asked my colleagues and I make it obvious you're seeking information of intelligence value while trying to recruit us. Diplomats either discuss irrelevant topics or try to craft a solution to a problem facing their nations that will be equally unappealing to both sides. Also, you have the same problem as other new operatives."

"What's that?"

"You're trying too hard, which means whoever you report to expects job performance. No one believes that a diplomat will accomplish much because, as I said, they're mostly into irrelevant conversations while appearing to be doing something important."

Sullivan was silent, knowing that Glazkov was correct in everything he'd said.

"A word of professional advice they don't give you at The Farm: everyone in this room, and at similar functions, is a professional, and they're not going to reveal anything of strategic value unless they lose control, have their backs to the wall, or decide you have something better to offer than what they're getting from their current employer. Moreover, if you believe you've turned someone, odds are they're leading you on to give unverifiable false information that will have the Agency chasing their tail."

"Are you speaking from experience?"

"I've had my share of fun with the CIA."

"You're assuming I work for the CIA."

"I know you work for Langley, which I confirmed when mentioning The Farm."

"Explain."

"As I made the reference, your facial expression didn't have the reaction of someone who didn't know what I was talking about. Also, you don't have the Ivy League stick-up-your-ass demeanor of a professional diplomat."

"Anything else?"

"You don't speak to those who I know are diplomats, focusing instead on persons your employer has told you are foreign operatives. Diplomats talk to each other to keep the relationship wheels greased so they can get minor concessions from one another to appear effective to their bosses and get promoted to better postings."

Sullivan countered with a question. "Are you with KGB, SVR, or some other intelligence service? I was told to assume you were KGB."

"That's correct," Glazkov said, stunning Sullivan, who now had something of intelligence value, even though it was marginal, that he could send to Langley. Figuring that as long as his foreign counterpart was answering questions, and knowing that the responses he received might be on the fuzzy end of truthful, he had several more he wanted to ask. However, he never got there because of what the Soviet said next.

"I understand you'll be returning to the States within a month," he told Sullivan, startling him.

"How would you know?"

Glazkov ignored the question. "They'll tell you next week when your replacement arrives. Your COS has told Langley you're ineffective."

"You seem unusually well-informed. But if what you say is true, which I doubt, what's the name of my replacement?" He asked, testing to see if he was bluffing.

The KGB operative told him.

Sullivan's facial expression betrayed his shock because the person mentioned was in his training class at The Farm.

"Call me sentimental," Glazkov continued, "but I'd rather deal with an adversary I know than one I don't. Give me a second," he said, removing a pen and small pad of paper from his coat pocket. After writing for a moment, he tore off the sheet and handed it to Sullivan.

"What's this?" The CIA agent asked.

"A lifeline. Are you familiar with the PFLP?" He asked.

"Vaguely."

"The terror group Popular Front for the Liberation of Palestine is a hardline organization based in the Gaza Strip and West Bank that doesn't recognize Israel and wants to establish a Palestinian state with Jerusalem as its capital. It attacks Western targets because it wants them out of the Middle East."

"Why are you telling me this?"

"Because they're going to hijack a TWA flight from Frankfurt. The flight number and other details are on the paper I handed you. They'll force it to land at Dawson's Field, a remote desert airstrip near Zarqa, Jordan, and demand an exchange of the crew and passengers for their comrades imprisoned in Germany. You'll need to act quickly because this will happen tomorrow."

"Not that I'm ungrateful, but why tell an intelligence agent who's on their way out and has no chance of reciprocating the favor?"

"You may have that opportunity later. And, as I said, I'd rather deal with an adversary I know than one I don't."

"This could be disinformation meant to destroy my career," Sullivan said, holding up the paper that Glazkov gave him.

"At this point, you have no meaningful career. But, given time, that will change."

"My COS will want to know the source of this intelligence."

"Give him my name. It'll be believable because the CIA suspects I'm a KGB agent, and those from your embassy have seen us speaking. Tell your COS that I let the information slip when bragging about our spying superiority and your country's inability to stop the spate of hijackings. Also, say I have additional information on terrorist activities and want to trade for it."

"KGB operatives are known to be tight-lipped unless they want something in return. He'll naturally be suspicious. So am I."

"It's not unusual for intelligence agencies to trade information, and his suspicion will be lessened when he sees the data I've given you is correct and has stopped a hijacking. Langley will want to know what else I have and will tell you to wring every bit of intelligence you can from me. Your replacement will stay in the States so you can become my best friend."

"You mentioned a trade. They'll ask what you want."

"Tell them a future favor. They're smart enough to know they can always say no, but in the meantime, they're getting actionable intelligence for nothing. What do Americans say? Don't look a gift horse in the mouth."

As predicted, when Glazov's information proved correct, the COS canceled Sullivan's replacement. During the next six months, the Soviet provided other actionable intelligence, further impressing Sullivan's bosses to the extent that when the Soviet diplomat/KGB agent was transferred to Turkey, he was reassigned to the US Embassy in Ankara because Langley didn't want to spook Glazkov by approaching him with another field agent.

The KGB agent continued to provide actionable intelligence for the next four months. Sullivan, who often wondered what he'd want in return, didn't ask because, as the KGB operative said, he didn't want to look a gift horse in the mouth. However, that one-way street ended in a meeting at a quiet café in Ankara.

"I've heard you're quite the celebrity at the CIA," Glazkov said.

"Thanks to you."

"How would you like to continue that rise, eventually getting into a senior position at Langley, perhaps even the directorship?"

"The answer is obvious."

"I could make that happen, but I need something in return."

"The favors."

"Precisely. Before I tell you what I want, consider that our intelligence agencies are similar in that we're independent of changes in ideology or political leadership. In our profession, knowledge is power, allowing us to protect our homelands and respective ways of life."

Sullivan remained silent, finding no disagreement with what was said because he viewed politicians as frequently putting their welfare ahead of the nation.

"The greater the threats, the greater the need to detect and counter them," Glazkov continued. "Both nations have enough missiles with nuclear warheads to initiate mutually assured destruction. Yet, we continue to develop new weapon systems, to the delight of your defense contractors and their shareholders and, in my case, state companies and government leaders. When one country develops a new technology, the other responds, eventually matching or countering the threat until equivalence is restored. The days of Khrushchev and the Cuban Missile Crisis are over because each nation knows the other's capabilities. Therefore, neither is ever going to lob a missile at the other. This equality creates stability."

"How does this relate to your favors?"

"I propose we share or nation's intelligence and technological advances to maintain this parity."

"Your favor is to ask me to commit treason."

"It's not treason for either of us if the information and benefits to our nations are even-handed. I'll provide you with intelligence that's beyond the CIA's reach. You'll know what we're developing and how to counter it before deployment. You'll reciprocate. Therefore, both countries benefit, and parity is maintained."

"Who within your government would know that I'm your source?"

"Three persons: me, the president, and the head of the KGB. You would only be referred to by a code name, which I've chosen to be Archangel."

"Why that name?"

"I was born in Arkhangelsk, in the northwestern part of the Soviet Union."

"Let's say I go along with this. Langley will eventually figure out that what I'm giving them is beyond the scope of your knowledge, making them very suspicious of what I'm providing you in return. They'll put me under a microscope, limiting my access to sensitive information until they can confirm I'm not bent. While we might agree on parity, many in the Agency will view what I'm doing as treason."

"Your superiors will trust you because I won't be the only KGB agent you'll turn," Glazkov said. "I'll arrange for you to recruit others. When I transfer to another embassy, the CIA will transfer you to the same city, just as they did here. There, I'll also provide you with someone you'll be credited with convincing to spy for your government. You can tell Langley that I'm helping you to recruit others. Over time, what comes from our relationship will give you the credibility and the accomplishments necessary to rise to the top of the Agency."

Because the intelligence flowed both ways, Sullivan believed that, even though Moscow would be learning his country's most valuable secrets, Washington would receive intelligence that it had no chance of otherwise obtaining, thereby maintaining, as Glazkov said, parity and the security of each nation. That intelligence windfall could also catapult him to the top of the Agency. He was all in.

After Turkey, he followed the Russian agent to Prague, where he served as Chief of Station, his field accomplishments continuing and resulting in his ascension to Director of the National Clandestine Service at Langley and, from there, to Deputy Director of the CIA. When a new administration came into the White House, his reputation within the Agency made him the unanimous choice of the president's selection committee to be the new Director of the Central Intelligence Agency. Four years later, with the next administration on the other side of the political aisle, he retired from public service and accepted the position of Chairman and CEO of Genesis Corporation, the nation's eighth-largest government contractor with annual revenues of seven billion dollars, and the developer of numerous classified systems for the Department of Defense, including Vigilant.

CHAPTER 18

"ARE THEY STILL IN the parking lot and watching the front entrance?" Laska asked Adamik, who met the colonel two blocks from Madam Irenka's.

"They're there, along with a second car that Calbot sent to watch the back door."

"I thought the front and back doors were the only ways to leave the house. How did you get away unseen?"

"Did you ever know a bootlegger who didn't have a way to escape a raid?"

"I never knew a bootlegger before Madam Irenka," Laska said.

"When I confronted her with my belief that there was a third way to leave the brothel and threatened to send officers into the surrounding area to look for that escape exit, she decided it was better that only I knew her secret rather than the entire department. Reluctantly, she led me to a hidden tunnel that ran beneath the parking lot and exited in the woods a hundred yards behind the house."

"What if Calbot's men, because you'll have appeared to be inside the brothel for some time, decide to enter the house and confirm if you're there?"

"I don't think that will happen because they'll believe I've settled in for the rest of the day. However, knowing it's possible, I asked Madam Irenka to cover for me."

"That's going to be unpleasant for whoever confronts her," Laska stated.

"It will be. She said they'd receive the same treatment as the building inspector, having the choice of being entertained by one of the girls or getting tossed out on their ass, to quote her."

"I'm glad she's on our side. You said you needed a ride to pick something up but didn't tell me what or where," Laska said.

Adamik gave him an address twenty minutes from them, explaining on the way what he needed and how it fit into his plan to kill Travis Sullivan.

"My predecessor and senior officials in our government have long suspected that the CIA, and possibly other foreign intelligence organizations, have tapped into Český Telecom, Vodafone, and other carriers that service Prague. If that's true, and I believe it is, they'll have a record of our calls and may even be able to listen to our conversations in real-time."

Adamik said he didn't doubt foreign governments had this capability, and because Prague was a vital intelligence hub for many of them, they'd long ago tapped into their telecommunications systems.

"Then they'll know where we're going and what you're after," Laska stated.

In response, the detective pulled a burner phone from his pocket.

"Your paranoia has its advantages," Laska conceded as they approached a row of retail establishments, parking in front of one whose sign read *KGB Museum*. It was six p.m.

Laska followed Adamik inside the museum, which had an extensive collection of weapons and devices used by the secret Soviet intelligence organization. The detective greeted the curator he'd spoken with earlier and followed him to a display case.

"Is this what you want?" The curator asked, removing a

two-inch-long pin from the display case and handing it to the detective.

"This is exactly what I want," Adamik replied. "I remember seeing it when I toured the museum years ago, but I never thought I'd ever need something like this. Does it still work?"

"That's anyone's guess because it's been on display for decades. I don't want to know why you need it; just return the item in the same condition and I'll treat this as the KGB would: what you're holding never left the display case. However, I have one request."

"What's that?"

"Considering its purpose, clean it before giving it back."

"I'll do that," Adamik agreed.

"Where's our next stop?" Laska asked as they got into his car.

"The morgue."

"To reserve us a spot for later this evening if your plan falls apart?"

The detective ignored the comment.

The two officers arrived at 6:30 p.m. As they exited the car, the building's rear door flung open and the medical examiner, who'd seen them arrive on one of the parking lot's security cameras, came outside and handed Adamik a vial containing an infinitesimal amount of purple-black liquid.

"Is this all I need?" The detective asked.

"Neurotoxins are, by definition, highly potent," the ME stated. "Use this to get the fluid," he said, handing Adamik a transfer pipette—a small pointed-glass tube with a red rubber bulb at the end.

"Was it difficult to extract?"

"Yes, but it was even harder getting the pufferfish. They're not easy to find because most places that retail seafood don't want the liability of selling their customers a fish in which certain organs, and even the skin if it's been thawed and the poison migrates from them, contain a neurotoxin that kills."

"Where did you find it?" Laska asked.

"I bought it from the only Japanese restaurant in Prague which had it on the menu. It cost me a small fortune because they're flown in fresh from God knows where, and the restaurant charges an unreasonable amount for each piece. I'll expect reimbursement," he told the colonel, handing him the receipt.

Laska's eyes widened when he saw the amount.

"Once I got the fish," the ME continued, "I removed the liver and crushed it using a mortar and pestle before adding a solution of one percent acetic acid in methanol and filtering it using Whatman number one filter paper."

"I don't understand what any of that means," Adamik said.

"It means it was a pain in the ass to convert a solid into a liquid, after which I spent half an hour cleaning and sterilizing the mortar and pestle to get rid of any trace amounts of the toxin," the ME replied, wanting the detective and colonel to understand how difficult it was to get what they needed.

"And you needed to take these precautions because there's no antidote to this neurotoxin," Adamik said, wanting to say that he should have thrown away the mortar and pestle and added it to Laska's tab, but thought better of it because the colonel was still staring at the receipt for the pufferfish.

"Correct. Once in the body, the neurotoxin paralyzes the muscles, including those controlling breathing, resulting in suffocation. The amount needed to cause death varies by individual, ranging from as little as two milligrams to as much as ten."

"I can't think in milligrams. How much is that in ounces?" Laska asked.

"Point zero zero zero three five ounces."

"That's not much," the colonel conceded.

"Were you able to get the ambulance?" Adamik asked.

The ME pointed to the far corner of the parking lot. "It's on loan until morning."

"I owe you a favor," Adamik said.

"I'll add it to the stack."

The Global Cyber Security Conference's last official function was a farewell social gathering that evening at the Prague Congress Center, the site of the conference. In addition to the attendees, invitees included business and civic leaders and other movers and shakers eager to meet the decision-makers from various governments and some of the world's largest companies who could stroke a check to buy or license their products.

Sullivan and his six bodyguards passed through the full-body scanning device, a requirement for everyone but law enforcement, and entered the massive room where the farewell social gathering was being held. As they did, Adamik was in the front seat of Laska's car. After slipping on a pair of latex gloves, and with the colonel holding a flashlight, he carefully uncapped the vial and pipetted the neurotoxin into the two-inch long pin, afterward putting it in his outside coat pocket. Five minutes later, he and Laska walked into the building and, showing their police credentials, bypassed the scanning stations. Iwinski greeted them as they entered the room.

"There are a lot of people here," the ambassador commented.

"Twenty-seven hundred," added Laska, who was responsible for assigning a sufficient number of officers to protect the venue and the VIPs.

"Sullivan is speaking to someone thirty feet to your right," Adamik told the colonel, who saw their target and his security detail.

"Any idea how we can get Sullivan away from the six pairs of eyes laser-focused on him?" Laska asked. "Because this needs to look like a heart attack and not an assassination; no one can see you stick him with the pin."

"Getting Sullivan away from his security detail will be complicated," he admitted.

"Speaking of complicated, look who just entered the room," Iwinski said. Laska and Adamik turned around and saw Calbot walking straight for them, ignoring two people along the way who unsuccessfully tried to get his attention.

"How'd you get out of the house unseen?" Calbot asked the detective.

"Let me have the satisfaction of keeping you guessing. How did you know we'd be here?"

"I didn't. I came to keep an eye on Sullivan. After all, we have a deal, and since he's returning to the States tomorrow, time is getting short for you to take him into custody and deliver the videos. Are you arresting him tonight?" He asked, shifting his gaze to Laska.

"To avoid a scene, we're keeping him under surveillance until he leaves the venue, at which point we'll arrest him."

"Do you have the warrant?" Calbot asked.

"If I obtained one for a person of this prominence, word would get out. That serves neither of us," the colonel replied.

The COS said that made sense and left the trio to speak with someone.

"That was quick thinking," Iwinski told Laska.

"It's only a reprieve."

"I need to use the restroom," the ambassador said.

"He's seventy-four years old," Adamik said to no one in particular.

"I'm seventy-two," Iwinski corrected.

"I was referring to Sullivan, not you."

"Why is that important, other than making the heart attack scenario believable?" Iwinski responded.

"Because all the septuagenarians I know have a prostrate the size of a grapefruit, and everywhere they go, the first thing they look for is the location of the restrooms because they constantly have to pee."

"He's right about that," Iwinski admitted. "When I come back, tell me why that's important," he said, striding toward the restroom sign at the back of the room.

"Tell me why Sullivan's prostrate is important," Laska said, not wanting to wait until Iwinski returned for the answer.

Adamik told him, also providing the answer to the ambassador when he returned. "His guards are probably used to his restroom trips," the detective continued, "with one or two accompanying him while the rest wait outside."

"Those with Sullivan still won't let anyone near him," Iwinski said.

"Almost anyone," Adamik countered, looking at the ambassador and explaining what he meant and everyone's part in what he intended to do.

When Adamik and Iwinski saw Sullivan and his security team briskly walking toward the restroom, they were waiting ten feet away and entered ahead of him. As predicted, two guards accompanied him inside and positioned themselves near the door, giving their protectee some privacy. When finished, he stepped in front of the only open sink, which was between Iwinski and Adamik, who were washing their hands.

"I don't believe we've been introduced. I'm United States Ambassador to the Czech Republic, Robert Iwinski," he told Sullivan. "You need no introduction because your reputation precedes you."

The encounter surprised Sullivan, who apologized for not coming to the embassy and meeting him earlier. As they chatted, both guards were in a relaxed posture as they watched the two septuagenarians talk. For years, they'd been accustomed to escorting the CEO to a restroom every sixty to ninety minutes and more frequently if he'd been drinking coffee or anything else containing caffeine, a diuretic that increased the frequency of urination. They ignored Adamik, who was two sinks away, believing he was associated with the diplomat because they'd seen the pair enter the restroom together. As everyone inside the building had passed through a full-body scanner, they were confident the pair near their protectee didn't have a weapon. Subsequently, as they focused on the two oldsters, neither saw Adamik casually slip his right hand into his jacket pocket and remove the poison pin, which was invisible in his cupped hand.

With the trio having coordinated the sequence of events earlier, Laska gave them several minutes before walking into the restroom for the finale. As the guards turned toward him to assess if he was a threat, Adamik seemingly tripped over one of the aluminum waste bins, fell forward into the CEO and, on his way to the floor, drove the tip of the needle through Sullivan's trousers and into his left calf, after which he pressed the plunger and returned the KGB weapon to his pocket. The CEO grabbed his left leg, believing the

259

brief pain he experienced came from striking the waste bin, but turned his attention to Adamik when the detective apologized for his clumsiness.

After hearing the noise that Adamik made when he kicked the waste bin, the remainder of the CEO's security team charged into the restroom.

"He's not usually this clumsy," Iwinski said before introducing Laska and Adamik.

The security team relaxed after hearing they were law enforcement and that the ambassador knew them.

"How long is it supposed to take?" Iwinski asked.

"The ME says the dose I injected should drop him in thirty to forty minutes," Adamik answered.

"That's good because we need him to collapse here, not in a car or hotel room," Iwinski said, watching as Sullivan conversed with others not far from them.

The effects of the neurotoxin first became apparent when the CEO's walk became unsteady and his breathing labored. Clearly in distress, two of his security team, each putting one of Sullivan's arms over their shoulder, brought him to a nearby chair where one loosened his tie. However, no sooner had he done this than the CEO collapsed unconscious onto the carpet. That was the cue for the trio to swing into action.

"Give him room," Laska told those beginning to encircle Sullivan, the colonel removing a lanyard with a police badge from his pocket and putting it around his neck. As he created a wide space around the motionless body, preventing the CEO's security team from performing CPR, Adamik called the medical examiner, who was waiting in a parking lot next to the Prague Congress Center.

"I've called for an ambulance," Adamik said loud enough to be heard by everyone in the area, including the security detail. As he said this, Calbot pushed through the crowd and came beside Laska.

"What happened?" The COS asked.

"We don't know. We were on the other side of the room when he collapsed and rushed over. His security detail might know more."

Calbot rushed to where the six were standing and was told that Sullivan had become disoriented shortly before gasping for breath and collapsing. "I've been with someone who experienced a heart attack. They had similar symptoms," someone from the team volunteered.

"Was he in good health?"

"As good as any seventy-four-year-old who's a workaholic, doesn't exercise, and drinks," he responded.

As Calbot returned to Sullivan, who was sprawled on the carpet and showing no signs of life, he saw an older person dressed in medical scrubs rushing into the room with a gurney. The medical examiner, who he presumed to be a paramedic, examined the unconscious executive, looking to see if his pupils were dilated, feeling for a pulse, and placing a stethoscope on his chest.

"There's no heartbeat. Don't any of you know CPR?" He asked, looking at the recalcitrant security detail. Although one wanted to say they were prevented from performing the procedure because the police ordered everyone to stay away, he remained silent because it served no purpose since the paramedic was now attending to their boss.

The ME grabbed a resuscitator bag from the cart and began manually squeezing it to push oxygen into Sullivan's lungs, asking Adamik to take over once he got the process started. As the detective was doing this, the ME took the defibrillator bag from beneath the gurney and, after ripping the septuagenarian's shirt open, told Adamik to remove the mask, putting a wooden depressor in the CEO's mouth to keep him from biting his tongue. He next positioned the paddles on the upper right and lower left side of the chest and administered three hundred sixty Joules of electricity. "Nothing," he said after putting a stethoscope on Sullivan's chest. "Let's try again." Following his second attempt to bring the CEO back to life, the paramedic again put a stethoscope to his chest and listened for a heartbeat. Finding none, he pronounced him dead. Despite the ME's pronouncement, Adamik placed the resuscitator bag over Sullivan's mouth and nose and continued pumping.

"Although I won't know for certain until after the autopsy, all signs point to a heart attack," he told Laska, loud enough for those in the surrounding area to hear.

"Which one of you is in charge?" Iwinski asked the security detail in a gentle voice.

"I am," one responded and stepped forward.

"Take my card," the ambassador said, handing it to him, "and give me your contact information."

Iwinski was handed the person's business card containing his cell number. The title below his name indicated he was a senior security consultant.

"I'll be your point of contact. The embassy will handle the paperwork for the repatriation of the body to the States on his aircraft and get you certified copies of the death certificate. If I can get the autopsy performed this evening, you can expect those documents tomorrow afternoon. Does he have a wife or next of kin I should inform, and who will give us their wishes for the disposition of his remains?" Iwinski asked, already knowing the answer.

"He has no siblings, never married, and his parents are deceased. I don't know if there is a next of kin."

"His attorneys can figure out who decides the disposition of the remains and where he's being buried."

The senior security consultant thanked the ambassador for taking control of the situation and lifting that burden from him.

Calbot, who was nearby, listened to their conversation and approached Iwinski once the consultant left. "I want those videos," he demanded.

Iwinski handed him a flash drive. "They're useless to you now that Sullivan is dead."

"On the contrary, I'll still get credit for uncovering one of the most damaging spies in our country's history. We'll begin the process of determining what information he gave the Russians and investigate whether he had accomplices."

"Do you think the Agency wants Congress, and when they eventually find out, the American people, because no congressperson I know can keep a secret, to ask how the former Director of the CIA got past the Agency's background checks, internal security protocols, lie detector tests and, for decades, passed sensitive information to the Russians without anyone finding out? You won't be able to count the number of investigations initiated by various committees in both Houses of Congress whose chairs want to make a name for themselves by crucifying the CIA, which you have to admit isn't the most beloved of American bureaucracies. You may get a bump in position, but only a few will know of your unmasking of Sullivan, limiting your ability to receive future promotions. The documentation on the discovery of Archangel and the videos on this drive will be put in a vault that only a few at Langley can access. Everyone will be told that Archangel is a Russian myth to get us to expend resources going down a rabbit hole to look for someone who doesn't exist."

"I don't disagree, but a bump up the ladder still furthers my career."

"It does, and I wish you well with whatever position you're given," Iwinski said. "However, as previously discussed, Adamik may still be in danger. Although he's no longer a threat to the Russians because their spy is dead, they may still want to kill him out of revenge or to keep their secret. Hell, the CIA may want him dead for that same reasons. Do you have a suggestion on how to keep him alive?"

"Because you didn't have to give this to me, but you did," Calbot said, holding up the drive, "perhaps I can see Glazkov before I leave and show him a snippet of its contents, suggesting that as long as Adamik is safe, the Agency won't leak what's on it."

"The Agency is soulless. They won't leak any of those videos to save Laska's detective."

"You and I know that, but they don't."

"Do you think that will work?" Iwinski asked.

"The Russians can't take the chance of me following through with that threat because of the political fallout that would follow the revelation of their armed aggression in international waters to obtain another nation's technology. If documented proof of that were disclosed, the only reason to harm the detective would be revenge.

That's too steep a price to pay for the consequences that would ensue because everyone would know the Kremlin was responsible for his death."

"Thank you. And I thought you were a heartless bastard."

"I am, so tell Adamik to keep that in mind if he thinks about breaching our agreement about who uncovered Archangel."

As Iwinski and Calbot spoke, the ME told Adamik to remove the resuscitator bag from Sullivan's face. He did, afterward helping Laska put the corpse in a body bag and lift it onto the gurney, which the ME pushed to the ambulance with the two law enforcement officers following. While the detective went to the driver's seat, the ME and Laska got into the back with the body; the medical examiner unzipped the body bag and intubated Sullivan by inserting a tube from an oxygenator through his mouth and into the trachea to deliver air into his body.

"What do you think?" Laska asked as the ME began an IV drip line and gave Sullivan an injection of atropine and dopamine.

"That creating the illusion of death is one thing, but getting him inside the ambulance took longer than expected," he said as he began vigorous chest compressions.

"Meaning what?"

"That his death may not be an illusion, and if the resuscitator bag didn't get enough oxygen to the brain, even if he survives, he'd have the cognitive ability of a carrot," the ME said as he continued chest compressions for several minutes before finally getting a faint heartbeat, after which he placed heart monitor leads on Sullivan's chest.

"I thought you said the resuscitator bag would give him enough oxygen," Laska stated.

"The brain can go without oxygen for three to five minutes. After that, its cells start to die. By my estimate, it took nearly that time to get him into the body bag, across a very large room that was thick with onlookers blocking our way, and into this ambulance. However, the issue of whether his brain received enough oxygen won't matter if we can't increase his heart rate. It's very close to being a flatline," the ME said, looking at the monitor to his left.

"Any idea why?" Laska asked.

"The neurotoxin may have caused bradycardia, meaning tissue damage to the heart, blood vessels may have become blocked, restricting blood flow, or the poison may have caused another disorder. It's hard to say. What I know for certain is that his heart isn't pumping enough blood through the body for his organs or brain to survive. Unless it gets stronger, leading him to breathe on his own where I can remove the intubation tube, he's functionally dead, and eventually, we'll have a flatline," the ME stated as he grabbed a syringe that was preloaded with a colorless liquid.

"It's important that he lives," Laska said.

"You went to an excessive amount of trouble to get this person, who hasn't committed any crimes against the Czech Republic or you would have arrested him, into this near-death state before trying to revive him. Why?" the ME asked as he injected his patient with epinephrine to increase his heart rate.

"It's complicated. Let's just say that the Americans want to interrogate him, but as you pointed out, since he hasn't violated Czech law, we can't arrest him. We also can't deport him, not only because the Americans don't want anyone to know of his misdeeds but also because of his influence within the United States government and the army of lawyers he employs," Laska answered.

"He's a spy," the ME stated.

"He's a spy."

"But if he's believed to be dead, he can be taken to a rendition site and questioned without reprisal."

"That's their thought," Laska said.

"This doesn't sound complicated. His death was faked so the CIA can interrogate him without interference."

"The CIA believes he's dead. A more highly-placed part of our government wants to find out what he knows and what stories he's told out of school," Iwinski, who'd gotten into the front passenger seat without them noticing and overheard their conversation, corrected.

"And after you've extracted everything you can from him, what then?" The ME asked as he looked at the monitor and saw that Sullivan's heart rate was beginning to increase.

"He'll be sent to a retirement home, although I don't believe I'd be one he'd choose."

"You're right, it's complicated," the ME said after redirecting his attention to Laska.

The ME was eventually able to stabilize Sullivan, and six hours after he collapsed on the floor, Archangel woke up strapped to a gurney in the cargo bay of a C-130 Hercules, with an IV in his arm and wearing an oxygen mask. The special operations aircraft, dispatched by the president, was en route from the Prague-Kbely Airport to a remote landing strip one hundred and eleven miles north of Warsaw, Poland. The strip of asphalt on which it would set down was adjacent to the Stare Kiejkuty prison, which doubled as a US government rendition site used to extract information from those who weren't especially eager to detail their misdeeds. Although the CIA and several other US government organizations also used this facility, prisoners were identified solely by number, and the information they provided was known only to the organization that sent them there. As a result, the CIA didn't know of his presence nor that his cell was near several of their detainees who were also undergoing interrogation. In the end, Sullivan provided a treasure trove of valuable information, all of which went directly to the DNI, Thomas Winegar.

CHAPTER 19

FOLLOWING THE PURPORTED DEATH of Archangel, Glazkov was transferred to Moscow. Medals were pinned on him by Putin and Abrankovich, and he was given a corner office at the Ministry of Foreign Affairs in recognition of having recruited his country's most valuable intelligence asset and the data that relationship provided. He viewed his return as a double-edged sword because, although he had a prestigious position within the ministry with what his colleagues considered significant perks, he was accustomed to the upscale lifestyle provided to embassy staff and the freedom of living in a foreign country on the generous expense account afforded to Archangel's handler. Now, he was in a gilded cage, his government apartment and office bugged to ensure he didn't brag or become talkative about his exploits, and a GPS device placed on his car and within his phone to keep track of his whereabouts. Consequently, while his peers believed his return to Moscow and promotion were rewards for his accomplishments, he viewed it as a way for the Kremlin to keep an eye on the only person besides Putin and Abrankovich who knew Archangel's identity.

Even though his asset was dead, Glazkov was certain that Moscow would have no qualms about killing him to protect Archangel's identity, a revelation that would cause the Americans to examine how Sullivan escaped detection for so long, afterward putting in place procedures and protocols to prevent a reoccurrence. That would expose the spies Moscow spent a great deal of time and money seeding throughout the United States government in anticipation that one or more would rise to become another Archangel. It would also heighten tensions between the nations, with the Americans likely responding by placing sanctions on the Russian Federation and getting their allies to respond in kind. Given the fabric of their economy was held together by painter's tape, the financial impact of multi-national sanctions would be consequential. Therefore, he believed that he was only allowed to live because Putin did the math and determined that rewarding him for his accomplishments, even though no one knew the specifics, had propaganda value in motivating his peers to succeed and receive the same recognition and perks. Afterward, once that propaganda value disappeared, he knew he was destined to succumb to an illness or an accident.

While Glazkov was staring out his office window reminiscing about the lavish embassy parties in which he'd no longer participate, Abrankovich was in Putin's office being verbally eviscerated for failing to obtain any of the Vigilant system which, because of Archangel's death and the cleverness of the Americans in discovering how it was being transported, was now beyond their reach. As Putin pointed out, the general's failure meant that the United States would have a strategic advantage over the Kremlin for the next decade, holding a knife to their throats until a counterbalancing technology was developed. Subsequently, Abrankovich was demoted three ranks from Army general, the second highest military rank, to major general, the lowest rank for a general officer, and reassigned to the FSB complex in Nenets Sabetta, the name translating to *the end of the world*. Situated on the Yamal Peninsula in Russia's Arctic region, it had the world's largest natural gas reserves and an enormous liquified natural gas processing center. However, within the Russian Federation, the area was famous for its consistently harsh environment, constant snow, and bitter cold rather than for its enormous natural gas deposits.

Watkins didn't have an easy time returning to Cabo Verde. Besides the imminent threat of the left wing ripping off the aircraft, the destruction of the C-17's port engines created a hydraulic leak, indicated by the red low-pressure warning lights on the cockpit's fault panel. The diminished pressure made The Moose increasingly challenging to control. Watkins realized that even if he made it to Cabo Verde, the hydraulic pressure might be too low to deploy the landing gear and flaps and operate the brakes, which were all crucial for landing safely. It wasn't hard to imagine a scenario where the lack of extension of the landing gear and flaps would force him to make a high-speed belly landing, where statistically, with an aircraft the size of a Globemaster, survivability was extremely low.

A C-17 can carry a maximum of thirty-five thousand five hundred and fifty gallons of fuel in fourteen integral fuel tanks, which equates to slightly more than two hundred thirty-eight thousand pounds. The Globemaster that Watkins was piloting was an extended range version which, due to the addition of a center wing tank, carried slightly more fuel, increasing the aircraft's range by nearly five hundred miles. During the long return flight, the pilots pumped fuel from the port to the starboard side of the aircraft, attempting to relieve stress on the damaged wing while not placing so much on the plane's right side that it would create excessive drag. However, when The Moose came within sight of the Cabo Verde airport, seven miles from the runway, the loss of hydraulic fluid resulted in its flight controls becoming marginally responsive, not unlike a car losing power steering fluid. Watkins understood he had one chance to set the aircraft down because he was rapidly losing control. Depending on when that control ended, the unresponsive plane would either crash into the runway or fly over it and strike the ocean, where it would be torn apart and sink like a rock, taking the crew with it. If he did manage to maintain control for the seven remaining miles, he didn't know whether there was enough pressure to drop his gear. As Durst went through their approach to landing checklist, he reached the item requiring dropping the gear.

"Let's see if we're scraping the concrete," Watkins said, Durst then pulling the lever that lowered the landing gear. However, when he did, instead of three green lights, he got three red, indicating that the two main and nose landing gears didn't drop and lock.

"Pull the manual release handle," Watkins told Durst, who activated the mechanical free-fall mechanism that disengaged the landing gear's uplocks enabling gravity to lower the main and nose wheels. This worked, and green lights replaced the red, indicating the landing gear was down and locked.

Watkins told him to try the flaps.

Durst did, receiving a red light indicating they wouldn't extend and knowing there was no manual way to lower them.

"What's our retracted flaps landing speed?" Watkins asked.

Durst looked that up in the flight manual and gave it to him. "Without lift augmentation, we're going to chew up a lot of runway, even if our brakes work," the copilot said.

The C-17 was the only plane currently flying with a high-lift device that directed engine exhaust over the flaps to increase lift, allowing the aircraft to land at a slower speed. However, because they were missing their left engines, they couldn't use the lift augmentation devices on the starboard side because this would produce asymmetrical lift, causing the plane to bank sharply to port. At their airspeed, that would result in the left wingtip striking the runway and causing the Globemaster to somersault.

"The airport approach chart says that Cabo Verde has an arrester barrier," Durst said, having brought up the chart on his screen now that they had the runway in sight.

The arrester barrier was a net that lay flat across the end of the runway. Held in place by a stanchion on either side, once raised, it enshrouded the plane. As the barrier was pulled from the stanchions, the large energy absorbers that were connected to it provided the resistance to brake the aircraft to a stop.

"What's its capacity?" Watkins asked.

"Forty tons. I don't think they have many aircraft this heavy landing here."

"Empty, we weigh one hundred twenty-eight tons, which should be close to our current weight, with fuel and two fewer engines. You might as well tell the tower to activate it," Watkins said. "It's better than nothing."

Durst called, and the controller pressed the button that raised the barrier.

With negligible hydraulic pressure, the Globemaster handled like an eighteen-wheeler from the 1940s, touching down at a substantially higher rate than its usual one hundred thirty mph. Although the barrier in front of them could absorb a ground speed of around two hundred mph, it wasn't designed for the massive weight of the aircraft. Subsequently, when The Moose engaged the barrier, it ripped out the stanchions and the cables connecting it to the energy absorbers, dragging the net and cabling with it as the aircraft went into the overrun—the area constructed at the end of the primary runway in the event of an overshoot or undershoot. The loss of inertia created by the now demolished barrier and the overrun area kept the aircraft from entering the water. However, the left wing, which had been hanging on by a thread the entire flight, separated from the airframe the moment the plane engaged the barrier. Fortunately, by then, Watkins had drained its fuel so that very little flowed from the detached wing onto the overrun. The small amount that did was immediately doused with foam from the airport's fire department, whose trucks were assembled to the side of the runway. Two hours later, The Moose was towed to a spot beside the hangar where the crew's previous aircraft was being repaired. The left wing, which a crane had lifted onto a flatbed truck, was parked beside the giant aircraft.

As Watkins watched the chocks being placed against the aircraft's tires, he was approached by the maintenance officer who'd flown from Andrews to supervise repairs to the other C-17—the same person who'd previously worked on the damaged Globemaster Watkins and his crew had flown from Spain following another Moretti mission.

"Tough day," the major said, looking at the aircraft with the missing left engines and the wing beside it. "What happened?"

"Surface-to-air missile."

"You're lucky to be alive. Getting this aircraft to Cabo Verde with two destroyed engines on the same wing, which obviously separated on landing, was an amazing feat of flying. Not many crews could have done that."

Watkins thanked him for the compliment.

"If I'm not mistaken, this is the third Globemaster you and your crew have tried to send to the boneyard in as many months. Let me guess. Moretti?"

"Moretti," Watkins confirmed.

Fifteen miles from Prague, Vitali Orlov entered the village of Okoř, which had less than one hundred permanent residents. As instructed, he drove a mile down a rural road at the south end of the village until he saw a vehicle parked to the side. Pulling behind it, he got out of his car and, opening the front passenger door of the other vehicle, got in.

"Are you sure you weren't followed?" Calbot asked.

"I know how to spot a tail. No one followed me. As promised," he said, handing the COS a digital camera memory card.

"How's the arm?" Calbot asked, seeing it was still in a sling.

"Healing nicely. You made me a hero."

"Here's a downpayment on our agreement," Calbot said, reaching into the cooler between them and handing Orlov a small tin of beluga caviar, a plastic spoon, two miniature bottles of alcohol, and a package of mints.

"As you requested, the memory card contains the Russian Embassy layout, including the entrances and exists for the tunnels beneath their grounds, as well as the organizational charts," Orlov said before savoring the caviar and taking a swig of vodka.

Calbot handed him a small rectangular piece of thick cardboard that looked like it had six thumbtacks pressed into it. Orlov, who was short a hand because of the sling, put his spoon down to accept it, then put it in his jacket pocket.

"What's this?" He asked after picking up his spoon and re-engaging the caviar.

"Micro recorders. Press them in inconspicuous places where embassy decision-makers assemble. Ensure you wear gloves so your fingerprints aren't on them."

"The embassy is swept daily for these types of devices," he said after finishing the first miniature.

"They're undetectable because they're passive recording devices that emit no electronic signals," Calbot responded, taking what appeared to be a Czech Koruna coin from his jacket pocket. "Press this on the tack for ten seconds. The data will automatically transfer and erase what's on the micro recorder. Each tack stores a surprising amount of information, but there's a limit. Therefore, daily downloads are preferable. I'll give you a replacement every time we meet," he said, slipping the coin into the spy's pocket.

"And if someone discovers the micro recorders?" Orlov said after finishing the caviar and placing the tin, the spoon, and the empty miniature in the cooler.

"That's the best part. These aren't US surveillance tools. They were developed by the FSB and manufactured in Russia. The microscopic serial number on the underside of each will verify this if they're discovered, and suspicion will fall on the FSB for planting them because they're tightly controlled within that organization."

"How did you get them?" Orlov asked, drinking the last of the vodka before placing the miniature bottle in the cooler and popping a couple of mints.

"Contact me in the usual way when you have half a dozen or more downloads," Calbot answered, ignoring the question "Dasvidaniya."

"Have a nice day," Orlov replied as he opened the car door.

The morning following Travis Sullivan's purported death, the medical examiner called a funeral parlor owner he'd known for more than a decade, saying that he was sending the remains of an American, along with his death certificate and other required paperwork, and that he wanted the body cremated, placed in an urn, and delivered as soon as possible to the ambassador at the US Embassy because it was going to be flown to the States later that day.

What struck the owner as unusual about this request was that neither the family nor their attorney was involved in determining whether he should be embalmed or cremated. However, he wasn't going to ask the ME for an explanation because the owner relied on the money he made from the repetitive business he received from the city for sending his three children to private schools and keeping his wife, who had expensive tastes, happy. Therefore, when the body arrived and he saw that the person looked Eastern European and that its condition indicated it'd been at the morgue for at least a week and was probably the remains of a Josef Novák, the Czech equivalent of John Doe, he ignored what he saw.

It took four hours for the cremation, which was the usual time for a body to turn into ash at eighteen hundred degrees Fahrenheit, and another two hours for it to cool enough to place into an urn. Therefore, it wasn't until three that afternoon that the remains were delivered to the ambassador. Once Iwinski took possession of the urn, he called the senior security consultant who'd given him his card. They agreed to meet at the airport's private terminal in approximately an hour, the time subject to Prague's unpredictable traffic.

One hour and twenty minutes later, after having picked up Laska, Iwinski drove to the private air terminal at Václav Havel Airport where he handed the consultant the urn and accompanying paperwork that would allow the incinerated remains to leave the Czech Republic and enter the United States.

"What the hell is this?" The senior security consultant asked.

"That should be obvious," Iwinski replied.

"You told me his body would be repatriated. This is ash. Why was it cremated? His attorney ordered me to bring the body home so there could be a second autopsy," he said in rapid succession.

"Unless the next of kin or someone in authority requests embalming and has a zinc-lined coffin that can be hermetically sealed to transport the body, cremation is standard," the ambassador replied.

"You didn't tell me this," the consultant angrily responded.

"The embassy doesn't make those decisions. That's left up to the family or others, such as the attorney or the executive assistant who is handling the affairs of the deceased. We take care of the paperwork and follow the procedures laid out by the Czech Republic to repatriate the remains back to the States."

Laska remained silent, knowing Iwinski had stretched the rubber band of truth to the breaking point, and that while cremation was standard in some situations, it wasn't in others, including this one.

"What do I tell his attorney?" The senior security consultant asked.

"That if he took the initiative and got involved when you spoke to him, there would be a coffin on the aircraft instead of an urn. He's an attorney, and you're part of a protective detail. You're not expected to know these things; he is," Iwinski answered.

"I like that," the consultant said before turning and taking the urn to the aircraft.

"Will you get any fallout from the cremation of the body?" Laska asked the ambassador as they returned to the vehicle.

"The president has my back. Genesis Corporation doesn't exist without government contracts. Since Sullivan has been declared dead by a competent medical authority, the executives below him will be in a feeding frenzy, contacting board members and back-stabbing each other to try to be the next CEO. In less than a week, Sullivan will be a memory as the board hurries to put someone at the helm who can calm shareholders and retain the DOD's confidence in their ability to get things done and deliver on their contracts."

"It sounds like you've been through something like this before."

"I have, and I'm glad that part of my life is behind me," Iwinski replied as they left the airport.

The next day, Adamik and Laska were seated in Madam Irenka's kitchen, each eating a large slice of Sekaná pečeně, the Czech version of meatloaf made with an equal amount of pork and minced beef, with a touch of bacon, onions, garlic, and marjoram.

"This has been a good week," Laska said.

"Except for my kidnapping, waterboarding, and nearly becoming the target for an FSB assassination, had Sullivan not been declared dead."

"Someone is always trying to kill you, Adamik."

"Not always. Were you able to fix Madam Irenka's problem with the court?"

"She faxed me the contractor's letter this morning. It contained an impressive array of buzzwords to certify the house complies with city engineering codes. I took it to the court clerk, who registered it as being inspected. Her operation is considered legal. By that, I mean the brothel is legal," Laska clarified. "Are you going to stay at Madam Irenka's?"

"Unless life changes."

"Did you get her parking tickets wiped off the books? They were dated, and her license will be suspected if she didn't pay the fines and missed any of her court appearance dates."

The look on Adamik's face told him that, with all that went on, taking care of the parking tickets slipped through the cracks.

At that moment, timing being everything in life, Madam Irenka could be heard coming toward the kitchen, yelling if anyone had seen that ničema, the Czech word for scoundrel. Her ladies understood she was referring to Adamik.

"Now might be a good time to take care of those tickets."

"Stall her while I get to my car," he asked, picking up his plate and putting it in the sink so she wouldn't know he was there and rushing toward the back door.

"Leave it to me."

As Adamik rushed out of the kitchen, Irenka entered carrying a letter from the court suspending her driver's license until she paid the fines and hefty late penalties.

"Where is that ničema?" she asked.

Laska smiled and pointed toward the back door.

AUTHOR'S NOTES

This is a work of fiction, and the characters, government, and corporate entities within it are not meant to represent nor implicate an actual person, entity, or organization. Representations of corruption, illegal activities, and actions taken by governments, agencies, corporations, persons, or institutions and their officials were done for the sake of the storyline. They don't represent or imply any illegality or nefarious activity by those who occupy or have occupied positions within them. Additionally, the actions purportedly taken by Putin and the FSB are fictional. In my first manuscript, I didn't use his name; instead, he was referred to as the president of Russia. However, that didn't make much sense because everyone would automatically associate Putin with that position. I should also note that since he and the FSB director don't include me in their planning sessions, their dialogue and actions, as with everything else between the covers, are from my imagination. That said, as written below, substantial portions of *The Archangel* are factual.

Even though the Vigilant system doesn't exist, UFPs do. The concept of UFPs, as outlined in the referenced article, is to have uncrewed, nonlethal systems in corrosion-proof high-pressure capsules that can remain for years on the deep-ocean floor. When activated, they release from the weights which anchor them to the seabed and "fall upward" to the surface. These capsules can contain a variety of weapons and systems. Although they're envisioned to house uncrewed aerial vehicles, it's not beyond the realm of possibility that they could hide missiles, torpedoes, or other weapons. The strategic advantage of UFPs is that they can be placed in remote areas that are logistically difficult and time-consuming to reach, enabling the military to respond quickly from these locations with lethal or nonlethal assets. They're also nearly impossible for an adversary to detect. You can find more information on UFPs at (https://www.darpa.mil/program/upward-falling-payloads).

The *Resolute Eagle* is fictional. However, it's logical to assume that the US government employs ships similar to it to conduct covert operations. One reason for this belief is the Glomar Explorer, whose construction was commissioned by the CIA as part of Project Azorian, an operation to retrieve the sunken diesel-electric Soviet nuclear missile submarine K-129 from the ocean floor at a depth of almost seventeen thousand feet. Wanting to keep the mission a secret, the Agency asked billionaire Howard Hughes to provide a cover story for the ship. The patriotic entrepreneur was happy to oblige and advertised that he was constructing a deep-sea mining vessel to extract manganese nodules from the ocean floor. While the construction cost for that ship in 1972 was $350 million, the expenditure in today's dollars would have been $2.37 billion. You can read more about Project Azorian at (https://www.smithsonianmag.com/history/during-cold-war-ci-secretly-plucked-soviet-submarine-ocean-floor-using-giant-claw-180972154/).

Although UFPs are designed to be released on command from the deep-ocean floor, a variant of this technology is the Ninox 103 underwater sub-to-air drone, which can be launched from a submarine while it's submerged and float to the surface in a capsule, where it can remain before deployment for up to twenty-four hours, giving the submarine time to leave the area to avoid the risk of detection and aggressive action taken against it. Once on the surface, and at a set time or on command, the capsule opens and launches a quadcopter. With four propeller-driven arms, the drone has a range of six miles and can remain airborne for forty-five minutes. During this time, it provides the submarine with imaging that's far beyond the range of an optical periscope, the video stream and data received by an antenna the submarine deploys while submerged. You can read more about this drone at (https://gizmodo.com/submarine-drone-nuclear-military-spearuav-quadcopter-pe-1849044843).

I was surprised by the enormous technological advancements in torpedoes, which extend beyond their use against ships and other submarines. As an example, Russia has developed the Poseidon long-range torpedo. Powered by a small nuclear reactor, it carries a 2-megaton nuclear warhead (one hundred times more powerful than the Hiroshima bomb) that's designed to destroy coastal cities and ports. Capable of attaining a speed of eighty mph, it can outrun every NATO submarine and any torpedo (at least those publicly acknowledged) employed against it, making this weapon technically impossible to defend against. You can read more about Poseidon at (https://www.popularmechanics.com/military/navy-ships/a42537023/russia-poseidon-torpedo/).

Drones have also undergone rapid technological advances, and are capable of being launched from an underwater platform, such as a submarine, and returning to it. One example is the Yellow Moray, which the US Navy uses to scout for mines and other hazards, gather intelligence, and improve a submarine commander's situational awareness. It's part of the REMUS series, which includes the Razorback and Kingfish, both capable of carrying sonar, cameras, and mission-specific sensors. These battery-powered UUVs (uncrewed underwater vehicles) have an endurance of twenty-four to seventy hours, depending on their battery size and the operational environment. While their published maximum depth is six hundred feet, I took the liberty of substantially increasing that operational limit in my manuscript. Razorbacks can be launched and recovered from a submarine's dry deck shelter, with newer versions said to be capable of deployment from a torpedo tube. Because it fit my storyline, I went along with the newer version although, since I'm not on the Pentagon's mailing list for classified Navy projects, this version may not yet be operational. You can read more about these UUVs at (https://hii.com/news/us-navy-submarines-drone-launch-torpedo-tube-remus-hii-2023/#:~:text=For%20the%20first%20time%2C%20a,surveillance%2C%20scouting%20and%20other%20missions.) and (https://www.thedrive.com/the-war-zone/navy-submarine-just-tested-a-torpedo-tube-recovered-drone).

The *USS Florida* is not one of the three operational Seawolf-class submarines (*USS Seawolf*, *USS Connecticut*, and *USS Jimmy Carter*). Because I would be sending an enormous number of problems their way and, at times, not making them look their best, I decided to use a fictional Seawolf-class submarine in deference to the crews of these three boats. Call me a softie!

Although their crush depths are classified, most of the articles I read believe this submarine class can descend to a depth of between two thousand four hundred feet and three thousand feet. I chose the less aggressive depth for this manuscript. The Seawolf class was designed to be faster and better armed than the Los Angeles-class nuclear-attack submarines it replaced. It's also significantly quieter, making less noise at twenty-five knots than its predecessor did when it was laid up beside a pier. The last Seawolf sub, the *USS*

Jimmy Carter, cost three and a half billion dollars. You can find more information on these submarines at (https://nationalinterest. org/blog/reboot/americas-seawolf-class-submarines-are-underwater-killers-194431) and (https://www.gdeb.com/about/oursubmarines/ seawolf/).

You've undoubtedly noticed that I refer to a submarine as a boat rather than a ship. One historical reason for this distinction is that the first submarines were small and manned only when used. Therefore, they were called boats. As they got larger and should have transitioned to being referred to as ships, the original term had already stuck and became a part of the Navy's tradition when referring to a submarine. Another reason for calling it a boat is that the earliest submarines were not technically sea-going vessels, as the article below denotes. Instead, used to send a torpedo into an opposing vessel, they were transported by ship to a maritime battle, boats being the term used for a vessel carried on a ship, whereas a vessel is a ship that goes to sea. Eventually, someone came up with the idea of submerging them for short periods as they approached their target. Today, most use the terms boat and ship interchangeably. However, many submariners cling to tradition and refer to their vessel as a boat, a term I used when describing the *USS Florida* and *Pantera*. (https://sailorsknowit. com/why-is-a-submarine-called-a-boat-and-not-a-ship/).

My description of the torpedo room and the procedures for firing a torpedo were generic since I couldn't find the checklists used by the crew of a Seawolf-class submarine, probably for good reason because the Navy doesn't want to publish their sub's operating manuals. Therefore, my respect and apologies to the old salts, meaning experienced sailors who served in the silent service, if I didn't get it exactly right. The data I used for torpedo room procedures were taken from the following:

(https://maritime.org/tech/torpfire.php#:~:text=When%20 the%20tube%20is%20flooded,is%20ejected%20from%20 the%20tube.), (https://www.quora.com/On-a-US-submarine- when-fire-is-shouted-does-it-mean-to-shoot-a-torpedo-or-to- warn-of-a-fire-on-the-ship), (https://www.navy.mil/Resources/ Fact-Files/Display-FactFiles/article/2169558/attack-submarines- ssn/#:~:text=Though%20lacking%20VLS%2C%20the%20 Seawolf,called%20the%20multi%2Dmission%20platform.).

Camp Peary is a nine thousand-acre military base near Williamsburg, Virginia, which hosts a covert CIA training center known as The Farm. This facility teaches spycraft to those connected with the CIA's Directorate of Operations, the DIA's Defense Clandestine Service, and other intelligence entities. The curriculum includes becoming an expert in 007-type skills as diverse as how to make brush passes and dead drops, surveillance detection, how to recruit assets, weapons training, parachuting, speed boating, driving techniques, how to withstand captivity and torture, including waterboarding, and other skills not shared with the public. The following articles provide a fascinating look at the training that's given at The Farm: (https://spyscape.com/ article/spy-school-confidential-cia-officers-spill-secrets-about- what-really-happens-at-the-farm), (https://en.wikipedia.org/wiki/ Camp_Peary), and (https://www.washingtonian.com/2019/10/13/ amaryllis-fox-how-you-train-spy-cia-most-elite-covert-unit/).

The Igla surface-to-air missile exists and, as stated, is believed to have a range of around three miles. Since the Russian military has not published the operational details of this weapon, my narrative cobbled together a CIA publication on the Igla (referenced below), and the launch procedures for the US Stinger man-portable infrared homing surface-to-air missile, which shares some similarities with it. Additionally, I left out several steps in how a Stinger is launched because it bogged down the flow of the story. Therefore, the takeaway is that the Inga and Stinger are similar systems intended to destroy low-flying aircraft entering their weapons envelopes. You can read more about them at (https://www.cia.gov/library/abbottabad-com pound/65/65B127CBF02A4667D8A8A229D6A5E87BIGLA.pdf) and (https://www.globalsecurity.org/military/library/policy/army/ fm/44-18-1/Ch3.htm).

Photonic masts are replacing the prisms and lenses of optical periscopes, providing imaging, navigation, electronic warfare, and communications functions. However, I couldn't confirm whether they're used on Seawolf-class submarines. Typically, there are two photonic masts in the ship's sail, each rising and lowering in a telescopic motion similar to a car antenna. The information and images from these masts are recorded and sent to two workstations and the commander's console. Each can be controlled via a joystick, keyboard, or trackball interface from these stations, with the information and images displayed on flat-panel screens. The description and technical information on how photonic masts work was taken from Kevin Bonsor's article published in *howstuffworks*. You can find this at (https://science.howstuffworks.com/photonic-mast2.htm).

I made the Genesis Corporation, a fictional company, the manufacturer of UFPs, although the US government awarded the Sparton Corporation phase one of the UFP project. (https://www.businesswire.com/news/home/20130816005064/

en/Sparton%E2%80%99s-Defense-and-Security-Systems-Awarded-DARPA-Contract-for-Upward-Falling-Payloads-Program). There is no intended comparison between Sparton and Genesis, nor of anyone who has been with or is currently at the company. After his career in government, I needed Archangel to be the head of a large defense contractor with innovative technology. I chose UFPs because I found the concept extremely interesting and something I could craft a story around. Therefore, Sparton's involvement shouldn't be implied. Although not mentioned by name, Martin Lockheed has a Manassas, Virginia plant that is believed to develop advanced undersea systems for the Department of Defense. However, there is no intended inference or involvement by Lockheed Martin, its employees, or its contractors to any incident mentioned in my novel. I needed the UFP to be a reasonable distance from Norfolk, and Manassas seemed to be the perfect location—Lockheed Martin and its plant incidental to that plot requirement.

Additionally, I cited the Office of Naval Research for their involvement in UFPs because I felt they were the perfect foil for what would occur, and I also needed someone from that office to be a part of the events that would unfold. The ONR has a focused and dedicated team with an extensive record of accomplishments, and their involvement in everything relating to my story is fictional.

The taking down of the Global Hawk drone by an EMP weapon was inspired by an August 29, 2021 article in *The National Interest* describing how Chinese engineers shot down a large drone using an EMP pulse, as well as a May 23, 2020 article by Brad Lendon in *CNN Breaking News*. An EMP device will inactivate anything that depends on electronic circuitry. The United States has a similar weapon named THOR—Tactical High Power Operational

Responder, which uses high-powered microwaves to defend airbases from swarms of drone threats.

A high-energy laser weapon destroys an object by hitting it with a massive number of photons that travel at the speed of light. I selected this weapon to take down the RQ-4 Global Hawk because I'd used an EMP pulse in *The Arrangement* to neutralize critical electronic equipment, and I wanted to employ another innovative means of technological destruction in this manuscript to avoid becoming repetitive. In reality, both systems would have taken the Global Hawk out of the sky. You can read more about these weapons at (https:// nationalinterest.org/blog/buzz/chinese-engineers-shot-down-large- drone-using-electromagnetic-pulse-192571) and (https://www. cnn.com/2020/05/22/asia/us-navy-lwsd-laser-intl-hnk-scli/index. html#:~:text=A%20US%20Navy%20warship%20has,said%20 in%20a%20statement%20Friday.)

The GBU-44 Viper Strike glide bomb is real and was developed as a replacement missile in situations where using the Hellfire would be overkill. Half the weight of a Hellfire, the Viper could be carried by lighter drones and, having a smaller blast radius, could be used closer to troops than other munitions. However, this lack of lethality led to its eventual withdrawal from usage. Although it was integrated for use with an AC-130 gunship, its deployment from a C-17 was solely in my imagination, as was having the copilot guide it to its target. Needing a way to disable the *Pantera* without rapidly sinking it and killing the crew, which would have occurred if I'd used a torpedo, cruise missile, or traditional air-to-ship missile, the Viper Strike seemed a plausible way to accomplish what I wanted. Its usage also required that Watkins get his C-17 low enough to deploy it, after which I could again significantly damage his aircraft with

Moretti, of course, getting the credit. The weapon's three-mile range and five-thousand feet height limitation were inserted for the sake of the storyline and doesn't reflect the operational limitations of the system. More information on the Viper Strike can be found at (https://nationalinterest.org/blog/buzz/meet-viper-strike-first-micro-missile-138342) and (https://ndiastorage.blob.core.usgovcloudapi.net/ndia/2009/psa_mar/Borden.pdf).

The C-17 is a flexible cargo aircraft that can carry up to 171,000 pounds of cargo in its cavernous interior, and has a maximum takeoff weight of 585,000 pounds. Designed to land on what the Air Force describes as austere runways, meaning those less than 4,000 feet long and 60 feet wide, each costs $366.2 million and has a cost-per-flight hour of $23,811. Although this is a big number, the USAF's largest transport aircraft, the C-5 Galaxy, costs $78,817 per flight hour. There are three crewmembers on a C-17—a pilot, copilot, and loadmaster. I refer to this last position as the aircraft's crew chief because I liked that description better than loadmaster, which implies this is their sole function. You can read more about this versatile aircraft, including the data used for my story, by going to (https://warriorlodge.com/pages/boeing-c-17-globemaster-iii#:~:text=With%20a%20payload%20of%20160%2C000%20lb%20%2872%2C600%20kg%29,sealed%20center%20wing%20bay%20as%20a%20fuel%20tank.), (https://apps.dtic.mil/sti/pdfs/ADA408125.pdf), (https://militarymachine.com/c-17-facts/), and (https://www.airforce-technology.com/projects/c-17-globemaster-iii-aircraft-us/?cf-view).

The costs associated with current and future submarines is, as mentioned in the story, accurate and taken from an October 10, 2019 article by Megan Eckstein in *USNI News*, which you can find at (https://news.usni.org/2019/10/10/cbo-navys-next-nuclear-attack-submarine-could-cost-5-5b-a-hull). The Navy anticipates that the next class of nuclear submarines will each cost $5.5 billion dollars as bigger boats are needed to meet future mission objectives. While a Virgina-class submarine displaces seven thousand eight hundred tons, the newer class of submarine is estimated to displace around nine thousand one hundred tons. The requirement for a larger class of submarines is because the Navy has shifted its focus from land-attack missions to blue-water warfare, which requires stealthier submarines that can deploy uncrewed vehicles, sensors, networks, and versatile weapons.

During my research, I discovered that six percent of fishing vessels turn off their automatic identification system or AIS, so their presence in illegal fishing areas can't be detected. In a study conducted between 2017 and 2019, over fifty-five thousand suspected disabling events occurred, obscuring five million hours of fishing vessel activity. Forty percent of these hours were in the Northwest Pacific Ocean and the Exclusive Economic Zones (EEZs) of Argentina and West African nations. In addition to disabling their AIS as they enter unauthorized locations to fish illegally, these vessels also turn off their system when transferring their catch to refrigerated cargo vessels. This allows them to secretly get their catch to shore and quickly resume fishing. You can read more about this at (https://www.theguardian.com/environment/2022/nov/02/at-least-6-percent-global-fishing-likely-as-ships-turn-off-tracking-devices-study) and (https://news.ucsc.edu/2022/11/unseen-fishing.html).

To the best of my knowledge, the Global Hawk does not have an augmented vision system that integrates with its cameras to view a ship's interior. However, given the current technology, it's not beyond reason that the military could possess this capability. I gave the RQ-4 this ability for the sake of the storyline to peer within a vessel's holds to discover if the Vigilant containers were within. The idea came from an article I read on Through-the-Wall-Sensors (TTWS), which are used by the military and law enforcement agencies. Although different systems, such as acoustic, radar-based, and thermal imaging, allow penetrable viewing, each employs energy waves to penetrate solid objects and create an image of what's on the other side. However, public data suggests that all have limitations, affected by the composition and thickness of what it's trying to look through. One system currently employed by police and government agencies that allows through-wall viewing is RANGE-R, which sells for around six thousand dollars. This system has been used by FBI hostage rescue teams, firefighters during collapsed building searches, and so forth. Although it can penetrate concrete, wood, glass, plastic, and other compositions, its distance-limited to two hundred thirty feet.

One concern as TTWS continues to become technologically more sophisticated is that, in the future, private drones may have this capability and offer it as a purchase option, allowing someone to look inside a residence without the occupants knowing they're being spied upon. You can find more information on TTWS at (https://www.kentfaith.com/blog/article_are-there-surveillance-cameras-that-can-see-through-walls_5022).

My description of Czech motorists is accurate. I've driven in many European and Asian countries, although I'll attribute my willingness to drive in Korea to my having a temporary bout of insanity. Decisively, the Czech Republic is a country where I'd never consider getting behind the wheel of a car. That's because the ordinarily pleasant and non-aggressive Czechs seem to take the opposite posture when they enter their vehicles, making the accident rate in their country twice that of Europe and the United States. Most Czech drivers don't stop at zebra crossings, and those who do won't wait for the pedestrian to finish getting across the street. Tailgating is commonplace, speed limits are ignored, and cyclists are viewed as obstructionists who are not entitled to any right of way. I'm told that one reason for this aggressive behavior is that both municipal and local governments don't, for the most part, enforce traffic laws. More information on Czech drivers can be found by going to (https://english.radio.cz/come-czech-republic-dont-try-crossing-road-8077615), (https://www.prague-guide.co.uk/drivers-in-prague/), and (http://www.pragprague.com/driving-car-in-prague/).

Besides the Senate Palace at the Kremlin, the president of Russia has offices at his residence in St. Petersburg, Sochi on the Black Sea, and Novo-Ogaryovo on the outskirts of Moscow. All are set up and decorated identically to confuse foreign intelligence and make it difficult to mount an assassination attempt. You can learn more about these offices by going to (https://nypost.com/2023/04/05/putin-has-replica-offices-around-russia-refuses-internet/).

Center 16, also known as the Center for Radio-Electronic Intelligence by Means of Communication, or Military Unit 71330, exists and oversees the FSB's signals intelligence capabilities. This includes communication intercepts, decryption, and data processing. Its various administrative functions are located in unmarked buildings around Moscow and forest enclosures, with this disbursement reducing the number of satellite dishes at a particular site, which draws attention to that location. Center 16 is credited with designing the world's most sophisticated cyber intelligence tool, the Snake, which has infected computers in over fifty countries, collecting sensitive intelligence from high-priority targets such as government networks, research facilities, and journalists. According to a May 9, 2023 article by the Cybersecurity & Infrastructure Security Agency, part of the Department of Homeland Security: *Snake has accessed and exfiltrated sensitive international relations documents, as well as other diplomatic communications, from a victim in a North Atlantic Treaty Organization (NATO) country. Within the United States, the FSB has victimized industries including education, small businesses, and media organizations, as well as critical infrastructure sectors including government facilities, financial services, critical manufacturing, and communications.* You can find more information on Center 16 and Snake at (https://www.rferl.org/a/russia-fsb-malware-snake-takedown/32407612.html#:~:text=The%20other%20is%20Center%2016,%2C%20decryption%2C%20and%20data%20processing.) and (https://www.cisa.gov/news-events/cybersecurity-advisories/aa23-129a).

References to the FSB planting listening devices in Prague restaurants and the State Department utilizing them to impart disinformation are fictional and done for the sake of the storyline as a way to give the FSB and those in the Kremlin what Adamik had discovered. As a side note, Bubeneč is a charming district in northwest Prague. Frequently called Little Moscow because of its proximity to the Russian Embassy and the congregation of their staff and support people in the area; it's primarily a quiet residential area dominated by parks, including Stromovka, the largest park in Prague. If you go there, try the pastry at Elvíra, and then walk across the street to Café Borzoi, a small espresso bar that serves locally roasted coffee. I found it a great way to start my day.

Information on the NSA's processing capabilities was taken from (https://nsa.govl.info/utah-data-center/), and a fascinating article by James Bamford that appeared in *Wired* magazine, the link to which is below. His article focuses on the Utah Data Center (UDC), a heavily fortified complex in Bluffdale that sits in a bowl-shaped valley with the Wasatch mountain range to the east and the Oquirrh Mountains to the west. The center is believed to receive data from National Reconnaissance Office satellites that record voice and data communications while over other countries. The UDC then cryptanalyses or breaks the unbelievably complex encryption systems employed by these governments to hide their voice and data communications, unmasking what's being transmitted.

(https://www.wired.com/2012/03/ff-nsadatacenter/#:~:text=10%20NSA%20headquarters%2C%20Fort%20Meade%2C%20Maryland%20Analysts%20here,also%20building%20an%20%24896%20million%20supercomputer%20center%20here). The UDC is said to be capable of storing yottabytes of information, with a yottabyte equal to 1,000,000,000,000,000GB, which is one septillion bytes, or a million trillion megabytes.

(https://www.cnet.com/tech/computing/nsa-to-store-yottabytes-in-utah-data-centre/).

In one of the articles I read, which purportedly divulged various functions within the super-secret National Security Agency that have been publicly disclosed, I learned about the existence of the NSA's Special Collection Service, codenamed F6. This joint NSA-CIA activity runs collection sites, which they call "denied" areas. Located on a seven thousand-acre property run by the Department of

Agriculture's Research Center in a complex next to a State Department communications facility referred to as the "Beltsville Annex," it can best be described as the ultimate testing and engineering center for espionage equipment. F6 is part of the black budget and has been referred to by some as similar to the Mission Impossible force in that, as some suspect, it develops cutting-edge espionage technology and conducts burglary, wiretapping, and breaking and entering operations to employ them in locations that the government would never admit to planting an electronic device. (https://greydynamics.com/special-collection-service-americas-mission-impossible-force/).

Additionally, in trying to keep current with the NSA's capabilities, I read a fascinating article by Sarah Taitz, published on April 11, 2023, titled: *Five Things to Know About NSA Mass Surveillance and the Coming Fight in Congress.* It concerned Section 702 of the Foreign Intelligence Surveillance Act, a statute enacted by Congress that permits the US government to conduct surveillance of an American's international communications, which includes emails, texts, phone calls, social media messages, and web browsing if the government is in pursuit of foreign intelligence targets. However, the definition of target is left vague, meaning that in addition to terrorists, spies, and criminals, the statute can be interpreted to allow the monitoring of communications of any American. The NSA divides foreign data collection into two surveillance programs: PRISM and Upstream.

PRISM obtains data on any non-US person the NSA wishes to monitor and orders US tech and social media companies, such as Facebook, Apple, Google, and Microsoft, to give them everything they have, not only on this person but on any of their communications with a US citizen. Upstream involves the NSA working with telecommunications companies like AT&T and Verizon to collect international internet communications. The NSA then uses their immense computer network to tie keywords, phone numbers, and other search parameters to their foreign target list.

The NSA keeps this information within its vast databases, which the FBI routinely accesses when examining the communications of individual Americans for a domestic investigation. Although Section 702 only allows the NSA to surveil foreigners abroad for foreign intelligence purposes, its data gathering necessarily casts a wide net and, just as in fishing when you're towing a net to catch a particular species of fish, you catch other species as well, only instead of throwing them back or, in this case deleting the information, the data collected is stored and can be accessed at any time for almost any reason. Many have a problem with the way Section 702 is written. However, the problem isn't with the NSA, whose DNA dictates it gathers as much data as it can and does a great job at trying to find the bad guys who want to destroy our great country. Instead, I believe the problem is with Congress because they haven't limited the legal boundaries for collecting and using this information. (https://www.aclu.org/news/national-security/five-things-to-know-about-nsa-mass-surveillance-and-the-coming-fight-in-congress#:~:text=Section%20702%20has%20morphed%20into,domestic%20investigations%20of%20all%20kinds.).

As long as I'm writing about the NSA, I should mention that they don't provide details on the functions of the various departments within their agency. Instead, they use generalities. Therefore, when I looked at their organization chart, which you can view at (https://viewer.edrawsoft.com/public/s/72cf2712204668), I had to take a stab at what departments handle the functions that were critical to my plot. For example, I had the IT Infrastructure Services System

Office find the terminal used to hack the ONR's computer because it sounded like a reasonable assumption. However, because I can't confirm that would be the responsibility of this office, that one's up for grabs. I also said the State Department's Bureau of Intelligence and Research (https://www.intelligence.gov/how-the-ic-works/our-organizations/424-state-department-bureau-of-intelligence-and-research#:~:text=Dept.-,of%20State%20Bureau%20of%20Intelligence%20and%20Research,Marshall%20established%20INR%20in%201947.) had an office at NSA headquarters. Again, that sounded reasonable, believing that other intelligence organizations could better coordinate with the NSA if they had a physical presence at the Agency. However, that's also up for grabs.

The examples of dead drop locations are accurate and lifted from the following articles (https://thehackernews.com/2012/11/new-dead-drop-techniques-used-by.html) and (https://spyscape.com/article/how-to-find-and-use-a-dead-letter-box#:~:text=Dead%20drops%20are%20a%20spycraft,have%20to%20meet%20in%20person.). I found the half-eaten peanut butter sandwich a particularly ingenious place to hide a flash drive, believing that not many would scrunch the peanut butter in a partially eaten sandwich to see if something was hidden within. However, not all dead drops go as planned. The CIA and KGB both used dead animals, such as large birds and rats, to hide information. The problem was that it didn't take long for scavengers to find and feast on these remains. One foreign intelligence agency cleverly tried to stop the scavenging by pouring liberal amounts of hot sauce on the dead animals to keep them from being devoured. However, I'm not sure if someone, especially a seasoned spy, would believe a dead animal hadn't been tampered with if they could see or smell the hot sauce on it. Another unusual dead drop I read about was a portable toilet, or Porta Potty, which works well if the exchange is made before they vacuum it out. In one documented instance, the timing was off and the information bag that was left got stuck in the vacuum hose.

As written, the Russian Embassy in Prague was the former headquarters of the Gestapo. Bought by Jiří Popper, a Czech banker in 1927, who fled to London in 1938, it and the surrounding property were confiscated by the Nazis the following year and used as the Prague headquarters for the Gestapo, who constructed a series of tunnels beneath it. After the war, the president of Czechoslovakia granted the property to the Soviet Union as a gesture of thanks for helping liberate the country. The property has remained under Russian control ever since. Because there's no public data where the tunnels run, although it's believed they provide a means to enter and leave the embassy without being seen, I took advantage of this ambiguity and had one run to Vyšehrad Park.

The Raven Rock Mountain Complex, or Site R, is located within the hollowed-out Raven Rock mountain, six hundred fifty feet below its fifteen hundred foot summit. This two hundred sixty-five thousand square feet bunker, approximately six miles from Camp David, Maryland, serves as the backup Pentagon and contains a series of buildings, some as tall as three stories. In the event of a catastrophe at the Pentagon, it can support the continuity of operation for the entire Department of Defense. However, it does not provide housing for members of the military or civilians stationed there, nor does it have a system, like I attributed to Nemesis, which mirrors the data from the numerous computer networks utilized by the government. I added the on-base housing for the sake of the storyline because it was easier to have members of the Nemesis team live there, so I wouldn't need to work around the transit times from their homes. I also required a way for Alexson and Connelly to search government databases without individually hacking them, which would have interfered with my timeline. You can read more about this complex at (https://whitehouse.gov1.info/raven-rock/about.html), (https://publicintelligence.net/raven-rock-mountain-complex-site-r/), and (https://www.warhistoryonline.com/instant-articles/raven-rock-the-u-s-governments.html).

Information on special forces techniques to board a vessel and the difficulties encountered is accurate. SEALs refer to the high-risk tactic of intercepting and boarding a ship at night as Visit, Board, Search and Seizure or VBSS. According to comments made by a SEAL in an article in NAVYSEALS.com, the link to which is below, "VBSS is *the sketchiest thing I did in the teams," he said. "Everything is slippery, it's dark, everything is moving, it's f**king cold so you can't feel sh*t. All agreed that the most dangerous moment of a VBSS raid comes during the initial boarding, often after a punishing, hours-long ride in a specially built speed boat or inflatable raiding boat. In often-rolling seas, SEALs climb from their boat onto the side of the target, often using a caving ladder, little more than a rope with handles. Several raiders at once might be on a ladder, clinging to wet bars a dozen or more feet in the air, as waves crash off the target boat and batter the SEAL's own delivery boat. A single slip could put a sailor, or several sailors, into the water, where they face the prospect of being lost in the dark or even pulled under one of the two boats.* Information on VBSS used in my manuscript was taken from a May 19, 2023 article in *Sandboxx* (https://www.sandboxx.us/news/career/training-and-promotion/vbss-a-navy-seal-walks-you-through-boarding-an-enemy-ship/#:~:text=This%20 is%20often%20accomplished%20via,deck%20of%20the%20 target%20vessel.), *Quora* (https://www.quora.com/How-do-Navy-SEALs-board-ships), and the quotes from (https://navyseals. com/5727/navy-seals-describe-how-boarding-a-ship-is-a-teams-sketchiest-mission/). The only easy day was yesterday.

The Russian laser weapon, known as Peresvet, exists and was named after Alexander Peresvet, a Russian Orthodox monk who fought the Tatar champion in single combat in the late fourteenth century. Both men killed each other. Legend has it that, although the Tatar champion fell from his saddle, Peresvet didn't. The Peresvet laser is portable and used for air and missile defense and to blind satellites. As little is known about it, I took liberties as to its scope of operation, making assumptions that I believed would align with its capabilities. You can find more information on this weapon at (https://military-history.fandom.com/wiki/Peresvet_(laser_weapon)) and (https:// www.techtimes.com/articles/275588/20220518/new-russia-peresvet-laser-test-shows-burn-drone-5-seconds.htm).

The technical information I used to describe pixelation was summarized, meaning I left a lot of technical jargon out so it wouldn't slow down the story. I decided to pixelate the face because it gave me numerous options to keep the reader in suspense about Archangel's identity rather than reveal it at the beginning of my story, which would have been a momentum-killer. Obscuring Sullivan's face also allowed Lisov to negotiate with the CIA, whom he didn't completely trust, compelling them, had he lived, to fulfill their word and get him to the United States. Respecting the NSA's enormous encryption and decryption capabilities, and because I wanted to make unblurring Sullivan's face nearly impossible, I used a one-time pad. The following articles will provide more information on pixelating (https://

iopscience.iop.org/article/10.1088/1742-6596/1008/1/012016/pdf) and (https://smallbusiness.chron.com/encrypt-pictures-50483.html).

As represented, a Black Hawk helicopter, even under minimal power, produces an eighty-five-decibel sound, which can be heard from a distance of five miles at night. When researching how sound emanates from a helicopter, because I needed Hunter and Moretti's Black Hawks to approach the *Antias* unheard, I read a very informative article by Ed Brotak in the February 25, 2021 edition of *Avfoil News*, which explained that all sounds are caused by a change in air pressure which produces vibrations in the ear. These are then converted to electrical impulses, which the brain recognizes as sound. While a Black Hawk engine isn't quiet, its sound primarily becomes noticeable when the aircraft is relatively close, with most of the noise that an approaching helicopter produces coming from the main rotor blades moving through the air. These generate thickness noise, created by the displacement of air moving through them, and loading noise, resulting from the lift and drag forces on the blade. As the helicopter approaches, we hear the airflow around a blade interacting with that of the next blade, producing vibrations that are directed downward, referred to as blade slap. Therefore, in trying to make the approach of Moretti and Hunter's Black Hawks as stealthy as possible, when the helicopters were throwing off 85db, it seemed logical that having them approach from an altitude below the deck of the ship would send the blade slap toward the ocean. If you'd like to read more about how a helicopter produces noise, please go to (https://www.avfoil.com/helicopter/the-science-behind-helicopter-noise-and-how-the-industry-is-working-to-reduce-it/).

The information on the *USS Dwight D. Eisenhower* is accurate (https://www.militaryfactory.com/ships/detail.php?ship_

id=USS-Dwight-D-Eisenhower-CVN69), with the exception of the location of the ready room and its bullseye address (3-95-2-P). The designation of *P* for the ready room might prove confusing to those who've served on an aircraft carrier because I could not find a code for the ready room, so I selected P.

I've been on a Navy cruiser, and I can say from experience that, even though this type of vessel is small compared to an aircraft carrier, it didn't take much for me to get lost in the ship's maze of passageways. In my defense, as weak as it is, I was in the Air Force and not the Navy, and there may have been some inter-service rivalry in letting me wander about the ship. You can read more about how to read a bullseye and navigate the passageways aboard a ship at (https://www.usni.org/magazines/naval-history-magazine/2018/december/bullseye-navigating-within-ship) and (https://www.quora.com/How-do-crew-members-not-get-lost-in-the-huge-interior-spaces-of-a-modern-aircraft-carrier#:~:text=Sailors%20certainly%20do%20get%20lost,first%20number%20indicates%20the%20deck.).

Adamik's analysis of where the shooter in Vyšehrad Park stood was accurate in determining that whoever killed Lisov and the two CIA agents wasn't at ground level because the wounds weren't circular. Instead, they were ellipse-shaped, meaning the killer fired at a downward angle. Given this, his determination of the killer's location was relatively easy because there were only two elevated places in the area where they could have taken the shots. However, I learned that tracking a bullet's trajectory is usually never this easy. It's complicated, particularly in environments where there are different elevations at varying distances, requiring a significant amount of data to be collected to determine where the shooter stood. One of the articles I read, which did an excellent job explaining this, can be found by going to (https://captainhunter.com/understanding-bullet-trajectory-the-definitive-guide-for-beginners/). It gets into such variables as muzzle velocity, spin drift, the Coriolis effect, and so forth that you'd likely see referenced on an episode of *CSI*. Additional information on trajectory analysis can be found at (https://www.crime-scene-investigator.net/bullet-trajectories-at-crime-scenes.html). My description of a body wound was taken from the information within a 2017 publication by Flinn Scientific, Inc., which you can find at (https://www.flinnsci.com/api/library/Download/274c70fa157f4e4b82b392846f), and an August 24, 2021 article in PathologyOutlines.com by Lorenzo Gitto, M.D., Robert Stoppacher, M.D. at (https://www.pathologyoutlines.com/topic/forensicsgunshotwounds.html).

For those who are Navy, Coast Guard, or otherwise nautically inclined, I apologize for the maritime liberties I took, especially in bringing the *Eisenhower* and the *Antias* together for the transfer of missile containers, necessitated by the factory ship listing heavily to starboard, the auxiliary generators onboard *Antias* having insufficient juice to power the ship's cranes, and the carrier not having a crane with enough reach to extract the missiles from the factory ship's holds. Therefore, the only way I could get the containers onto *Ike* before the *Antias* met its fate was to bring both vessels alongside each other. In my research, I saw that experts have always stated that putting vessels in contact with one another at sea is a very bad idea because, even if the ocean is calm, the ships would still grind together, the amount of damage escalating with an increase in the wind or sea swells. However, because of my storyline, that's precisely what I did. You can read more on why it's a bad idea to bring ships together at sea by going to (https://www.

marineinsight.com/marine-navigation/mooring-methods-ships/) and (https://worldbuilding.stackexchange.com/questions/125853/ is-it-possible-to-bind-multiple-ships-together-on-open-water).

The GIUK (Greenland, Iceland, United Kingdom) gap is a naval choke point in the Northern Atlantic, and its control is considered critical to protecting what the military refers to as sea lines of communication (SLOCs) and the supply lines between NATO's European members and the United States. Additionally, because most of Russia's naval assets in the North Atlantic are deployed from the Kola Peninsula, the gap is an essential focal point for the United States Navy. More information on Russia's extensive military capabilities on the Kola Peninsula, including the information I incorporated into my manuscript, can be found in a March 23, 2020 brief published by the *Center for Strategic & International Studies*, and written by Joseph S. Mermudez Jr., Heather A. Conley, and Matthew Melino. You can find this brief at (https://www.csis.org/ analysis/ice-curtain-modernization-kola-peninsula). Information on the GIUK gap can be found in a January 23, 2023 article by John Grady in *USNI News* (https://news.usni.org/2023/01/26/russian- arctic-threat-growing-more-potent-report-says) and at (https:// en.wikipedia.org/wiki/GIUK_gap).

In creating a sense of urgency to get the fictional *USS Florida* to its rendezvous with Moretti and his team in the GIUK gap, I had Captain Quinn go to one hundred ten percent power, recalling a scene from the movie *The Hunt for Red October*, where Captain Viktor Tupolev, the Commander of the Konovalov, a Soviet Alfa class submarine, orders his boat to go to one hundred and five percent power on the reactor. I just upped it by five percent. Wanting to understand what this meant because I have a problem with anything exceeding one hundred percent of power, believing that if it did, the higher power number would be the new one hundred percent rating, I began researching nuclear reactors. Surprisingly, my reasoning wasn't far off, discovering that a nameplate rating, the normal maximum full-load sustained output, is considered the baseline for one hundred percent power. However, if the system is upgraded to create greater efficiency and power, that rating is revised. References to capacity use the original design specifications, not the output from upgrades, which increases the production efficiency beyond the original design. Subsequently, it's possible to exceed one hundred percent, the extent and length of time you remain there determining the possibility of a meltdown.

(https://theaviationgeekclub.com/us-navy-nuclear-propulsion-plant-operator-explains-when-a-submarine-reactor-can-be-run-at-higher-than-100-and-why-the-105-on-the-reactor-ordered-in-the-hunt-for-red-october-movie-would-not-be-worth-a/), and (https://www.reddit.com/r/askscience/comments/9rn49y/how_is_it_possible_for_a_nuclear_power_plants/?rdt=49172).

The Akula-class nuclear submarine *Pantera*, sometimes referred to as submarine K-317, exists and is assigned to Russia's Northern Fleet. With all Russian submarine designs named after fish, akula translates into shark. Because this is a work of fiction, the actions attributed to the vessel and crew are from the author's imagination, and although they made sense to me, they would probably cause a submariner to visit their local bar. Additionally, as the Russian Navy doesn't publish data on the thickness of its hulls, at least none that I could find, and knowing the thickness of the hulls on subs are said to vary between four and ten inches, I crafted one for the outer and pressure hulls that fit my storyline.

As long as I'm addressing my failings, and because I'm also not an expert in nuclear submarine propulsion systems, I thought a plausible way to get *Pantera* to surface was to damage its propulsion system by sending two Razorback UUVs into its screw, believing that one wouldn't do the job. Once I came up with this idea, I did a significant amount of research to see if there was data on the effect of sending a non-explosive projectile into a submarine's propeller. However, I came up empty. Instead, I discovered that if one submarine shoots at another, it's to destroy and not to disable it. Therefore, without information on the damage a non-lethal projectile would cause when it gets entangled in a submarine's propeller, the more technical aspects of what I described may fall short of what the Navy knows would happen in such a situation, although I think I came close. If you go to *alanrefkin.com* and click on *story settings*, you'll see photos of the equipment, locations, and other items used in this novel, including pictures of *Pantera,* photonic masts, and so forth.

You can find more information on submarine hulls at (http://www.madehow.com/Volume-5/Nuclear-Submarine.html) and (https://medium.com/@bob.davis_5265/how-thick-is-a-submarines-hull-what-material-is-it-made-out-of-2533bd3aee8e#:~:text=The%20 thickness%20of%20a%20submarine's,(4%20to%2010%20 inches).).

Bodies of water are made up of layers, each determined by temperature; the top layer is referred to as the epipelagic zone, sunlight zone, or ocean skin, which reacts with the wind and waves. The thermocline is at the bottom of this layer, and is the transition between this warmer surface layer and the cooler water below. Between three thousand three hundred feet and thirteen thousand one hundred feet, the water temperature remains constant. Below that, the temperature will gradually decrease until it gets to just above freezing. (https://oceanservice.noaa.gov/facts/thermocline.html) and (https://www.boatsafe.com/thermocline/). You can read more on how submariners use thermoclines to their advantage by going to (https://www.quora.com/How-does-the-thermal-layer-in-the-ocean-provide-protection-to-a-submarine-from-the-detection-by-enemy-sonar-search).

The United States employs a number of undersea detection systems, such as the Integrated Undersea Surveillance System (IUSS), Sound Surveillance System (SOSUS), and the Deep Reliable Acoustic Path Exploitation System (DRAPES). As stated, the undersea environment imposes significant technological hurdles on listening devices below the ocean's surface. These challenges occur because the devices are at various depths and subject to differences in pressure and temperature; the systems software and hardware needing to compensate for these non-standard conditions in its analysis of sound waves, and the acoustic reflection from the surrounding underwater topographical seascape. Therefore, detecting and tracking a submarine is far from being a certainty. I found that the best explanation of these systems was in a paper by the Australian government's Department of Defence, titled *Remote Undersea Surveillance*, which you can find at (https://www.dst.defence.gov.au/sites/default/files/events/documents/Insights%20Paper%20-%20Remote%20Undersea%20Surveillance%20F1.pdf). You can read about the Navy's undersea threat detection array at (https://maritime-executive.com/article/navy-invests-in-subsea-threat-detection-array).

It's long been known that the Central Intelligence Agency stations its employees in American embassies, providing them with State Department titles that provide diplomatic immunity. In the past, Agency personnel were stationed at an embassy for an extended period. Because their job was to spy and recruit, and they performed no meaningful function within the embassy, it wasn't long before everyone knew they were CIA operatives. Therefore, operatives are now intermingled with legitimate outside specialists, such as computer software engineers, auditors, and so forth, who are sent to the agency for a limited period. Also, CIA facilities outside the United States are not limited to embassies. Shadow businesses or international organizations also provide cover. During my research on the CIA's presence in embassies, I used the following articles: (https://www.quora.com/Is-a-CIA-station-typically-located-within-an-American-embassy-If-so-wouldnt-every-diplomat-basically-know-who-the-spies-are), (https://www.washingtonpost.com/archive/politics/1979/12/05/diplomatic-titles-often-used-to-protect-intelligence-aides/e57eec6c-e41e-4e6d-b193-1ebab1341dad/), and (https://www.cia.gov/readingroom/docs/CIA-RDP78-04722A000300030018-3.pdf).

The description on how to pick a lock is accurate and was taken from a May 19, 2022 article by M.W. Byrne in *The Coolest* (https://www.thecoolist.com/how-to-pick-a-lock/), a July 29, 2021 article by Brett in *Manly Know-How, Skills* (https://www.artofmanliness.com/skills/manly-know-how/how-to-pick-a-lock-pin-tumbler-locks/), and *wikiHow* (https://www.wikihow.com/Pick-a-Lock#:~:text=A%20professional%20lock%20picking%20kit,%2C%20picks%2C%20and%20raking%20tools.&text=You'll%20also%20need%20a,bobby%20pin%20or%20a%20paperclip.). After researching how easy it was to pick the average lock, I now know it takes only a couple of minutes if you have the proper tools, which are not against the law to own or carry as long as you're not trying to illegally use them to enter someone else's business or residence. Push-button combination locks seemed a better alternative, where putting in a code releases the turning knob. However, thieves have discovered a way around this by slipping a particular type of shim behind it to avoid the buttons and open the door, because the drive-shaft, which retracts the latch, is not locked (https://www.lockpickworld.com/products/2pc-bypass-lock-shanks). Therefore, security systems seem a prudent supplement to locked doors.

Prague does have a KGB museum (https://www.atlasobscura.com/places/kgb-muzeum), which has an excellent collection of KGB memorabilia. These include spy cameras, concealed weapons, electrical "interrogation equipment," and other items employed by this foreign intelligence and domestic security arm of the Soviet government, which operated from 1954 to 1991, the year it was dissolved and succeeded by the Foreign Intelligence Service (SVR), which later became the FSB or Federal Security Service. The pin used by Adamik to administer the neurotoxin is not a museum exhibit. Instead, the idea came to me while reading an article about the umbrella used in the assassination of Bulgarian dissident writer Georgi Markov. Now referred to as the Bulgarian umbrella (https://en.wikipedia.org/wiki/Bulgarian_umbrella), which had a hidden pneumatic mechanism that, upon contact, injected a small poisonous pellet containing ricin into the victim. As I couldn't have Adamik stroll around an exclusive social event carrying an umbrella, I decided to use a poison pin that was referenced in a PBS article (https://www.pbs.org/opb/historydetectives/investigation/poison-pin/index.html).

In my research, I was surprised to see how small an amount of pufferfish toxin it took to cause death, ranging from 2 mg to 10 mg (.00035 ounces). Because there's no antidote, it was eye-opening to discover that the mortality rate isn't one hundred percent (https://www.sciencedirect.com/topics/agricultural-and-biological-sciences/puffer-fish). Although symptoms typically appear between thirty minutes to four hours after ingestion, death has been known to occur in as little as seventeen minutes. The survival rate varies from seven to sixty percent and depends on an array of variables. These include the amount of toxin ingested, the time it takes afterward to be placed on breathing equipment and receive oxygen, the removal of unabsorbed toxins by gastric lavage (suctioning gastric contents through a nasogastric tube), the administration of intravenous fluids, and the injection of atropine for bradycardia and dopamine to manage hypotension. In other words, if you ingest enough of the toxin, it will take a lot to save you.

You can read more about tetrodotoxins at (https://www.quora.com/Is-it-possible-to-survive-Fugu-poisoning#:~:text=Fugu%2C%20or%20pufferfish%2C%20contains%20a,an%20antidote%2C%20survival%20is%20possible.),

(https://www.theguardian.com/science/blog/2016/apr/21/thus-with-a-kiss-i-die-how-a-shakespeare-poison-has-parallels-with-pufferfish#:~:text=This%20poison%20has%20been%20known,liver%20and%20ovaries%20of%20pufferfish.), and (https://www.ncbi.nlm.nih.gov/books/NBK507714/#:~:text=There%20is%20no%20known%20antidote,within%2060%20minutes%20of%20ingestion.), and (https://www.theguardian.com/science/blog/2016/apr/21/thus-with-a-kiss-i-die-how-a-shakespeare-poison-has-parallels-with-pufferfish#:~:text=This%20poison%20has%20been%20known,liver%20and%20ovaries%20of%20pufferfish.).

Unlike in the James Bond movie *Casino Royale*, where the use of a defibrillator restored the secret agent's heart rhythm and allowed him to retake his seat at the gambling table and financially wipe out his opponent, defibrillation is ineffective for this type of poisoning (https://www.sciencenordic.com/denmark-health-heart/introducing-the-poison-that-inspired-van-gogh-and-almost-killed-james-bond-digoxin/2060566). Also, although one of the procedures employed for someone who's been poisoned is to empty their stomach, it was unnecessary to do this with Sullivan because he was injected with a toxin and removing his stomach contents would have no effect.

Extraordinary rendition is the transfer, without legal process, of someone to the custody of a foreign government for the purpose of detention and interrogation (https://www.justiceinitiative. org/voices/20-extraordinary-facts-about-cia-extraordinary-rendition-and-secret-detention#:~:text=At%20least%20136%20 individuals%20were,documents%20may%20reveal%20many%20 more.). The rendition site at Stare Kiejkuty was taken from a July 24, 2014 article by Amnesty International, although it seems to have only operated between 2002 and 2005 (https://www.amnesty. org/en/latest/news/2014/07/landmark-rulings-expose-poland-s-role-cia-secret-detention-and-torture/). Some articles suggest that the CIA has agreements for extraordinary rendition sites in fifty-four countries, although there's obviously no way to verify this.

Nenets Sabetta exists (https://www.dailysabah.com/travel/2020/ 02/16/sabetta-a-frozen-russian-town-at-the-edge-of-the-world) and, as written, literally translates to *the end of the world*. The environment is harsh, having only twenty-seven and a half days of sunshine (658 hours), snowing an average of one hundred twenty-six days a year, and rain for sixty-five. Because it presides over the world's largest natural gas reserves, this town grew from nineteen persons in the early 2000s to over thirty thousand, half employed by the Yamal LNG plant and the nearby seaport. One of the more interesting facts I read when researching Nenets Sabetta was that residents are not allowed to smoke, even in their homes, on the streets, or in their offices, which makes sense given what's around and beneath them, the town constructing smoking huts for those so inclined. The FSB does have an office in the town, referring to it as its Arctic complex (https://thebarentsobserver.com/ru/node/1022), and that its purpose is to bolster security along the Arctic frontier. I sent Abrankovich there because I believed that Putin would want to denigrate him by stripping the general of his previous rank and reassigning him from his lofty position as head of the FSB to *the end of the world*.

ABOUT THE AUTHOR

Alan Refkin has written fifteen previous works of fiction and is the co-author of four business books on China, for which he received Editor's Choice Awards for *The Wild Wild East* and *Piercing the Great Wall of Corporate China*. In addition to the Matt Moretti-Han Li action-adventure thrillers, he's written the Mauro Bruno detective series and Gunter Wayan private investigator novels. He and his wife Kerry live in southwest Florida, where he's working on his next Matt Moretti-Han Li novel. You can find more information on the author and the locations used in his books at alanrefkin.com.

Printed in the United States
by Baker & Taylor Publisher Services